STEPHEN LEATHER

STILL STANDING

HODDER

First published in Great Britain in 2023 by Hodder & Stoughton
An Hachette UK company

This paperback edition published in 2023

1

A CIP catalogue record for this title is available from the British Library

Paperback ISBN 978 1 529 36755 3

Typeset in Plantin Light by
Palimpsest Book Production Ltd, Falkirk, Stirlingshire

Printed and bound in Great Britain by Clays Ltd, Elcograf S.p.A.

Hodder & Stoughton policy is to use papers that are natural, renewable
and recyclable products and made from wood grown in sustainable forests.
The logging and manufacturing processes are expected to conform to the
environmental regulations of the country of origin.

Hodder & Stoughton Ltd
Carmelite House
50 Victoria Embankment
London EC4Y 0DZ

www.hodder.co.uk

STILL STANDING

CHAPTER 1

Pete Green peered out of the Chinook's window at the Syrian desert just a hundred yards below. At least he assumed it was the Syrian desert, the Chinook had taken off in Turkey and there had been no indication that he had crossed any border. There was just sand and rock, a forbidding land-scape as alien as the moon.

Green was the only SAS trooper in the cabin. He was in his late twenties, his fair skin tanned from overexposure to the fierce Middle Eastern sun that had bleached his mousy-brown hair. His eyes were a piercing blue and he had a tendency to smile when he was nervous. He was smiling now. The other nine men were Navy SEALs, armed to the teeth and ready for action.

The Navy SEAL on his right winked at him. 'You okay, Pete?' His name was Jessie Dean Cooper but everyone called him JD. JD was tall and thin with olive skin and high cheek-bones. His father was American but his mother – who had died giving birth to him – had been Vietnamese.

'I'm good, JD. Locked and loaded.'

JD grinned and flashed him a thumbs up. JD had been Green's buddy since he had first been embedded with the Navy SEALs. He had shown him the ropes during training at the SEALs' base at Virginia Beach and had bunked with him on missions in Iraq and Syria.

Green was on a three-month attachment with the Navy SEALs as part of a programme to increase cooperation between the two units. In return, the SEALs had sent one of their people over to Stirling Lines to be shown the British way of doing things. Both Green and the Navy SEAL in the UK were combat medics and Green had a full battlefield medical kit in his backpack.

Sitting across from them was the highest-ranking officer on the Chinook – Lieutenant Ricky 'Tom' Hanks. But the operation was being overseen by a captain seven thousand miles away in Creech Air Force base in Nevada. Thousands of feet above the Chinook, circling in the darkness, was an MQ-9 Reaper drone which had been launched from the Incirlik Air Base in Turkey hours earlier. The Reaper was a beast of a drone with a twenty-metre wingspan and a top speed of almost five hundred kilometres an hour. Once the drone was in the air, control had been handed over to the ground control station in Nevada where Captain Joe Haschka functioned as the Mission Intelligence Co-ordinator, assisted by a pilot and sensor operator.

The Reaper was carrying a minimum weapons payload, so it could stay up for almost thirty hours at an altitude of up to fifteen thousand metres. Long-term loitering is what they called it, which always made Green think of unsavoury characters hanging out on street corners. This Reaper was carrying two Hellfire missiles but they weren't going to be used – it was a capture mission and the drone was there for surveillance only. Captain Haschka would be making any operational decisions. That was one of the things that Green had learned from his attachment – the Navy SEALs were all about command structure, whereas in the SAS it was the troopers who tended to call the shots once a mission was underway.

The Chinook had been specially fitted out for the SEALs. It was the MH-47G variant and it came with two M134 7.62mm air-cooled Miniguns and two M240 7.62mm belt-fed machine guns mounted on either side of the fuselage. It was equipped with a full range of defensive aids including a missile warning system, an integrated radio frequency countermeasures suite and dark flares that were designed to protect the helicopter against surface-to-air and air-to-air heat-seeking missiles. The MH-47G also came with a fast rope insertion system for dropping SEALs into hot spots, and for extracting them, but for this mission the helicopter would be opening its rear ramp and the men would be running out.

The mission was simple enough on paper, and the CIA officer who had carried out the briefing at Incirlik Air Base seemed to have been almost bored by it. She was a blonde woman in her mid-thirties wearing a pale blue safari suit and Chanel earrings. She hadn't bothered to introduce herself, or to say who she worked for, but she was clearly CIA. The target was Shafiq Ali Rafiq, a senior ISIS leader and bomb-maker who had been top of the CIA's most wanted list for more than six months. The CIA had learned that Rafiq's mother was in the late stages of bowel cancer and had maintained twenty-four-seven surveillance on the old woman, figuring that at some point the dutiful son would want to say goodbye. That had indeed come to pass and Rafiq had turned up at his mother's house in the village of al-Humaira, about four kilometres from the Turkish border. He had arrived with a full security team in four pick-up trucks, and they were holed up in two nearby cottages. Rafiq had intel that the CIA needed, and so the decision had been taken to launch a capture mission rather than simply destroy him with a Hellfire missile.

Two Chinooks would fly from Incirlik Air Base, along with two Black Hawk gunships, and wait close to the border until Captain Haschka gave the go order. The Chinook that Green was in was to go in first and take out the security teams. The Chinook would land about half a mile from the cottages, on the other side of a hill that would absorb much of the noise of the helicopter's turbines. The SEALs would take out the security teams at which point the second Chinook would be called in. It would land next to the house where Rafiq was staying, protected by the two Black Hawks. Rafiq would be taken and flown back to the base in Turkey. Job done. The CIA woman had made it sound like a walk in the park.

Green had had a few questions, but he had kept them to himself. When the SAS proposed a mission, everybody involved was listened to, and there would be a Chinese Parliament where every man's view would be taken into consideration. But the SEALs didn't work that way, and it was clear from the briefing that the CIA woman was calling the shots. When she had finished her briefing, the woman asked if there were any queries, but her tone suggested that she hoped there wouldn't be. She got her wish.

Once they were armed and ready to go, the two Chinooks – accompanied by the two Black Hawks – flew to a landing area a few kilometres from the border. They had waited there until Captain Haschka had given the go order. Green had been surprised to find that both pilots of the Chinook were women. They were with the Army's 160th Special Operations Aviation Regiment, known to the SEALs as 'The Night Stalkers', and they had greeted several of the SEALs by name.

Green and JD were both holding Heckler & Koch 416 carbines, as were most of the SEALs, though all had been adapted with personalised stocks, grips, optics, lasers and lights. The sniper on the mission, a lanky Texan by the name of Bobby Hawkins, was cradling a McMillan TAC-50, a weapon that was responsible for the longest recorded sniper kill ever made: by an unidentified Canadian sniper who killed an Iraqi insurgent at a distance of 3,540 metres.

The SEALs carried a range of sidearms including Glock 19s, HK45s and SIG Sauer P226s and P320s in a variety of holsters. Green had a Glock 19 in a nylon holster on his right thigh.

The Chinook slowed as it came in to land. JD pulled a set of steel dog tags from under his ballistic vest and kissed them. It was his thing, his lucky charm. The SEALs carried a set of two black dog tags. US soldiers had carried two dog tags since 1916, if the soldier was killed then one set stayed with the body and the other was used for record keeping. British soldiers were issued with circular identity discs that carried the same information – name, service number, blood group and religion. But JD had a second set of dog tags around his neck – they belonged to his father who had done three tours of Vietnam in the Seventies. JD figured that if they had got his dad through Vietnam, they must be lucky, so he always took them with him whenever he was deployed.

The Chinook landed and almost immediately the back ramp started to lower. The SEALs undid their harnesses and stood up. There was a decent-sized moon overhead, so they had decided against using night vision gear. JD slapped Green on the back and they headed down the ramp. Lieutenant Hanks checked them all off, then pointed in the direction of the cottages where the security teams were holed up. They began to jog, their boots thumping on the desert floor.

They had only gone a couple of hundred metres when there was a deafening explosion off to Green's right. JD had trodden on a landmine that sent him spinning through the air, blowing off most of his left leg. Green raced over to him and applied a tourniquet but it barely stemmed the blood that was pumping from the remains of the limb. Jagged pieces of broken bone protruded through bloody flesh, glistening in the moonlight.

'Shit, shit, shit,' said JD.

'You're okay, JD, just stay with me.' He tightened the tourniquet and the blood flow finally slowed. JD was in shock, which is why he wasn't screaming in pain. But the injury was catastrophic and Green didn't see how it could be survivable. He pulled out his XStat syringe. It injected sponge-like pellets into a wound, they would expand over fifteen seconds or so to block severed blood vessels. It wasn't best suited for a full amputation but it was better than nothing.

He did the best job he could with the XStat, then undid JD's vest and ripped open his shirt. He stuck a circular IV device onto the middle of his chest. He found the sternum and pushed the IV hard so that the needles penetrated. In combat there was no time to fumble around with a needle and hunt for a vein, the patch was put in position and hit hard. Job done. He began feeding ketamine through the IV.

Lieutenant Hanks knelt down next to Green. 'How's he doing?'

'We need to get him back to the airbase now.'

'Sure, yes. I just need to get confirmation from Captain Haschka.'

'Fuck that,' said Green. 'This mission is over. We're in the middle of a minefield, we're not going anywhere. We need to get JD to hospital, now!'

The lieutenant nodded, then waved two more SEALs over and they carried JD back to the Chinook and up the ramp. The rest of the SEALs joined them, taking care where they put their feet as they retraced their steps.

As soon as all the Navy SEALs were on board, the ramp came up and the rotors began to spin.

JD lay on the floor between the seats. His face was ashen and his eyes were wide and staring. He grabbed Green's arm. 'Pete.'

'I'm here, mate. Don't worry.'

'Pete, go see my dad, okay?' His voice was little more than a whisper and Green had to put his ear near the man's mouth to hear what he was saying. 'Take him the dog tags. Tell him I love him.'

'You can tell him yourself, JD.'

JD shook his head. 'Swear. Swear you'll do it.'

The Chinook lifted off the ground and turned west, towards Turkey.

'You're going to be okay, JD.' Green patted the man's hand. It was cold and the life was fast fading from his eyes. He wasn't going to be okay, and they both knew it. 'I'll go and see him in Ho Chi Minh City. Hell, all the stories you've told me about him, I feel like I know him already.'

JD forced a smile, shuddered, then released his grip on Green's arm and went still.

The lieutenant looked at Green hopefully, but his face fell when Green shook his head.

'Shit,' said the lieutenant.

'Somebody needs to have a word with that CIA lady when

we get back,' Green shouted above the roar of the turbines. 'She sent us into a bloody minefield. How does that happen?'

'That's a good question.'

'Yeah? Well, I just hope that somebody asks her for an answer. Though my guess is we won't see her again. Not if she knows what's good for her.' He reached out and gently took both sets of dog tags from around JD's neck.

'Will you go and see JD's dad?'

'Hell, yes. I promised. This Captain Haschka, he's a SEAL, right?'

The lieutenant nodded. 'He's a good guy.'

'You need to tell him what happened to JD. And then you need to tell him to get that Reaper to unleash a Hellfire missile and blow that bastard Rafiq to Kingdom Come. If he does that, at least some good will have come from this shit storm.'

'I'm on it,' said the lieutenant.

CHAPTER 2

The Hercules taxied off the main runway and over to a large grey hangar where three white SUVs and a large military truck were waiting. SAS Sergeant Matt Standing peered out of the window. 'Welcome to Mărculeşti International Airport,' he said.

'You been here before?' asked Jack Ellis. He was tall and lanky with soulful brown eyes and a drooping moustache. He had picked up the nickname 'Thing One' to differentiate him from his twin brother, Joe, who had joined the regiment a year after Jack and was promptly designated 'Thing Two'. Joe was sitting on the other side of the cabin. Between them was a stack of wooden boxes containing the equipment they would be using in Moldova. They were all wearing desert camouflage fatigues and had holstered Glocks. It was a military flight and there had been no Border Force checks on leaving Brize Norton. There were four SAS troopers with Standing – Jack and Joe Ellis, Billy Green and Alan Sage. Billy Green was a medic and was the only trooper that Standing hadn't worked with before.

'Never had a reason,' said Standing. 'Moldova is a tiny country, about the same size as Belgium, with a population of about three million. In the grand scheme of things it doesn't account for much. If it wasn't for what Putin did in Ukraine,

HMG wouldn't give a toss. But after the Russian invasion of Ukraine, the powers that be decided they needed to strengthen the rest of the former USSR countries.'

'You think that's a smart move?' asked Alan Sage. He was in his mid-thirties, a former Para who was cultivating a long bushy beard in anticipation of being sent to Syria. 'Remember all the training and equipment we gave to the Afghans? At the first hint of trouble they dropped their weapons and ran for the hills. Coming soon to a dinghy near you.'

'I think they're hoping the Moldovans will be more like Ukrainians and less like the Afghans,' said Standing. 'You've got to admit, the Ukrainians put up a hell of a fight. But yeah, it makes sense that we offer what help we can. If we don't, there's no telling what Russia might try next.'

The Hercules came to a halt and the engines powered down. It had been a five-hour flight and Standing had slept most of the way. Like soldiers the world over he had learned to grab food and sleep whenever it was available. The loadmaster, a big bruiser of a Cockney with a shaved head, operated the mechanism to lower the main ramp. Standing's team unclipped their harnesses, stood up and stretched.

'Where will we be kipping?' asked Billy Green as he grabbed his backpack.

'That'll be up to our hosts,' said Standing. 'But we're only here for four nights. Some basic anti-tank training and you can spend a day with their medics, showing them our gear and how best to use it. And Sagey can show them our comms systems.'

'These guys are special forces, right?' said Jack Ellis. 'How special can they be with a population so small?'

'That's what I was told,' said Standing. 'But yes, it's a good point. Their army only has seven thousand men.' He shrugged. 'Ours not to reason why.'

The ramp was down now. Standing and his team headed out. The loadmaster was preparing his lifting trolley and he nodded at Standing. 'Can you check that their truck's ready, Matt? We're on a tight schedule today.'

'Will do, Dave.'

Standing walked down the ramp. Waiting for him were two big, barrel-chested men wearing camouflage fatigues. They both had Russian-made AK-74 assault rifles hanging from slings and Makarov pistols in holsters. The larger of the two men stepped forward. 'Which of you is Standing?' he asked in a heavy accent. He had a square chin that looked as if it would have no problem in shrugging off a punch, and a heavy brow over a spreading nose. He would be a hard man to take down in a fight.

'To be fair, we're all on our feet,' said Jack Ellis.

'Seriously, Jack?' said Standing scornfully. He raised his hand. 'I'm Standing.'

'We're all Standing,' said Jack Ellis.

'I'm Spartacus,' said his brother.

'Guys, give it a rest,' hissed Standing. 'Show some respect.'

'I am Colonel Damian Rusu,' said the Moldovan. He nodded at his companion. 'This is Captain Leonid Melnic.' Melnic nodded curtly.

'We have transport to our camp, are you okay to start work today?' the colonel asked.

'Absolutely, sir,' said Standing. 'We're here to work.'

'The camp is about two hours away, not far from the border with Transnistria. That's where our problems lie, so I thought it best we train there.'

'Sounds good,' said Standing.

Transnistria was a breakaway region of Moldova, close to Ukraine, where Russia stationed up to two thousand soldiers, in addition to the region's own troops. The presence of so many Russian soldiers in Transnistria was one of the reasons the UK government was interested in helping to support the Moldovan armed forces.

The loadmaster brought the first four of the boxes down the ramp on the lifting trolley. The colonel waved over at the truck and motioned for it to come closer to the plane. He grinned when he saw the writing on the side of the boxes. 'Excellent,' he said. 'How many Javelins did you bring?'

'Eight, plus a training model,' said Standing. 'I'm told there are more on the way.'

'You know they are $80,000 each?' said the colonel.

'That's what I heard.'

'It sounds expensive until you realise that each Javelin can destroy a four-million-dollar tank. That makes it a bargain.'

'I guess so,' said Standing.

The truck stopped by the side of the Hercules. The driver climbed out and opened up the rear of the truck. Four men climbed out of one of the SUVs and jogged over to help the loadmaster with the boxes.

Standing introduced his team to the colonel. 'Billy is our medic, Jack and Joe have had a lot of experience with the Javelin and Alan is our communications expert. We'll be showing you how to access real-time satellite imagery on the battlefield.'

'I'm looking forward to that,' said the colonel. He looked quizzically at the Ellis boys. 'So you are twins?'

'Peas in a pod,' said Jack Ellis.

'That's very unusual,' said the colonel. 'To see twins in special forces.'

'Well, Billy here is a twin as well,' said Standing. 'His brother is also an SAS medic.'

'Real twin or fake twin?' asked Joe Ellis.

'What's the difference?' asked Green.

'Identical or non-identical?' said Jack Ellis. 'Non-identicals don't really count as twins, they're just siblings who shared a womb.'

'We're identical,' said Green.

'You first or second?' asked Joe Ellis.

'Second. Pete was in a rush to get out and he kicked me in the face. Broke my nose. He's been in a rush ever since.'

The men loaded the first of the Javelins into the back of the truck while the loadmaster took the trolley back up the ramp.

'When's your brother back?' asked Standing.

'Couple of weeks,' said Green. 'But we don't usually see much of each other even when we're both in the country. For some reason they wouldn't put us in the same squadron. Plus he's boat troop and I'm mountain troop. And we're both medics and that's another reason to keep us apart.'

The SAS was divided into four squadrons – A, B, D and G – each made up of about seventy men and commanded by a major. Each squadron was in turn divided into four troops of sixteen men and a small HQ section. Each troop specialised in an area of warfare. Air Troop were specialists in different parachuting techniques, Boat Troop had maritime skills, Mountain Troop specialised in fighting in the cold and Mobility Troop were trained to fight in the desert and were also skilled motor mechanics. The troops were further divided into four patrols, each of four men, each of them having a special skill, such as demolitions, signals, languages or medicine.

Jack Ellis laughed. 'Yeah, they tried to keep me and Joe apart but we weren't having it.'

'They were probably worried that twins would fuck with the officers,' said Standing.

'And they were right,' said Joe Ellis. 'Anything goes wrong and we just blame each other.'

'You mean I blame you,' said his brother. 'I never fuck up.'

'If only that were true.'

The soldiers finished loading the final boxes into the truck. The loadmaster went over to Standing. 'That's us,' he said. 'We'll see you in four days, right?'

'Hopefully. Thanks for your help.'

The loadmaster went back into the hold of the Hercules and the ramp slowly closed.

'If you and your men go with Captain Melnic, we'll go straight to the camp,' said the colonel. 'We can eat there and start the training.'

'Excellent,' said Standing.

The colonel nodded and went back with his men to the SUVs. Captain Melnic took Standing and the team over to the nearest SUV and they climbed in. The captain started the engine as Standing got into the front passenger seat and Green, Sage and the Ellis boys climbed into the back. There were three rows of seats, so plenty of room for them to stretch out.

The colonel's SUV led the way, followed by the truck. Another SUV full of soldiers followed and Standing's SUV brought up the rear of the convoy.

Melnic's English turned out to be not great and none of the

SAS team spoke Romanian – the main language spoken in Moldova – so they took the opportunity to grab some sleep.

In just over two hours they arrived at their destination, a cluster of four long wooden huts in a compound surrounded by a chainlink fence. More than a dozen SUVs and trucks were parked in the middle of the compound. It didn't appear to be a military base and there was no obvious security. They drove through an unmanned gate and it wasn't until they were parking that anyone appeared. Two young men in camouflage fatigues came out of one of the huts, carrying AK-74s.

Colonel Rusu climbed out of his SUV and spoke to the men. Standing and his team got out and looked around. 'What is this place?' asked Green.

'Our base for the next three days,' said Standing.

'It's a bit basic,' said Sage.

'We're not here on holiday,' said Standing. 'Grab your gear.'

They pulled their backpacks from the rear of the SUV. The colonel came over. 'I'll show you your barracks and then we can eat in the mess,' he said. 'You can give the men a presentation after we've eaten, then I thought we could do a live firing. I have had some targets prepared.'

'Perfect,' said Standing.

The colonel took them to one of the wooden buildings and showed them inside. There were eight double bunk beds and a large bathroom. It was basic but clean and would do the job.

They chose their bunks and dropped their backpacks, then followed the colonel to another hut where a dozen tables had been pushed together to allow two dozen men to eat together. The colonel sat at one end and pointed for the SAS team to sit around him. More men in fatigues joined them, and two cooks in white uniforms emerged from a side door and began serving food – bowls of pork stew, fried vegetables, stuffed bell peppers and stuffed cabbage meals. It was good, hearty food and they devoured it greedily.

'So what is this place, Colonel?' asked Standing.

'It used to be used by scouts,' said the colonel. 'They were disbanded during the Communist years. They got going again after the USSR fell but this place was never used, so the Army took it over. It's too small for most units but it suits special forces just fine. And it's close to Transnistria, which is extremely useful for us.'

They finished their food and the chefs cleared away the plates and dishes. 'I thought you could give your presentation here,' said the colonel. 'I'll get the men to move the tables and give you some space.'

The Ellis boys went off to fetch their Javelin training unit as the Moldovan soldiers moved the tables to the side of the room and laid out the chairs in rows.

When they returned, there were almost thirty men in fatigues sitting and waiting, most of them smoking.

Jack Ellis gave them a quick guide to the Javelin, the American-made fire-and-forget missile that had all but made tanks redundant during the Russian invasion of Ukraine. The Americans had shipped more than seven thousand units to Ukraine and the Ukrainians had made good use of them.

The missile could be fired directly at buildings and even low-flying helicopters, but its top attack system was what made it so effective against tanks. Tanks had most of their armour on the sides, so the missile was designed to fly up to one hundred and fifty metres in the air before diving down onto the target, hitting the tank's weakest point – its roof.

The missile had two warheads – the first to detonate any

explosive reactive armour, then a main charge to penetrate the tank's primary armour. The Javelin was pretty much the perfect tank killer, and the colonel was practically salivating while Jack Ellis explained how it worked.

'The manufacturer says they have an effective range of two thousand five hundred metres, but we've used them at four thousand metres with no problems at all,' said Jack Ellis. 'I think our longest hit has been four thousand five hundred, so I would personally ignore the two thousand five hundred metre figure and go with four thousand, or two and a half miles.'

Joe Ellis ran through the various parts of the missile system and explained how they worked, then he demonstrated the individual controls. It was almost idiot-proof – the operator pointed the unit and locked onto the target using a small video screen. Once the target was locked in, a simple pull on the trigger launched the missile. Once launched, there was no further input required from the operator, the missile took care of business itself. It really was fire and forget.

The Ellis boys let the soldiers play with the controls until they were all familiar with the unit, then the colonel announced that they were all to head outside.

The men went out into the compound and climbed into the SUVs. Standing and his team rode with the colonel, who insisted on driving. 'I have set up some targets in a field not far away,' said the colonel. 'I couldn't get tanks but we have several old vehicles we can use.'

They drove out of the camp and along a narrow road between ploughed fields. The sky was darkening but there were still a couple of hours of daylight left. The colonel led the convoy past a wooded area and then stopped. He wound the window down and pointed at three rusting saloon cars that had been abandoned in a field. 'Are they suitable?' the colonel asked.

'They'll be fine,' said Standing. 'The sensors can lock onto anything.' He pointed at a hill more than a mile away. 'We need line of sight to fire, can we use that hill over there?'

'Not a problem,' said the colonel. He put the SUV in gear and ten minutes later they were parking at the base of the hill. Standing and the colonel climbed out of the SUV. The colonel's men got out of their vehicles and gathered around him as he explained what was going to happen. The Ellis boys fetched one of the Javelin boxes from the truck.

Sage was scanning the surrounding countryside through a pair of binoculars. He looked over at Standing. 'Matt, we've got visitors.'

Standing frowned. 'What?'

'Eight quad bikes, heading west. About two kilometres away.'

'Who the hell are they?' said Standing. Sage gave him the binoculars and Standing scanned the area. There were eight quad bikes cutting across a field in the distance. They were big vehicles, each with a rider and a rear-facing passenger. All the passengers were cradling AK-74s.

He looked over at Colonel Rusu. 'Who would they be, Colonel?'

Standing gave the binoculars to the colonel, who muttered under his breath as he checked out the intruders. 'Bad news,' he said. 'They're Wagner Group.'

Standing frowned. 'You're sure?' The Wagner Group was a Russian paramilitary company that functioned as a private army, almost always carrying out missions that the Russian government wanted to keep at arm's length. The organisation was thought to have been behind the assassinations of several Ukrainian leaders during the Russian invasion of Ukraine.

The colonel nodded. 'They've come over a few times recently. They're based in Transnistria.' He gave the binoculars back to Standing.

'To do what?' asked Standing.

'To make a nuisance of themselves. Anything that will keep pressure on the Moldovan government. They carry out attacks here and in Transnistria. They want Moldova to crack down on the Transnistria rebels so that Russia will have an excuse to invade.'

'So they carry out false flag operations?'

Colonel Rusu nodded. 'Both ways. Sometimes they make it look as if Moldova is attacking Transnistria, other times it's Transnistria attacking Moldova. Anything to keep tensions high. So they sneak over the border and blow things up here or assassinate local politicians. But recently they blew up broadcast towers and shot at a Russian munitions depot in Transnistria, and Ukrainian infiltrators were blamed. But I ask you, why would Moldova want to provoke Russia? We've seen what happened to Ukraine. There's nothing to be gained by poking the Russian bear.'

'So what do you think they're up to today?'

'They're probably going to disable the electricity substation. We are totally dependent on Russia for our energy. All our natural gas is imported from Russia and three quarters of our electricity comes from Transnistria, and of course they use Russian gas to generate it. The substation is an easy target. They disable that and most of the country will lose power.'

Standing looked through the binoculars again. The quad bikes were heading for a squat grey concrete building surrounded by transformers and circuit breakers. Power lines reached out across the fields and the site was surrounded by a high wire fence.

'Do you want to stop them, Colonel?'

'They'd see us coming across the fields. There'd be a lot of casualties. And there's always a risk of the Russians using any armed confrontation as an excuse for invasion.' He shrugged. 'If lives were at risk, we would intervene, but if they are only damaging property, my standing orders are not to get involved if it means putting my men at risk.'

Standing grinned. 'You're missing something, Colonel.' He gestured at the Javelin boxes.

The colonel frowned, then he smiled as realisation dawned. 'You're okay with that?'

'Colonel, they're your weapons, we're just here to advise.'

'Then let's do it.'

Standing turned towards Sage. 'How far away are they, Alan?'

'Just under four thousand metres.'

'We can do it from here, Colonel,' said Standing. 'Do you want to do the honours?'

'Definitely.'

'Joe, Jack, can you prepare a Javelin?'

'Sure,' said Jack Ellis. He and his brother opened one of the Javelin boxes.

Standing used the binoculars again. The eight quad bikes were now parked and the riders had dismounted. They were gathered together about fifty metres from the quad bikes. One of the men, presumably the leader, was pointing towards the substation.

The Ellis boys finished preparing the Javelin and positioned the launcher on the colonel's shoulder.

Standing watched as the colonel aimed at the quad bike in the centre of the group. He selected the target and nodded at Standing. 'Yes?'

'Looks good, sir,' said Standing.

'Okay to fire?'

'Okay to fire.'

The colonel pulled the trigger. There was a whooshing sound and the missile leapt from the tube. Once the missile was about fifty feet away, the main thruster unit kicked in and the missile accelerated and headed up into the sky. It levelled off at a hundred and fifty metres above the ground and streaked towards the electricity substation.

The Moldovan soldiers were shielding their eyes with their hands as they followed the missile's progress through the sky.

The Wagner mercenaries didn't hear the missile's approach until the last second. A few of the men turned to watch as it transitioned into a dive. The missile hit its target and instantly exploded in a ball of flame. Most of the mercenaries threw themselves to the ground but some stood transfixed in shock.

'A perfect shot, Colonel,' said Standing. 'Well done.' The missile had destroyed all the quad bikes but it didn't look as if any of the men had been injured. The Javelin was designed to minimise collateral damage so that tanks could be destroyed in civilian settings.

The colonel's men punched the air in triumph and cheered.

Jack Ellis took the launcher from the colonel and placed it back in the box. It would be recycled later.

'I can see why it's a game changer,' said the colonel. 'Just a few men armed with Javelins could take out an entire tank battalion.'

'We'll run various strategies by you that can achieve that

objective,' said Standing. 'What do you want to do about the mercenaries?' He gave him the binoculars.

The colonel studied the men in the distance. They had turned away from the substation and had begun walking across the fields, back the way they had come. 'They have a long walk ahead of them,' he said.

'Do you want to go after them, sir?'

The colonel smiled. 'I don't think so,' he said. 'Let them return to Transnistria and explain how they lost all their vehicles.'

'You don't want to capture them?'

'At this stage it's not a good idea to poke the bear,' said the colonel. 'That time will come, but not today.'

'You know best, sir.'

CHAPTER 3

The SAS trooper had his Heckler up at his shoulder and his knees slightly bent as he edged towards the doorway. The room was full of smoke and the full-face respirator he was wearing protected his lungs and eyes but restricted his peripheral vision, so he was moving his head from side to side. Matt Standing was tucked in behind him. Standing's respirator was misting up, which was a pain, but there was nothing he could do about it.

The trooper's name was Eddie Longworth but everyone used his nickname, Short Arse, and he was happy enough to answer to it. He spotted a figure in the corner of the room. A big bald man holding an AK-47. Short Arse swung around and put two rounds in the man's chest, a perfect double tap, or it would have been if the man hadn't been wearing a bullet-proof vest.

'Head shot!' shouted Standing, and Short Arse put two in the man's face.

'Sorry, Sarge,' said Short Arse, but Standing ignored him. They headed to the left, to another doorway. The smoke was thicker there and Short Arse hesitated. Standing gave him a slight push, it was important to keep the momentum going. Short Arse bent lower and went through the door. He tracked to the left and immediately spotted the target – a tall, thin man

with a moustache, holding a shotgun. Short Arse fired immediately, two shots to the chest, dead centre. Perfect.

Short Arse was already tracking to the right. There were
two figures behind a cheap plastic sofa. A woman, short and
dark-haired, and next to her a snarling man with a black-and-
white headscarf, holding a gun to her throat. It was always a
tough call but there was enough of the man's chest visible to
put in a tight double tap and that's what Short Arse did before
moving towards the far doorway.

Standing reached out to touch the trooper's right shoulder
and eased him around so that he could see the figure crouched
in the corner, a swarthy bruiser of a man with an AK-47 up
to his shoulder. Short Arse muttered under his breath and put
two shots into the man's chest.

'Sorry, Sarge,' he mumbled, but Standing again ignored the
apology.

Short Arse moved forward, hesitated for a second at the
doorway, then quickly crossed the threshold, sweeping left until
he saw that the area was clear, then sweeping right where he
immediately saw two targets. The first was a middle-aged,
bearded man, his right hand clenched on a black object, next
to him a blonde girl with both hands on a revolver. Short Arse
aimed his gun at the man's chest, clocked that he was holding
a mobile phone, and put two shots in the blonde girl's chest.
He checked the remaining corner of the room, and headed for
the exit.

Standing picked up the cut-out target of the man with the
phone and followed him out.

The next room was bare, with a large sign on the wall saying
EXERCISE OVER, MAKE WEAPONS SAFE.

Short Arse lowered his Heckler, clicked the fire selector

to the safety position and pushed open the door marked EXIT.

There were three other troopers waiting for him and they cheered as he pulled off his respirator. They had been watching his progress on a series of CCTV monitors on one wall.

Standing closed the door and took off his own respirator and put it on a table to his left. Short Arse put his Heckler in a rack by the door. Like the other three troopers he had a holstered Glock on his right thigh. Standing's weapon was higher up, on his hip. The four men frowned as he put the wooden target on the floor, facing them.

'That was all pretty good, guys, you're starting to get a feel for it,' he said. 'Just remember to keep moving. The moment you stop, you make yourself a target.' He looked at their faces and grinned. 'And you all made the same mistake in the final room. Every one of you.' He turned and gestured at the cut-out of the Arab man holding the phone. 'All of you double tapped the woman with the handgun, and kudos for that. Man, woman, or even child, if they're pointing a gun at you they're fair game. And all of you spotted that this guy was holding a mobile and not a gun, so you gave him a free pass. But take a closer look.' He stepped to the side and pointed to the man's open jacket. Underneath were blocks of explosive and pieces of coiled wire.

'Oh, for fuck's sake,' said Smart Arse. 'You tricked us.'

'And that's a problem because terrorists are never devious?' said Standing. 'You spotted the phone, but not the suicide vest. And that phone is probably what sets off the explosive. He pushes one button and you're all dead. So what do we do?'

'Head shots, quick double tap to the face,' said Smart Arse. 'Not a chest shot because . . .'

'Because it might set off the vest.'

'Exactly,' said Standing. 'And you have to be constantly assessing your targets. Ideally you want a double tap in the centre of mass, bang bang to the heart, but if you see a suicide vest you go straight for a head shot. Ditto a Kevlar vest.'

'Sarge, why not go for the head every time?' asked one of the recruits. The other three troopers grimaced. Questions generally weren't welcomed in the regular Army, other than asking 'how high?' when told that they had to jump. Questioning a sergeant in the Paras would more than likely be met with a tirade of abuse, but the SAS worked differently. Success in the regular Army came when soldiers followed orders, but in special forces it was more important that the men thought for themselves, and providing a question was sensible it would be treated with respect. In this case, the question posed by Richard 'Spotty' Baxter, a lanky Geordie with an over-large Adam's apple, was a valid one.

'Your head is about a third of the width of your chest, so it's a much smaller target,' said Standing. 'And it takes a lot more effort to move the chest out of the way. So it's an easier shot, and at your skill level that's important. You'll see the old-timers going solely for head shots but by that stage they've fired tens of thousands of rounds. Your average SAS trooper fires more rounds in a year than a Para will fire in their whole military career, so eventually they reach the point where they can pull off head shots every time. But you guys, good as you are, are some way off that. A loose round in the CQBH means you hit a wall, but do that in a crowded plane or a shopping centre full of screaming civilians and you're going to ruin somebody's day.'

Baxter nodded. 'Got it, Sarge.'

'Okay, guys, grab a bite and I'll see you over at the shooting range.'

The four troopers nodded and headed over to the mess hall. Standing looked up at the sky and sighed. He had been up since dawn, jogging around the Stirling Lines base for forty minutes followed by an hour in the gym, then showering before devouring two bacon rolls and a mug of coffee in the Sergeants' Mess. He had spent the rest of the morning running the new recruits through the Close Quarter Battle House. The guys were young and enthusiastic, but they had a lot to learn.

The SAS was having something of a recruitment crisis. The Regiment usually had between four hundred and four hundred and fifty men, and needed to recruit up to thirty men annually just to stay at that level. There were two selection courses a year, with most applicants coming from the Parachute Regiment. Up to one hundred and twenty candidates applied and about ten per cent made it through the rigorous selection procedure. The problem was that the powers that be wanted to get the Regiment up to six hundred men, and it was proving difficult to draw in the extra recruits. Many soldiers simply didn't want to join the special forces group, they knew how demanding the job was, and how it often played havoc with relationships. SAS soldiers could be sent anywhere in the world at a moment's notice and be away for months at a time. And most regular soldiers just weren't interested in the SAS's regime of non-stop training and deployment, disparagingly referred to as 'the wheel of death'.

As a result, those recruits who did make it through Selection had to be trained quickly, and there was a lot to learn. That meant that literally the day after arriving back from Moldova, Standing had been tasked with training four recent additions to the Regiment. They were all full of vim and vigour and fit as the proverbial butcher's dog, but while most of them had been in combat with the Paras in Syria, Afghanistan and Iraq, being in the SAS required a whole new set of skills.

There was another reason for teaching the recruits to go for chest shots. Most of the time Paras fought at a distance, it was rare for them to be involved in close quarter fighting. More often than not they'd be in cover taking shots at the enemy hundreds of metres away. But the SAS often dealt with their opposition up close and personal, and shooting a man in the head at short range meant that you were looking into his eyes when you pulled the trigger. That was a big thing. A very big thing. And if a trooper wasn't used to it, they would hesitate, no matter how committed they were. They'd see the look of panic and terror in the target's eyes and there'd be a brief moment when their conscience would kick in and they'd worry if they were doing the right thing, and that merest hesitation could cost them their own life. Better to stick to chest shots until killing became second nature. Even then, as Standing knew from experience, it was never easy to look into a man's eyes as you took his life. But that wasn't something he'd be comfortable explaining to the new recruits.

As Standing walked towards the Sergeants' Mess, he saw Billy Green pacing up and down outside one of the massive beige hangars that dotted the thousand-acre site. 'Are you okay, Billy?' Standing shouted, but Green didn't react.

Standing walked over to him. 'What's wrong, Billy?'

Green shook his head but didn't reply. He turned away, his head down. Whatever it was, it was bad. Standing put a hand on the man's shoulder. 'What is it, maybe I can help?'

Green shook his head again. 'It's Pete.'

A cold hand gripped Standing's heart. The way Green was behaving could only mean one thing, but that didn't make sense because Pete Green wasn't in a trouble spot, he was away on leave.

'He's dead, Matt. He's fucking dead.'

Green shuddered. Standing pulled Green towards him and hugged him. He didn't know what to say. He'd lost comrades before and that was devastating enough. But Green had lost a brother, and more than that, he'd lost a twin, and Standing couldn't imagine how that felt. 'I'm sorry, mate,' he said.

'I can't fucking believe it.'

Standing had a stack of questions, but he knew that Green didn't need to be interrogated, not just then anyway. 'You need a drink,' said Standing. 'We both do.'

He put his arm around Green's shoulders and walked him to the Sergeants' Mess. The place was empty, so Standing put Green at a table by the window and went behind the bar, where he grabbed a bottle of Johnnie Walker Black Label – Green's drink of choice – and two glasses. He joined Green at the table and poured two large measures of whisky. Standing picked up his glass. 'He was one of the good guys,' he said. 'The best.'

Green nodded and picked up his glass. 'Cheers, Matt.'

'He'll be missed, mate,' said Standing. He clinked his glass against Green's and the two men drank.

'I can't fucking believe it,' said Green, shaking his head. 'I just can't get my fucking head around it. Pete was always one of the lucky ones, you know? I was the one who acted like a fucking magnet for rounds. He never got hit, not once, and he'd been in some sticky situations.'

'What happened?'

Green didn't reply. He refilled his glass and took another drink. Standing took the opportunity to take out his phone to text Alan Sage and Terry 'Paddy' Ireland. SERGEANTS MESS. NOW. He sent the same message to Joe and Jack Ellis.

Standing sipped his whisky and watched Green over the top of his glass. People dealt with death in different ways. Green was generally calm and collected but he had a Glock strapped to his leg and sometimes people reacted violently.

'You okay, Billy?' It was a lame question, but Standing couldn't think of anything else to say.

Green forced a grin. 'I'm not dead, so that's got to be worth something. Fuck, Matt. I just feel numb. Like, I'm processing it but it doesn't feel real.'

'How did you find out?'

'My sister just phoned. The British embassy in Bangkok called our mum and told her. Mum's in bits. Obviously.'

'What was he doing in Bangkok?'

'He wasn't in Bangkok, that's where the embassy is. He was in a place called Koh Chang. One of the islands.' Green drained his glass. 'The embassy said Pete had killed himself. Suicide.'

'Bollocks,' said Standing.

'That's what I said. Pete would never top himself. He was due back next week.'

'What was he doing in Koh Chang?'

'I don't know. Last time we spoke he was in Vietnam.'

'Holiday, right?'

'Yeah. Who kills himself on holiday, Matt? Nobody, that's who.'

'What did the embassy say happened?'

'Just that he killed himself. And that they can recommend a company who will ship his body back to the UK if that's what we want. My mum doesn't know what to do.'

'Sorry, mate.' Standing took a sip of his whisky.

Alan Sage appeared at the door. 'What's up?' he asked as he walked over to the table. He was wearing desert fatigues and like Green had a Glock in a holster strapped to his thigh.

'Pete's dead,' said Standing.

'Get the fuck out of here.'

'Billy's just found out.' He gestured at the bar. 'Get yourself a glass. Grab one for Paddy, he should be on his way.'

Sage put his hand on Green's shoulder. 'Sorry, mate,' he said, then walked over to the bar.

A captain walked by outside, then he stopped when he saw them sitting at the table. He was a recent arrival at Stirling Lines. Standing had met him a few times, his name was Clive Tomlin and he had transferred in from The Rifles. Troopers and sergeants could stay in the Regiment for as long as they could carry out the job, but officers came and went, usually staying for between two and three years. The officers were generally referred to as Ruperts, but Tomlin had earned the nickname Upchuck after throwing up in the Killing House. They were initiating the young officer into the delights of being under live fire. Tomlin had been placed between two terrorist targets and told to stay put. Two troopers had then run into the room, guns blazing, and had emptied their magazines into the targets, the rounds only inches away from the captain. The captain had stood his ground, albeit with a lot of flinching, but immediately afterwards had bent over and emptied his stomach.

Tomlin frowned as he spotted the bottle of whisky. Standing stared at the officer, narrowed his eyes and gave a small shake of his head. Tomlin's frown deepened, then he obviously realised that something was going on that he'd best stay out of, so he nodded and walked away.

Sage returned with two glasses. He sat down, poured whisky into one of the glasses and raised it into the air. 'It's not the years in your life that count, it's the life in your years.' He drained his glass and refilled it.

'Who said that?' asked Standing.

'Abraham Lincoln,' said Sage. 'So what the fuck happened?'

'Pete was on holiday in Thailand,' said Standing. 'The embassy says he topped himself.'

'Bull-fucking-shit.'

'That's what I said.'

'No way would Pete do that,' said Sage. 'So what did the embassy say?'

Standing looked over at Green, who was staring into his glass. 'I didn't get any details,' said Green. 'The embassy just told my mum that he was dead and that we should arrange to ship his body home.'

Terry Ireland walked in. He was wearing a black Nike track-suit and his face was bathed in sweat. 'What's going on?' he asked in his strong Norfolk accent. He was tall and broad-shouldered and had recently shaved off his beard, leaving pale patches of skin around his chin.

Sage poured a whisky and handed him the glass. 'Pete's dead,' he said.

'Fuck.' Ireland took the glass and knocked the contents back in a couple of swallows. 'Fuck,' he said again, and sat down. Sage refilled his glass.

Green stood up, catching them all by surprise. 'I've got to go to Thailand,' he said.

'Sit down, Billy. We need a plan.'

'I told you what my plan is, I'm going to Thailand to find out what happened to Pete.'

'That's fine, that can be arranged. But we need a plan. You can't just go off half-cock.'

'Fuck you, Matt. He's not your brother.'

'No, but he was a good mate and I want to find out what happened as much as you do.'

Green sneered at Standing. 'Not the same,' he said. 'Nowhere near the same.'

'Billy, I'm on your side here. We're all in shock. Whatever we do has to be done with a clear head. Now sit down.'

'Fuck you,' said Green, and he reached for his gun.

'Whoa!' shouted Sage. He jumped to his feet and grabbed Green's gun arm.

Standing was also up in a fraction of a second, and he put his hands on Green's shoulders. There was a blood lust in the man's eyes and Standing shook him. 'Billy, get a grip.'

Green gritted his teeth and his nostrils flared.

'Billy!' said Standing, louder this time, and he tightened his grip on the man's shoulders.

Green strained against Sage, who was holding his elbow with both hands, and then he suddenly relaxed and the rage faded from his eyes. 'Sorry, Matt,' he said quietly.

'It's okay,' said Standing, letting go of his shoulders.

Green looked at Sage and smiled. 'I'm okay, Alan.'

Sage released his grip on Green's elbow and Green raised both his hands. 'I'm good.' He sat down and picked up his glass.

Sage and Ireland both looked at Standing and the message was clear – was it a good idea to let Green keep his weapon? Standing would have preferred to have taken the Glock off him, but that was a big step, akin to saying that Green wasn't to be trusted.

Green saw the look of concern on Standing's face. 'I'm okay, Matt. Really.' He picked up his glass and drank his whisky. 'I'm going out there. To Thailand.'

'Okay,' said Standing.

'I want to find out what happened. And I want to bring Pete back. He belongs here.'

'No argument there,' said Standing.

Sage refilled their glasses. Ireland raised his glass. 'We'll miss you, Pete. One of the best.'

'One of the best,' repeated Sage.

'Gone too soon,' said Standing.

Green nodded and drained his glass. The other three men followed his example.

Standing got to his feet. 'I'm going to talk to the colonel,' he said.

'I'll come with you,' said Green. He pushed himself up but he was unsteady and swayed back and forth before dropping back onto his chair.

'You stay with the lads,' said Standing. He gestured at the half-empty bottle of whisky. 'There's more behind the bar if you need it.'

On the way out he bumped into Jack and Joe Ellis. Standing brought them up to speed and they disappeared into the Sergeants' Mess as he headed over to the admin block.

CHAPTER 4

Standing strode along the corridor towards the office of Colonel Davies. His secretary was sitting at her desk and his door was closed. Debbie Gilmore was married to one of the Regiment's longest-serving sergeant majors and was rumoured to be a cordon bleu cook. She looked up from her computer and smiled. 'Hi, Matt, the colonel has said he doesn't want to be disturbed.'

'Sorry, Debbie, this is important,' he said, and strode past her desk. He grabbed the handle to the colonel's door and pushed it open.

'Matt!' Debbie shouted, but he was already in.

Colonel Davies was sitting back in his chair with his boots on his desk, talking into his phone. He frowned in annoyance when he saw Standing.

'I need to talk to you, boss,' said Standing.

The colonel continued to glare at Standing. He was in his fifties, not an ounce of fat on him, with close-cropped grey hair. His nose and cheeks were flecked with broken blood vessels and he had a five o'clock shadow, but he still looked a good decade younger than his true age. He had been due to retire the previous year but the MoD had persuaded him to stay on, allegedly at the insistence of the Prime Minister. 'I'll call you back,' the colonel snapped, then he slammed down the phone.

'I'm sorry about this, boss, but it's important.'

The colonel stood up. His fatigues were the four-colour woodland pattern DPM – disruptive pattern material – and he had a SIG Sauer on a holster on his waist. His eyes narrowed. 'Have you been drinking, Matt? You smell like a distillery.'

Standing held up his hand to cut the colonel short. 'Pete Green is dead. Billy has just found out. He's in the Sergeants' Mess, Sagey and Paddy are watching him.'

The colonel sat down heavily, shaking his head. 'What the fuck happened?'

'They're saying he killed himself.'

The colonel screwed up his face. 'Impossible.'

'Yeah, that's what we all think.' He quickly explained about the phone call from the British embassy in Thailand.

'Thailand? He was supposed to be in Vietnam, wasn't he?'

Standing nodded. 'That's right.'

'He should have notified us if he was heading to another country. Do we know what he was doing there?'

'Billy thought he was on holiday. We all did.'

'There's no suggestion he was doing some off-the-books freelance operation?'

'Pete wasn't the type, boss.'

The colonel rubbed the back of his neck. 'How's Billy taking it?'

'He's calm enough but he's literally only just found out. You know how close they were. Peas in a pod. Look, boss, Billy is going to want to go out there. There'll be no talking him out of it.'

'Fair enough.'

'I want to go with him, to make sure he doesn't get into trouble.'

'What sort of trouble?'

'Any sort. I just want to keep an eye on him.'

The colonel grimaced and Standing knew exactly what was running through his mind. Trouble spots were popping up all over the world at a time when the Regiment was finding it increasingly difficult to find suitable recruits. The SAS was especially short of sergeants, and Standing was due to fly out to Finland to help train Finnish special forces units on the border with Russia. Pete Green had also been drafted into the assignment, which would leave the colonel two men short. The colonel waved a hand as if brushing away his reservations. 'Billy needs to go and you're right, you should go with him. But, Matt, no vigilante nonsense, okay? If you find out that anything untoward happened to Pete, you go straight to the authorities.'

'Understood, boss.'

The colonel nodded. 'And tell Billy to drop by before you head off. I want to give him my condolences.'

'I will do.'

'When will you go?'

'He wants to go right away but I'm suggesting he waits until his head is clear, so tomorrow. We'll fly to Bangkok, that's where the embassy is, and I guess we need to talk to them first. But Pete died in a place called Koh Chang. I figure that's where Pete's body is. But we'll see what the embassy has to say.'

'What a nightmare,' said the colonel. 'Okay, Matt, do what you have to do. But check in with me, every day.'

'Will do, boss.'

'And please, stay out of trouble.'

'I'll do my best, boss.'

CHAPTER 5

The Thai Airways plane landed five minutes earlier than scheduled but Standing and Green had been in the rear of the economy section, so they were the last off. The upside was that the flight wasn't busy, so they each had a row to themselves and could lie down and get some sleep; the downside was that it took them more than an hour to get through immigration.

Standing had spent most of his time at Heathrow gathering intel on his iPhone while Green knocked back glasses of Johnnie Walker Black Label.

Koh Chang was Thailand's third largest island, behind Phuket and Koh Samui, some three hundred kilometres east of Bangkok. There was no airport on the island and no bridge, the only way to get there was on a ferry which only operated during daylight hours. The island was just over two hundred square kilometres with unspoiled beaches and rainforests and rugged mountains in the middle, most of which was a national park. The population was a little more than eight thousand. Tourism had been hard hit by the Covid pandemic, but the island had started to recover and most of the restaurants and bars had reopened.

Standing had phoned the British embassy in Bangkok and had arranged to meet the official who had contacted Green's mother, so as soon as they had passed through immigration they went to the taxi line and headed for the British embassy. They had no bags to collect – Green had a North Face ruck-sack that he had carried on board and Standing had a black Samsonite cabin case.

The taxi drove on a ten-lane motorway to Bangkok. From a distance they could see what looked like a grey dome almost half a mile high covering the entire city. Standing frowned, wondering what sort of weather phenomenon it could be, then realised it was pollution.

Green had noticed it, too. 'That can't be good for the lungs,' he said.

'We won't be here long,' said Standing.

They were soon driving between the tower blocks, and while the air looked clean enough, Standing knew that the pollution they had seen from the motorway was now deep in his lungs, albeit cooled by the taxi's blistering air conditioning.

'I didn't realise it would be as modern as this,' said Green, looking around. 'If it wasn't for the signs in Thai, this could be any modern big city in the world.'

'What were you expecting?'

'I dunno. Rickshaws and wooden shacks, I suppose.'

Standing laughed. 'Rickshaws were Chinese and even in China I think they went out a hundred years ago,' he said. 'This is a big city. Population ten million.'

'What's London?'

'A bit less.'

They pulled up at a red traffic light. On the building to their left was a huge LED screen showing video adverts. A pretty girl in a green uniform was holding out a credit card. She was replaced by a large Ford pick-up driving across the desert leaving plumes of dust in its wake.

Standing looked to the right. There was another screen there, this one on a pole. And beyond it, halfway up a tower block, was another, much larger, screen, maybe fifty metres high. As the minutes ticked by and the light stayed on red, Standing realised why there were so many screens – they had a captive audience. Though as he looked around he saw that most drivers were ignoring the screens and were busy on their smartphones.

The traffic was heavy, but other than at the traffic lights it was moving smoothly. Motorbikes and scooters were weaving in and out of the cars, half of them working for food delivery companies. The red, white and blue striped Thai flag seemed to be flying from every building and there were pictures of the King and Queen of Thailand wherever they looked.

Eventually the driver pulled up at the kerb and stopped the meter. Standing and Green looked out of the window. They were in front of a large office block.

'No, we want the British embassy,' said Standing.

The driver nodded enthusiastically. 'Yes, British embassy.'

Standing peered at the building. It was a regular office block. According to a large glass and metal sign it was the AIA Sathorn Tower. And to the left of that sign was another for a big leading accountancy firm. 'This can't be right,' he muttered, but he paid the driver and he and Green climbed out with their bags. They looked up at the tower. There must have been almost thirty floors, no way was it an embassy. The building was facing a huge station on the city's Skytrain network and a train rattled by overhead. 'We've been scammed,' said Green.

'Maybe not,' said Standing. He pointed at a small sign on the wall to the left of the building. It was the crest of the British embassy.

'Curiouser and curiouser,' said Green. They took their bags

into a large atrium. Ahead of them was a row of glass and metal turnstiles leading to a left lobby. To their right was a reception desk and several rows of chairs. To the left was a smaller reception desk, this one with a sign saying BRITISH EMBASSY.

'There we go,' said Standing.

A burly Thai man in a grey suit nodded as they headed to the roped-off entrance. Standing explained who they were and that they were there to see Ian Butcher of consular services, and he waved them through. Standing had to run through his explanation again to a young Thai woman in a dark suit and she tapped on a computer and asked to see their ID. They handed over their passports which she photocopied and returned to them, then she asked them to sign the copies. She gave them keycards. 'You are to go up to the twelfth floor,' she said. 'You will need the cards to access the lifts.'

They thanked her and headed to the turnstiles. They had to tap their cards onto a reader to get the lift to work and they rode up to the twelfth floor. The doors opened onto another reception area, behind which was a large framed portrait of the King Charles. A balding man in a grey suit was waiting for them. He was in his forties with black-framed spectacles hanging on a chain around his neck. He was carrying a manila folder.

'Mr Green?' he said, looking at them.

'That's me,' said Green, raising a hand.

'I'm so sorry for your loss, Mr Green,' said Butcher. He offered his hand and they shook.

'This is Matt Standing, he was a good pal of Pete's,' said Green.

'I'm sorry for your loss, too,' said Butcher, and he shook Standing's hand. 'I have a room this way we can use.'

He took them down a grey-carpeted corridor and pushed open a door that led to a small room with a table and four chairs. Butcher sat down and Green and Standing took the chairs opposite him. 'You've come straight from the airport?' he asked, nodding at their bags.

'Strike while the iron's hot,' said Green.

'I wasn't expecting the embassy to be halfway up a tower block,' said Standing.

'Nobody's happy about it,' said Butcher. 'Up until 2019 the embassy was a colonial building on a beautiful site in the middle of the city with mature trees and a lake, but the Foreign Office sold it for more than four hundred million pounds and moved the staff here. They're building a huge shopping mall on the site and the ambassador's residence is now in the Four Seasons. Another tower block.' He shrugged. 'The way of the world, I suppose.' He opened the file and looked down at a typewritten sheet. He put on his glasses and sighed. 'Again, I am so sorry about your loss. A death overseas is aways difficult, but suicide just makes it worse for everybody left behind.'

'My brother wouldn't kill himself,' said Green.

'The police are quite definite,' said Butcher.

'Can you tell us what happened?' asked Standing.

Butcher took off his glasses and sat back in his chair. 'I really don't have much in the way of detail, I'm afraid, just that Mr Green was out drinking at a local bar, he returned to his hotel just after midnight, alone. When the maid opened the door to clean the room the next morning, he was dead.'

'There's no way my brother would kill himself,' said Green.

'I can only tell you what Police Colonel Kittisak told me. And he is an experienced officer.'

'So you didn't go to Koh Chang yourself?' said Green.

'No. That's not what we do here.'

'So you don't actually know what happened. You're just repeating what this Colonel Kit Kat told you.'

'Colonel Kittisak,' said Butcher. He shifted uncomfortably in his chair. 'In situations such as this, the embassy really acts as an intermediary between the Thai authorities and the British citizen, which is yourself. A conduit, so to speak.'

'A conduit?' repeated Green.

'Exactly. We talk to the authorities on your behalf and then pass on any information you require. And what I'm telling you is that Police Colonel Kittisak will have any information you need, and that he is based at the Trat police station.'

'Trat?' repeated Standing. Where is that? On the island?'

'Trat is the main town on the mainland close to the island,' said Butcher. 'Koh Chang itself is quite small, population-wise, and there isn't much crime there, so there's not much of a police presence. Anything major is handled by the Trat station. I've already sent him an email, so he is expecting you. You can liaise with him about the repatriation of your brother's body.' He took a sheet of paper from the file and gave it to Green. 'These are his contact details.' He slid a second sheet across the table. 'And this is the consular letter you'll need to give him so that they can release the body for burial, cremation or repatriation, whichever you decide to do.'

Green folded the sheets and put them into his jacket pocket. 'What about the post mortem?' he asked.

Butcher frowned. 'Excuse me?'

Green's eyes hardened. 'The post mortem. Pete died suddenly and unexpectedly, there has to be a post mortem.'

'To be fair, Mr Green, even in England a post mortem wouldn't necessarily be held in the wake of a suicide. A coroner might well decide that one isn't necessary. And this is Thailand, not the UK.'

'So there was no post mortem? Is that what you're saying?'

'My understanding is that there was no dispute about the cause of death. Your brother – I'm sorry to say – took his own life. The police are quite sure of that.'

Green shook his head. 'My brother wouldn't kill himself.'

'I understand that, Mr Green. But a lot of people do commit suicide in Thailand. Literally hundreds of British citizens die each year. Some are in hospital, some are accidents, but a lot are people, usually men, who decide to end their lives.' Green opened his mouth to speak but Butcher raised his hand to silence him. 'Sometimes it's drug or alcohol related, often it's linked to a relationship going sour. We have so many Brits throwing themselves off balconies in Pattaya that they refer to it as the Pattaya Flying Club.'

'You think this is funny?' said Green, getting to his feet.

Standing grabbed his arm. 'Easy, Billy.'

Green shook him off and continued to stare at the embassy official. 'My brother wouldn't kill himself. He just wouldn't. Push him the wrong way and there's a chance he'd kill you, but he would never, ever, top himself.'

Butcher's cheeks had reddened and his eyes flicked nervously between Standing and Green. 'I hear you, Mr Green. But please, don't shoot the messenger. I'm just relaying to you what the Thai police have told me. There were no suspicious circumstances surrounding your brother's death. If you want more information, I'm sure Police Colonel Kittisak will be able to help you.'

He opened the file and took out another printed sheet. 'This is a list of companies who can ship your brother's body back to the UK. It is worth asking for estimates as the charges do vary. Or you might think about having him cremated here in Thailand.'

Green shook his head. 'He'll be buried back in England.'

'Then you'll be needing this list,' said Butcher, sliding the sheet of paper across the table. 'And once again, Mr Green, I am very sorry about your loss. If you do have any issues when you're in Trat or Koh Chang, feel free to give me a call.'

'I do have one question for you,' said Green.

Butcher's jaw tightened. 'Sure,' he said. 'What is it?'

'Why did you phone my mother?'

Butcher frowned. 'She'd be next of kin, surely?'

Green shook his head. 'No, I'm his ICE, his In Case of Emergency number. And he's mine. You should have called me.'

'We didn't have his phone,' said Butcher. 'The police had his passport and they emailed us a scan. From that we got an address from the Passport Office and that led us to Mrs Green.'

'So where is Pete's phone?'

'That I couldn't tell you,' said Butcher. 'You can raise that with Colonel Kittisak.' He pointedly looked at his watch. 'I'm really going to have to draw this meeting to a close,' he said.

'Sure, because you've got more important things to deal with than the death of my brother,' said Green.

'Leave it, Billy,' said Standing. He stood up and flashed Butcher a smile. 'We are grateful for everything you've done,' he said. 'As you can imagine, it's a stressful time for everyone.'

Butcher smiled gratefully. 'Thank you,' he said. 'And as I said, if you run into any problems, I'll be here.'

Green was about to say something, but Standing put his arm around his shoulders and guided him out of the room.

'He thinks it's a fucking joke, does he?' hissed Green as they walked to the lifts. 'Pattaya fucking Flying Club?'

'He was nervous,' said Standing. 'I think he thought you were going to punch his lights out.'

'The thought crossed my mind,' said Green. 'I need a drink.'

'I hear you,' said Standing. 'But maybe we need a clear head at the moment.'

They reached the lifts and Green turned to look at Standing. There was a blankness to his eyes and his jaw had clenched. 'I didn't say I wanted a drink, I said I needed a drink.'

'Okay, Billy. Just chill.' He pressed the lift button and one opened immediately. They went in and down to the ground floor.

The W Hotel was a short walk away, on the other side of North Sathorn Road, but Standing figured it was probably a bit too upmarket for an SAS trooper with a thirst on. Standing took out his phone and checked Google Maps. The red light area of Patpong was only a fifteen minute walk away.

They crossed the main road, walked by the huge tower block that was the W Hotel and actually reached Patpong in ten minutes. Most of the bars hadn't yet opened but the Tip Top restaurant was open and they walked in.

A waitress with a braided ponytail smiled, put her hands together as if in prayer and dipped her head. 'What is that?' Green asked Standing. 'What's she doing?'

'It's a way of showing respect, or thanks,' said Standing. 'They call it a wai.'

'A what?'

Standing laughed. 'Who's on first base? It's called a wai. You'll see it a lot.'

'You've been to Thailand before?'

'A few years ago. We were on an exercise in Cambodia and stopped off for some R&R for a couple of days.'

'Have fun?'

Standing chuckled and shook his head. 'I spent both days in hospital, I got a cut on my leg in the jungle and it went septic. I was on an antibiotic drip for two days while the rest of the lads were blowing off steam.'

They sat down at a table and the waitress gave them two plastic-covered menus with photographs of the food on offer, Thai and Western. 'Two beers,' said Green.

'We have Chang, Singha or Heineken,' said the waitress.

'Chang?' said Green.

The waitress nodded. 'It means elephant.'

Green leaned towards her. 'So what does Koh Chang mean?'

She smiled, showing brilliant white teeth. 'Elephant Island,' she said.

'How about that?' Green said to Standing. 'That's where we're going, right? Elephant Island?'

Standing grinned. 'Mate, if you'd done some intel gathering instead of hitting the whisky bottle, you'd know that.'

'Nobody likes a smart arse, Matt,' said Green.

'That's Sergeant Matt to you, trooper,' said Standing.

Green smiled at the waitress. 'Two bottles of Chang beer, darling,' he said. He settled back in his chair and studied the menu as the waitress walked away. 'I'm not really a fan of Thai food,' he said.

'They've got burgers. And steak.'

'Yeah, a burger will do me.'

Standing nodded. 'Yeah, sounds good.'

When the waitress returned with their beers, they asked for two burgers and chips. Standing sipped his beer as she walked away. 'We're going to have to decide what to do, Billy,' he said. 'Trat is a four- to five-hour drive. So we can either sort out a car and drive now and stay in a hotel in Trat. Or we can bunk down in Bangkok and drive first thing in the morning.'

Green took a mouthful of beer and shrugged. 'Six of one.'

'I don't know what the roads are like but I'd prefer not to drive at night. I'm thinking we get a room here. Pick up a car first thing and drive to Trat. If we leave here at oh nine hundred hours, we'll be there by fourteen hundred hours at the latest. The last ferry to Koh Chang is eighteen thirty hours.'

'Better we get to the cop shop early,' said Green. 'We don't know how long that'll take, so if we cut it close we might miss the ferry. Why not get a car tonight and then we can head off early doors tomorrow?'

Standing nodded. 'Okay, that'll work.' He took out his phone and looked for car rental places. He smiled when he saw that there were offices of both Thrifty and Hertz just a short walk from where they were, back on the North Sathorn Road. 'We're in luck,' he said.

CHAPTER 6

Standing and Green finished their burgers, paid the waitress who gave them another wai, and walked back to North Sathorn Road. The Thrifty outlet had a full range of cars and Standing chose a grey Toyota Fortuner, a big beast of an SUV that appeared to be based on a pick-up truck. In less than fifteen minutes an earnest young man had photocopied Standing's driving licence and passport, run the total through his credit card, shown them the vehicle and waved them on their way. Standing had paid for a GPS and Green set it up. 'So what now?' he asked when he'd finished.

Standing looked at his watch. It was coming up to 7 p.m. 'I know it's early but I'm for getting some shuteye,' he said. 'Then we can set off at dawn tomorrow.'

'I'm up for that,' said Green. 'There's a hotel,' he said, pointing off to the left. It was a two-storey building with a sign that said HOTEL 888.

'My lucky number,' said Standing. He indicated and turned into the hotel entrance. A man in a red shirt with the hotel logo on the chest appeared from nowhere and waved for them to follow him. He took them away from the main entrance down a path at the side of the hotel. There were rooms with doors leading onto the path, with a paved area in front where cars could be parked. Standing frowned when he saw that curtains had been drawn around the cars that had already been parked there. 'What's that about?'

'Keep them clean, maybe?'

Standing shrugged. The man stopped and pointed at a parking space in front of one of the rooms. 'I guess it's more like a motel,' he said. He turned, guided the SUV into the spot and switched off the engine. The man pulled the curtain around the car.

Standing climbed out and the man hurried over to him. 'Room, yes?' said the man, smiling broadly. A small Buddha figure was hanging from a gold chain around his neck

'Room, yes,' said Standing. 'Just one night. How much?'

'Three hundred baht,' said the man. He pulled open the door and waved for Standing to go in.

'That's cheap,' said Standing. Three hundred baht was less than ten pounds.

Green climbed out of the passenger seat. 'A bargain,' he said.

'Three hundred baht one hour,' said the man. 'Five hundred baht two hours.'

'We need it all night,' said Standing.

'All night, no problem. One thousand baht.'

'That's still only about twenty quid,' said Green. 'What's the catch?'

Standing stepped into the room and laughed. In the middle of the room was a circular bed with black sheets and two black pillows. There was a circular mirror on the ceiling above the bed, and two of the walls were mirrored. The only furniture in the room was a black chair that looked as if it belonged in a gynaecologist's office, the back at an angle and with two stirrups where the feet could be placed, and a red plastic sofa against one wall. There was a small TV up near the ceiling, by a door that led to a bathroom.

Green followed him in and snorted. 'What the fuck?'

'It's a love hotel, short-time hotel, whatever you want to call it,' said Standing.

The Thai man peered into the back of the Fortuner. 'You have girls?'

Standing turned to look at him. 'No,' he said. 'No girls.'

'No problem,' grinned the man. 'I can get girls for you. One girl, two thousand baht. Two girls four thousand baht. You want a party? Three girls? Four?'

Standing couldn't help grinning. 'No, no party. Just the two of us.' He took out his wallet and gave the man a thousand-baht note.

The man was frowning now. 'No girls?'

'No girls,' said Standing.

'Boys?' said the man, hopefully.

Standing ushered the man out and closed the door. Green was staring at the chair. 'That is some sick shit,' he said. 'Are we really staying here?'

'It's cheap. We'll be out of here in a few hours. If it makes you feel any better, you can have the bed and I'll take the sofa.'

'I was thinking of trying out the chair,' said Green. He picked up a remote and switched on the television.

Standing went into the bathroom. It was clean and functional with a walk-in shower, though the mirrored ceiling suggested that more than ablutions went on in the room. He'd slept in far worse places.

'And there's footie to watch,' said Green. He dropped onto the bed and chuckled when he realised the circular mattress was filled with water. 'We gotta give this place five stars on Tripadvisor,' he said.

CHAPTER 7

Standing and Green woke at five thirty. They showered and shaved and changed into clean clothes and were in the Fortuner heading east by six, just as the sun was coming up. Standing had programmed the Trat police station into the GPS and most of the route appeared to be motorways. He was pleasantly surprised by how good the Thai roads were, though the quality of the drivers was a different matter. Indicators were rarely used and traffic lights were treated as voluntary. Half of the drivers had mobile phones in their hands. Motorcycles weaved in and out of the traffic, almost never indicating.

Driving skills didn't improve much when they reached the motorway. Most vehicles ignored the posted speed limits, and lane discipline didn't seem to be a thing, cars were weaving across the lanes and undertaking at will, and more often than not the drivers wouldn't bother using their indicators, preferring instead to flash their lights and sound their horns.

There were pick-up trucks loaded with labourers in the back, shielding their heads from the burning sun with floppy hats or towels. Other pick-up trucks were piled high with bales of straw or sacks of produce, the loads often five or six times the height of the cab.

There were toll booths at irregular intervals along the

motorway. Some cars had electronic tags that allowed them to drive through, but Standing and Green had to join the queues for the cash booths, where women with face masks held out their hands for the fee – usually the equivalent of about a pound.

They stopped off once to buy fuel. As soon as they pulled up at a pump a young man ran over and asked what they wanted. Standing had him fill the tank. 'Why don't they do this in the UK?' asked Green. 'We don't even have to get out of the car.'

'They probably pay them peanuts,' said Standing. 'But yeah, in the UK they make us do it ourselves. And then we have to queue to hand over our money. This is so much more civilised.'

The young man filled their tank and took Standing's money, giving him a heartfelt wai when Standing said he could keep the change. They drove over to a toilet block, which was far cleaner than Standing had expected. There were food shops, an Amazon coffee shop, and a 7/11 convenience store. They bought soft drinks and bottled water, and Green grabbed a couple of bananas and a pack of biscuits.

They decided that Green should drive, so he took the wheel for the rest of the journey. Once they reached Trat province they began to see roadside stalls selling a strange-looking fruit, varying in colour from green to brown and covered with spikes. Some of them had been split open to reveal the yellow flesh inside. In some places there were half a dozen of the stalls, a hundred feet or so apart, each staffed by a woman wrapped up against the fierce sun with a large floppy hat, a scarf over her face and gloves covering her hands.

Eventually the GPS took them off the motorway and into the town of Trat. The police station was much bigger than

Standing had expected, consisting of a couple of sprawling two-storey buildings next to a pair of massive communication pylons covered with satellite dishes and aerials. The building on the left was white concrete, dotted with air-conditioning units. The one on the right was brick and concrete and had a ramp and steps up to the entrance.

The kerb outside the station was painted red and white to prohibit parking, and midway along the pavement, between the two buildings, was a large pagoda shrine with a golden buddha. There were police vehicles lined up in the car park – saloons and pick-up trucks and a row of radio-equipped motorcycles – but there were plenty of available spaces.

Green parked and climbed out. Standing joined him. All the signage was in Thai but Standing figured the ramp suggested it was for public use, so he gestured at the building on the right. The two men headed up the steps and pushed open the glass doors that led to a large reception area. Standing went over to a counter where a uniformed woman in her thirties smiled at him and said, 'Good morning, how can I help you?' Standing was surprised that she had spoken to him in English. He had anticipated having a problem explaining what he wanted and so was already holding the sheet of paper that Butcher had given them, but instead he just told her who he wanted to see. 'Please take a seat,' she said.

They sat by the door. There were more than a dozen Thais waiting, most of them dressed in cheap clothes and plastic flip-flops. Almost all of them were bent over their phones.

'I can't believe we're here,' said Green. 'Two days ago I'm in Stirling Lines and all's well with the world. Now . . .' He shrugged and left the sentence unfinished.

'You okay?'

'I don't know, Matt. I'm still breathing, so that's good. But I just can't believe that Pete's gone.' He sighed. 'They say twins have a special connection, right? So why didn't I feel anything when he died?'

'Did you have that sort of connection?'

'When we were kids, yes. We always knew what each other was thinking. And we'd always finish each other's sentences. When we were at primary school we had our own language. Made up words that only the two of us could understand.'

'I never heard you two doing that.'

'We stopped when we were teenagers. It was as if we grew apart. Or maybe we wanted to grow apart so that people could see we were different. He was a Spurs fan, I followed Chelsea. I drank lager and he drank beer, and when we were older I drank whisky and he went for vodka. I also went for busty blonde girls and he dated redheads. He'd been out here a few times. I never saw the attraction but he loved Vietnam, Thailand, Laos, all those places. Me, I preferred Spain.' He leaned back in his chair and stretched out his legs. 'I always thought that if something bad happened to him, I'd know. But I didn't. My mum called me and it was a bolt from the fucking blue.'

'How's she taking it?'

Green smiled thinly. 'She's as tough as old boots, my mum,' he said. 'She raised me and Pete and our two sisters single-handed after our dad left. Worked two jobs most of the time we were kids. Went to bat for us whenever we were in trouble, but gave us a clip behind the ears when we deserved it. Old school. She would have made a good sergeant major.' He sighed. 'Pete was the one who always kept in touch. He rang her every Sunday, no matter where he was, even if it was just a few minutes to check that she was okay. Me, I'd go for weeks without calling.' He folded his arms. 'I'll call her from now on.'

'Every Sunday.'

Green nodded. 'Every Sunday.'

The woman from reception walked over and smiled at them. 'Please, follow me,' she said. She led them down a tiled corridor to an office where a young female officer was tapping on a computer. The older woman said something in Thai and the younger woman nodded and replied.

'I will leave you here,' the older woman said to Green and Standing. 'If you could just wait until Colonel Kittisak is free.' She gestured at two chairs against the wall.

They thanked her and sat down. She went back down the corridor. The minutes ticked by. 'He's obviously a very busy man,' said Green.

Standing wrinkled his nose. 'He just wants to show us how important he is,' he said.

The young female officer continued to tap away on her computer. Standing folded his arms and stretched out his legs. Another five minutes ticked by. And another. He took a deep breath. Patience wasn't one of his virtues. He didn't mind being on a job and having to wait. He'd spent days on surveillance missions, and once had spent an entire week dug into the side of a hill in Afghanistan waiting for an al-Qaeda convoy to appear so that he could call in a bombing raid. But being forced to sit in an office because somebody was too busy to see him was a whole different experience. He wanted to get up and ask the junior officer what was taking so long, but he concentrated on some square breathing instead. He started by slowly exhaling until his lungs were empty. Then he gently inhaled through his nose to a slow count of four. Then he held his breath for another count of four. Then he gently exhaled through his mouth for another four seconds. At the bottom of the breath he paused and held it for another count of four. It was a technique he often used when he could feel himself starting to get angry. Just the act of focusing on his breathing and counting off the seconds calmed him down.

He was on his fifteenth circuit when the phone on the junior officer's desk rang. She answered it, nodded, and put the receiver down before getting up and walking over to Standing and Green. 'Colonel Kittisak is free now,' she said.

Standing smiled up at her. 'Excellent,' he said.

They stood up and followed her over to a door. She knocked on it and opened it and spoke to Police Colonel Kittisak in Thai, then she motioned for Standing and Green to go through.

They walked into the office and she closed the door behind them. Police Colonel Kittisak was sitting behind a large modern desk on which there was a sleek computer monitor, a wire basket of papers and files, and a large brass plaque with his name and rank and the insignia of the Royal Thai Police. On the wall behind him were more than a dozen framed photographs of him meeting various Thai dignitaries, including two of him with the King of Thailand.

Kittisak was a large man with glossy slicked-back hair, dark-framed glasses and a tight-fitting uniform with a row of medals on his chest. He had a squarish face, and jowls that rolled over the collar of his shirt. He waved at the two metal chairs facing his desk. His own seat was a high-backed leather executive model that swivelled as he reached for a pack of cigarettes decorated with a photograph of someone suffering from throat cancer. As the two men sat down he tapped out a cigarette and offered the pack to them. They both shook their heads. Kittisak looked out of the window across the car park to the road as he lit the cigarette with a gold Dunhill lighter and blew smoke up at the ceiling. He frowned as if he was trying to get his thoughts together, then spun around to look at them. 'So, first of all let me say I am sorry for your loss,' he said. He had a heavy accent but he spoke confidently. 'We will try to make this process as pain-less as possible for you.'

'Where is my brother's body?' asked Green.

'It is being held on Koh Chang, awaiting a consular letter,' said the colonel.

'I have that,' said Green. He reached into his jacket and took out the letter that Butcher had given to him.

Green gave it to the colonel, who studied it for almost a minute and then placed it on his desk. 'And I will need your passports.'

Green and Standing produced their passports. The colonel called for his secretary and spoke to her in Thai. She took the passports and the consular letter into her office, photocopied them and brought them back. The colonel had Green and Standing sign the copies of their passport, then he sat back and smiled. 'Now that I have the letter the body can be released. What are your plans?'

'Plans?' said Green.

'Do you want to have the body cremated here? Or buried? That can be arranged but most bodies are cremated in Thailand. Or you can arrange to have the body taken to England, though that is very expensive and requires a lot of paperwork.'

'I'm taking him home,' said Green.

'That is fine,' said the colonel. 'But you will need a company to represent you. It is not a simple matter. Preparations have to be made and as I said, there is a lot of paperwork.'

'The embassy gave us a list of firms who can take care of it for us,' said Standing. 'It's not a problem.'

'Excellent, I will assist you in making the arrangements. Where are you staying?'

'We're on our way to Koh Chang,' said Green.

'There's no need, we will have your brother's remains brought here.'

'We want to see where it happened,' said Green.

The colonel grimaced. 'I am not sure why you would want to do that.'

'Everybody keeps telling us that Pete killed himself, but that's just not possible.'

The colonel frowned. 'Why not?'

'Because Pete wasn't the type.'

'There is no doubt that your brother's death was suicide,' said the colonel. 'No doubt at all.'

'Did you see the body?' asked Standing.

'No, I didn't.'

'But you went to the crime scene?'

'There was no crime, it was a suicide.'

'But did you see what had happened?'

'I didn't go to Koh Chang, if that is what you are asking.'

'Why not?' asked Green.

'Because there was no need. Captain Somchai is perfectly capable of coming to a conclusion without me looking over his shoulder. He was the investigating officer and I have every faith in him.'

'So you didn't have any part in the investigation?' said Standing. 'You didn't even go to Koh Chang?'

The colonel stubbed out his cigarette. 'What is your job?' he asked.

'I'm a soldier.'

'Mister Pete was, too?'

Standing nodded. 'We all are.'

'Then you understand how rank works. What rank are you?'

'I'm a sergeant.'

'Then the men under you obey you. Give them a task, and they do it. You do not carry out those tasks yourself. And if a captain wants something done, he will tell you and you will do it. He will not do it himself. And if a colonel tells the captain to do something, the captain does it, or gets you to do it. I heard an expression. Why have a dog and then bark yourself? You have heard that expression?'

Standing smiled. 'Yes, I have.'

'And I heard another expression. Shit rolls downhill. Have you heard that one?'

Standing laughed out loud. 'Yes, I have.'

The colonel smiled and nodded. 'Then you understand exactly what I am saying. The maid found the body. A police officer attended and pronounced the death as suicide. The police officer informed his sergeant who informed the captain on Koh Chang who in turn informed me. That does not mean that I have to attend the scene. And nor does the captain. There is a chain of command.'

'I understand, sir,' said Standing.

'Understanding doesn't make it right,' said Green.

'Billy . . .' said Standing. There was no point in antagonising the colonel, there was clearly nothing they could say that would change his mind.

Green shook his head fiercely. 'This is bullshit, Matt. No

way would Pete kill himself. Either someone didn't do their job or there's been a cover-up.'

'If there's a problem, we can address it on Koh Chang. The colonel wasn't there, he doesn't know what happened, there's no point in lashing out at him.'

'Fucking Ruperts,' said Green. 'More trouble than they're worth.'

'Leave it, Billy.'

Green opened his mouth but Standing flashed him a warning look. Green grunted and folded his arms.

Standing smiled at the colonel, who was watching them both with cold eyes. 'I apologise,' Standing said. 'It's been a very stressful time.'

'I understand.' Colonel Kittisak took another cigarette from his pack and lit it. He blew smoke up at the ceiling before continuing. 'It's clear that you have questions that you need answering, and I hope Captain Somchai can answer those questions for you.' He smiled at Standing but his eyes stayed cold. 'But I would suggest you do not use that tone with Captain Somchai. He might not be as understanding as I am.'

Standing nodded and forced himself to smile. 'We will definitely bear that in mind,' he said.

'If you do want to see where it happened, I am sure Captain Somchai can arrange that for you.'

'What about my brother's stuff?' asked Green. 'His things?'

'They would be at the Koh Chang police station.'

'And what about Pete's body?'

'You will have to check with Captain Somchai, I would assume it would be kept at a temple as they have storage facilities. Thailand is a very hot country, so bodies have to be kept cold.' The colonel opened a small brass box and took out an embossed business card. He handed it to Standing. 'If you have any problems while you are on Koh Chang, my cell phone number is on my card.'

Standing thanked him. He looked over at Green, who was clearly still unhappy. Standing narrowed his eyes and gestured with his chin. Green got the message and thanked the colonel, though his eyes gave away his true feelings. Billy Green was not a happy man.

CHAPTER 8

'This is fucking bollocks,' said Green as he climbed into the passenger seat of the Fortuner.

'I know,' said Standing. He fastened his seat belt and put the key in the ignition. They had decided that Standing would do the driving to Koh Chang. 'But pissing off a police colonel won't get us anywhere.' They had only been in the police station for half an hour but the Fortuner was already red hot inside, so Standing turned the air conditioning on full blast.

'Yeah, I know,' said Green. 'I saw *Midnight Express*.'

'That was Turkey. But yeah, the same principle applies. Cops out here run by different rules. They can be a law unto themselves.' He gestured at the GPS. 'Can you put the ferry terminal in?'

Green programmed the terminal into the GPS as Standing drove out onto the road. It showed up as a forty-minute drive, due west.

Once they left Trat they were driving through rural areas, farms and scrubland, the soil a rusty orange colour. If it hadn't been for the GPS they would have missed the turn-off for the ferry terminal, if there was a sign in English they didn't see it and it was only when the GPS told them to make a U-turn that they realised they had driven by it.

They went back, found the turn and drove down a narrow

road to the terminal. As they reached it, they saw a line of brightly coloured tour buses parked on a dusty patch of land, then a sign in English pointing to a ticket office. The Fortuner joined a line of cars waiting for tickets. There was only one booth but the young girl taking the money was efficient and took only a few seconds to handle each vehicle.

Standing paid and a woman in a large wide-brimmed hat and sunglasses wearing a hi-vis jacket pointed for him to join a line of cars off to the right. There were several lines and his was in the middle. The line on the far right was moving towards the ferry under the watchful eyes of more staff in hi-vis jackets. Once the line was on board it was the turn of the line next to the Fortuner, eight cars in all, mostly saloons. Once they had all boarded it was their turn. Standing followed the car in front of him until a man in a hi-vis jacket pointed for him to go to the right and park behind a Honda CR-V. Standing stopped about three feet from the Honda but the man started waving urgently, telling him to move forward. He didn't stop waving until the Fortuner was inches from the Honda's rear bumper. To their right was a pick-up truck, less than a foot away, and a Toyota saloon pulled up on their left, just two feet away.

'How are we supposed to get out?' asked Green.

'It's only a five-kilometre crossing, we'll be over in thirty minutes.'

'What if I need the toilet?'

'Do you?'

'No, but if I did?'

'Use a bottle. Or a plastic bag.' He grinned. 'It wouldn't be the first time, would it?'

The last of the cars had pulled up on the ferry. More than

a dozen motorbikes were allowed on, easing their way through what spaces there were until they were all on board.

'I don't see any lifejackets, do you?' asked Green.

'You can swim.'

'Not if I can't get out of the car, I can't.'

'Mate, if you can't get out of the car, a lifejacket's not going to be any use to you.' He grabbed a bottle of water, unscrewed the cap and drank. He nodded at the GPS. 'See if you can program in the Koh Chang cop shop.' The ferry's engines vibrated as the vessel began to move away from the pier.

The GPS showed two police stations on the island, a Tourist Police station on the west side, and an HQ building on the east. 'Headquarters?' said Green.

'I guess so.'

Green started the route and they were able to follow the progress of the ferry on the small screen as it moved slowly towards Koh Chang. They could see the island ahead of them, or at least the mountainous jungle-covered peaks in the centre.

The crossing was smooth and in less than thirty minutes they were driving off the ferry. They followed the GPS route, but it was easy enough as there was only the one road, which went east and west from the terminal and then south, following the coastline on both sides of the island. They took the east route.

Koh Chang was a far cry from the bustling metropolis of Bangkok. The road was just two lanes and narrow, and when they met oncoming traffic there were only inches to spare. Most of the buildings they passed were little more than wooden shacks using electricity supplied by wires strung along concrete poles running alongside the road. To the left they caught occasional glimpses of the sea, but there were no hotels or bars, just homes belonging to people who clearly didn't have two pennies to rub together.

They passed Koh Chang hospital on the right, pretty much in the middle of nowhere, and then they saw the police station, next to a small wooden shack with a few tables and chairs under a sloping plastic roof that looked as if it might be a restaurant.

The police station was a two-storey building with a flat roof, a fraction of the size of the one in Trat. A Thai flag on a pole twice the height of the building fluttered in the breeze, and behind the station was an even taller communications pylon.

There was a large concrete yard in front of the station but most vehicles were parked under two long canopies on either side which offered some shade from the blistering sun. Standing edged the Fortuner into a space and the two men climbed out.

There was a wide flight of concrete steps leading up to the entrance. All the signs were in Thai, they clearly weren't geared up for dealing with foreigners. The main door was open and they walked in. There was a counter to the left and two rows of white plastic seats to the right. Two large wood-bladed fans turned slowly overhead. There were two men in brown uniforms behind the counter. The older of the two, bald with horn-rimmed spectacles, looked at them and frowned.

'We're here to see Police Captain Somchai,' said Standing. He held out the business card that Colonel Kittisak had given him. 'Colonel Kittisak sent us.' The man examined the card carefully, then looked over the top of his glasses and nodded at the plastic seats. 'Sit,' he said. Standing didn't think the man was being rude, he just didn't speak much English, so he smiled and nodded and went over and sat down with Green.

The overhead fans had little effect on the muggy air and they were both sweating by the time a young girl came out of a door and went over to the counter to talk to the bald policeman. She was in her mid-twenties with waist-length jet-black hair, wearing a beige uniform with TOURIST POLICE flashes on her shoulders. There was a Glock pistol in a brown leather holster on her right hip. The policeman gave her the business card and pointed over at the chairs. She turned to look at them, and then frowned before turning back to talk to her colleague again. He nodded as she spoke to him, and eventually she walked over, her heels clicking on the tiles, her hair swinging from side to side. She was smiling but she seemed nervous and she clasped her hands together.

'My name is Fah,' she said. 'I will take you to Captain Somchai.' She held out the card and Standing took it. 'I will give you my card, too,' she said. She took out a small wallet and gave him another business card.

'I'm Matt Standing,' he said. He nodded at Green. 'This is Billy Green. You know what this is about?'

'Ah. Mister Billy. I did not know Mister Pete had a twin,' she said. 'Police Colonel Kittisak already phoned to say that you were coming. Captain Somchai's English isn't great, so I will translate for you.' She smiled sympathetically at Green. 'I am sorry for your loss.'

'Thank you,' said Green.

She gave Green one of her cards, then took them through the door and along a corridor. Captain Somchai's office was at the far end of the corridor. The door was closed and Fah knocked quietly, then opened it. Captain Somchai was sitting behind a desk, peering at a computer screen. He was wearing a dark brown uniform and had a Glock in a nylon holster on his hip. He was in his thirties with jet-black hair and cheeks pockmarked with old acne scars. There were large framed paintings of the King and Queen of Thailand on the wall behind him. To the left were two metal-framed windows over-looking the road. He grunted and pointed at two wooden chairs facing his desk.

'Please, sit down,' said Fah. She went to stand between the two windows as Standing and Green sat.

'Thank you for seeing us,' said Standing, and waited while Fah translated. The captain grunted again. 'Colonel Kittisak said you would be able to explain the circumstances of Pete Green's death.' Again Fah translated, then she listened as the captain replied at length in Thai.

When he had finished, she smiled at them both. 'Captain Somchai says he is sorry for your loss. His own brother killed himself several years ago, so he understands the grief you are feeling.'

Green opened his mouth to interrupt but Standing put his hand on his arm and squeezed, then gave him a small shake of the head.

'Mister Pete was found in his room by a maid who had come to clean it,' continued Fah. 'His body was cold and he had been dead for some time. Mister Pete had been drinking and had decided to take his own life.'

Standing nodded. 'How? What did he do?'

Fah translated and again the captain spoke at length in Thai. Fah asked a few questions and the captain answered. Eventually Fah turned to look at Standing and Green. 'He suffocated himself. He put a plastic bag over his head.'

'Bollocks,' said Green.

'That sounds unlikely,' said Standing. 'He would have tried to take the bag off, surely? You can't kill yourself that way.'

'I said that but Captain Somchai said that your friend tied his hands behind his back.'

'That doesn't make any sense at all,' said Green. He was almost shouting, but he lowered his voice when Standing threw him a warning look. 'How could he put a bag over his head if his hands were tied behind his back?'

'I asked that,' said Fah. 'It happens a lot, he said. People put the bag over their head and use tape or string to make it tight around the neck. If the bag is loose there is enough air for one or two minutes, which is sufficient time for them to put on handcuffs or tie a noose around their hands.'

Green shook his head scornfully. 'Never happen.'

'No, it does happen, really.'

'With Thais, maybe, but that's not how Westerners kill themselves.'

Fah frowned. 'Really? How do Westerners kill themselves?'

'If they're soldiers they swallow their gun. Or they drive their car into a tree. Or they jump in front of a train. But nobody, least of all my brother, would put a bag over their head and tie their own hands behind their back.' He looked across at Standing. 'Am I right, or am I right?'

'Yeah, you're right.' He smiled at Fah. 'But please don't tell your boss what we said.'

'I won't. I do understand what you mean. I have heard of Westerners killing themselves but I have never heard of Westerners killing themselves like this.'

'Pete wouldn't kill himself, period,' said Green. 'But if he did, he wouldn't fuck around like that.' He gritted his teeth and grunted. Standing could see that he was having difficulty keeping his anger in check.

'Do you have Pete's belongings?' asked Standing.

Fah translated and Captain Somchai replied. She nodded and headed out of the room, returning after thirty seconds pulling a blue hard-shell wheeled cabin bag. She gave it to Green who put it on the floor and opened it. There were clothes inside, and a washbag, a pair of boots and a pair of trainers. There were two paperbacks – a Chris Ryan thriller and a field guide to the birds of Thailand – a passport, a pair of Nikon binoculars and a Breitling watch. Green moved the clothes and found a set of keys, including a key fob. He dropped the keys back into the case. 'Where's his phone?'

Fah spoke to Captain Somchai and he replied. 'There was no phone,' said Fah.

'He had a phone. An iPhone 12.'

Fah and the captain had a conversation. 'There was no phone in his room,' said Fah eventually.

'Then someone must have taken it,' said Green. He looked over at Standing. 'Someone stole Pete's phone.'

'Is his wallet there?' asked Standing.

Green looked through the case and pulled out a black leather wallet. He opened it and showed Standing the contents. There were several credit cards and a wad of Thai baht. Standing nodded. A thief would have taken the wallet, the watch and probably the binoculars. They looked expensive. Green showed the wallet to Captain Somchai. The policeman shrugged, then spoke to Fah. She headed for the door.

'What did he say?' asked Green.

'He said I'm to get your brother,' said Fah. She hurried out into the corridor.

'What the fuck?' said Green, looking at Standing. 'What the fuck is going on?'

Standing looked over at Captain Somchai but he was staring out of the window.

Fah returned with a cardboard box, two feet long, a foot wide and a foot deep. She was holding it with both hands. Standing and Green realised immediately what it was. 'You have got to be kidding,' said Green. 'No fucking way.'

He stood up, took the box from Fah, opened it and looked inside. There was a white cloth bag, tied with red rope at the top. He loosened the rope and peered at the contents, then moaned like an animal in pain and sat down, the box on his lap.

'Please, it is okay,' said Fah. 'He was burned.'

Standing took the box from Green and gently eased apart the cloth. He grimaced when he saw the ashes.

'Burned?' said Green. 'What do you mean, burned?'

The girl frowned as she struggled to find the correct word. 'Cremated,' she said, and smiled with relief. 'He was cremated.'

'Cremated where?'

'Here on Koh Chang. At the Wat Salak Phet.'

'What the fuck is the Wat Salak Phet?' said Green.

'A temple. A very famous temple. Your brother was cremated there.'

Green stood up so quickly that his chair fell back and hit the tiled floor. Captain Somchai flinched and pushed himself away from the desk. A young cop appeared in the doorway brandishing a revolver.

'Easy, Billy, easy!' said Standing.

'I'm not the one waving a fucking gun around,' said Green.

The young cop shouted at Green in Thai. He was holding his gun with both hands and his finger was on the trigger.

Green pointed at the young cop. 'You'd better kill me with the first round because I will rip your fucking head off!' he shouted.

'Billy, calm the fuck down!' shouted Standing. He moved between Green and the cop with the gun, still holding the cardboard box.

Captain Somchai was trying to get his gun out of its holster but was having trouble.

'It's okay,' Standing said to Captain Somchai. 'My friend is upset. He doesn't mean any harm. He's just got a lot to process, that's all.' He looked at Fah. 'Please, translate for me. No one needs to get hurt here.'

Fah nodded and began to speak to Captain Somchai in rapid Thai. He listened and nodded, then replied. She listened and then turned to Standing. 'Captain Somchai understands that your friend has a lot to deal with but he needs to sit down and act calmly.'

'He will,' said Standing. 'You heard the lady, Billy. Sit down and behave.'

Green continued to sneer at the cop with the gun.

'Billy, come on. These guys aren't the problem, they're just doing their jobs.'

Green grimaced, then sat down next to Standing. Standing gave him the box and he put it on his lap.

'Tell Captain Somchai I'm sorry,' said Standing. 'Tell him I'm very sorry.'

Fah translated and Captain Somchai nodded. He barked at the young cop, who holstered his gun and backed out of the room.

'We weren't expecting for Pete to have been cremated so soon,' said Standing. 'It's a bit of a shock to be given his ashes.

We were expecting to take Pete's body back to England with us.'

He paused while Fah translated. Captain Somchai listened and nodded.

'Can Captain Somchai explain why Pete was cremated?' Standing asked.

Fah spoke to Captain Somchai, who shrugged and then spoke for several minutes. When he eventually finished he leaned back in his chair. Fah flashed Standing a tight smile. 'The body was sent to Wat Salak Phet. They were to look after it until it was decided what was to be done. For some reason the body was cremated yesterday and the ashes were delivered here this morning. If you want to know why the body was burned – cremated – then you should talk to the abbot.'

'Okay,' said Standing. 'But I don't understand why the body wasn't held for evidence. And I don't understand why no post mortem was carried out.'

Fah frowned. 'Post mortem?'

'Autopsy. When a doctor examines a body to see what happened.'

'I understand.' She spoke to Captain Somchai, who clearly wasn't happy with the question. He sneered at her before answering, and she was smiling as she listened as if she didn't want to antagonise him any further. Eventually he stopped and Fah turned to look at Standing. 'Okay, so there was no doubt that it was suicide. Mister Pete killed himself. That was clear. So there would be no reason for an . . .' She hesitated over the word. '. . . autopsy. The body was taken from the resort to the wat. The temple.'

Standing nodded and smiled. 'Please thank Captain Somchai for all his help. We are very grateful. The thing is, Fah, we

know almost nothing about what happened to Pete. Can we
have a look at the file?'

'There would be no point,' she said. 'It will be in Thai.'

'Could you go through it with us? Explain what happened?'

'Translate the file, you mean?'

'It would be a big help for us, so that we can understand
what happened.'

She nodded and then spoke to Captain Somchai. It was
clear from his body language that he wasn't happy with the
idea, but she lowered her head and smiled a lot and kept
nodding and eventually he nodded along with her. He spoke
to her gruffly and gestured at Standing and Green. 'Captain
Somchai says yes, I can go over the file with you, but only on
the computer and you mustn't take any photographs.'

'That's fine,' said Standing. He smiled at Captain Somchai.
'Thank you so much,' he said, and gave him a wai. Captain
Somchai seemed taken aback by the gesture, he sat up straight
and gave him a wai back.

CHAPTER 9

Fah gave Standing and Green bottles of water and two paper cups, then sat down at her computer and logged on. Standing and Green were sitting either side of her. Green didn't bother with his cup and gulped straight from the bottle. A wood-bladed fan turned slowly overhead but Fah had a much more efficient floor-standing fan in the corner of her office. The breeze rippled her hair as her red-painted nails clicked on the keyboard. Eventually a file popped up onto her screen. Standing leaned towards it but it was in Thai and he couldn't make head nor tail of it. The box containing Pete Green's ashes was on a table by the door.

As Fah scrolled through the report, she reached a drawing of a room. There was a square which obviously represented the bed, and on it the outline of a body.

'Stop there,' said Standing, and he leaned forward again to get a better look. 'Who drew that?' he asked.

'The officer who was first on the scene,' said Fah. 'Police Lance Corporal Chayaphon.'

'So Captain Somchai didn't actually visit the crime scene?'

'Mister Matt, it wasn't a crime scene. It was a suicide scene. So there would be no need for the captain to attend.'

'Okay, but the officer who drew this picture. Why didn't he take photographs?'

Fah frowned. 'Why would he take a photograph?'

'For evidence. To show what the crime—' He grimaced and corrected himself. 'To show what the room looked like. When they found Pete.'

'We wouldn't normally do that.'

Standing opened his mouth to argue but realised there was no point. If things were done differently in Thailand, arguing about them wouldn't change anything. 'So what happened?' he asked.

'A maid opened the door to clean the room. She had knocked and no one had answered. She called the police and Police Lance Corporal Chayaphon attended on his motorbike. He saw the body and realised immediately that Mister Pete had killed himself.'

'That's the way it works here? The first officer on the scene decides what happened?'

'In the case of suicide, yes.'

'But what about a doctor? Did he call a doctor?'

Fah frowned. 'Why would he call a doctor? Mister Pete was already dead.'

'In England, a doctor has to sign a piece of paper giving the cause of death. He is called in before the body is taken away.'

'That doesn't happen here. A death certificate is usually issued one or two days later.'

'What does the report say happened?'

'Just that Mister Pete put a plastic bag over his head and suffocated. He had clearly been dead for several hours before he was found.'

'And the report says that his hands were tied behind his back?'

Fah peered at the report, scrolled back, read some more, and then nodded. 'He used a plastic tie. A zip tie.'

'Where would Pete have got a zip tie from?' asked Green.

'You can buy them,' said Fah.

'What, they have a shop here on Koh Chang that sells zip ties?' said Green. 'I don't think so.'

'Where is the zip tie?' asked Standing.

Fah frowned. 'What do you mean?'

'Someone must have cut the tie off. The smart thing to do would be to dust it for prints.'

'They didn't do that,' said Fah.

'So no one checked for forensics?'

'There isn't a forensics team or laboratory on Koh Chang,' said Fah. 'They would have to send one from Trat. And for anything like DNA they would have to send the samples to Bangkok for analysis. But in a case like this where it is clearly suicide . . .' She shrugged and left the sentence unfinished.

'So everyone just takes the word of a single policeman?' said Green. 'This is bullshit.'

'This hotel where Pete was staying,' said Standing. 'Where is it?'

Fah scrolled through the report, then nodded. 'It's a resort in Lonely Beach.'

Standing laughed. 'Lonely Beach? Seriously?'

'That's what it's called. It's one of the quiet beaches. It's on the west side of the island. Very popular with backpackers. What is it you say? Cheap and cheerful.'

Green smiled. 'That sounds like Pete. Short arms and long pockets.'

Fah frowned, not getting the reference. 'It means he was careful with his money,' explained Standing.

Fah tilted her head on one side, then she laughed. 'I see, his arms are too short to reach his money. That's funny.'

'Yeah, that was Pete,' said Green.

'What's the resort called?' asked Standing.

'The Best Friends Resort,' said Fah.

'How long to drive from here?'

'Half an hour, maybe more. You have to go north and then around the west side of the island.'

'And the temple where they burned Pete?'

Fah stood up and went over to a large map on the wall. It was a map of the island and a chunk of the mainland. She pointed at the top. 'This is the ferry terminal,' she said. 'From there you can drive west and south, or east and south.' She ran her finger to the left and down. 'This is the main tourist area, White Sand Beach, and further south is Lonely Beach. At the end of the road is Bang Bao Pier and fishing village.' She put her finger back on the pier at the top of the map. 'The east side of the island has fewer tourists.' She ran her finger down the road on the east side of the island. 'This is where we are, and if you drive further south you will come to Wat Salak Phet and beyond it the White Buddha Viewpoint. Wonderful for photographing the bay. The problem is there is no road between Bang Bao on the west and Salak Phet on the east. It is only a few miles but there is no road. You have to drive all the way up to the top of the island and back down.'

'Why is there no road at the bottom of the island?' asked Standing.

'No one knows for sure,' said Fah. 'The government approved it years ago but nothing happened.' She shrugged. 'Probably corruption.' She went back to the computer and sat down. She looked at the screen. 'The report says Mister Pete had booked in to the resort four days ago. According to his passport he had arrived in Thailand the day before he checked in, on a flight from Vietnam. The hotel staff said he had no visitors and that he had driven there in a rented car.'

'Where is the car now?' asked Standing.

Fah scrolled through the report. 'It doesn't say. Maybe it is still at the hotel. Somebody will have to come from Bangkok to collect it.'

'What sort of car is it?'

She checked the file. 'A Ford Ranger pick-up truck. A red one.'

Standing looked over at Green. 'What do you think, Billy? Temple first or the hotel?'

Green looked at his watch. 'It'll be dark soon,' he said.

'The roads can be dangerous at night,' said Fah. 'They are narrow and very steep in places.'

'Hotel, then,' said Standing. 'We can check in to the Best Friends and ask around. Then first thing tomorrow we can drive over to the temple.'

Green nodded. 'Sounds good to me,' he said.

Standing smiled at Fah. 'Well, thank you for all your help,' he said. 'Is there anything else in that report that you think we should know about?'

She finished scrolling down the report, then shook her head. 'It's just like Captain Somchai said. Mister Pete was found alone in his room, he didn't have any visitors, and he was dead when Police Lance Corporal Chayaphon arrived. I am sorry for your loss but it does look as if Mister Pete took his own life.'

Green opened his mouth, but Standing glared at him and shook his head. The girl was doing her best to help, and if there was a problem it wasn't down to her. 'Thank you, Fah,' he said. 'Your name, does it mean something?'

'It means sky,' she said. 'Or the colour blue.'

'It's a nice name,' said Standing. He and Green stood up. Green picked up the cardboard box.

'Matt is a nice name, too,' she said. 'Does that have a meaning?'

'Yeah,' growled Green. 'It's something you wipe your feet on.'

Fah frowned in confusion and Standing chuckled. 'He's just joking,' he said. 'Thank you again for all your help.'

'No problem,' said Fah. She put her hands together and gave him a wai.

Standing returned the gesture, then grabbed the carry-on bag and followed Green out of the office and down the corridor. Green opened the door to the reception area. 'This is all bollocks, right?' said Green. 'No way Pete topped himself.'

'You're preaching to the converted, mate. But there's no point in making waves here. The cops have made their decision, nothing you or I can say is going to change that.'

Green held up the box. 'And what the fuck is this about? Someone wanted rid of the evidence, right?'

Standing nodded. 'I think so, yes. Let's see what they have to say at the temple. Until then, all we have is guesswork and supposition. We take this step by step, Billy. Once we've got all the intel we need, then we'll make a plan of attack. We need to stay calm. Focused. No flying off the handle.'

Green flashed him a sly smile. 'You'd know all about that, right?'

Standing grinned. It was a fair enough comment. Standing had had more than his fair share of flying-off-the-handle moments, and twice he had lost his sergeant's stripes for letting his anger get the better of him. Standing's problem was that he tended to react instinctively and the reactions that served him well while under fire tended to cause issues when he wasn't in combat. When pushed he tended to push back, and to push back aggressively, but anger management courses and the threat of being thrown out of the Regiment had helped him bring his anger under control – most of the time.

Standing put the carry-on bag into the back of the Fortuner. Green put the cardboard box next to the bag and Standing closed the door.

They climbed into the vehicle and Standing started the engine. He was just about to pull away from the kerb when Fah came running out of the police station.

Standing wound down the window as she ran up to the vehicle. 'Mister Matt, wait. Don't go!'

'What's wrong?' asked Standing.

'My boss says I can go with you,' she said.

'Go with me?' Standing repeated.

'To help with you. I can translate for you.'

'Okay, that's great.'

'But I have to go home to change. He says I cannot wear my uniform. It cannot be official, so I have to take holiday leave.'

'That's crazy.'

'No, he doesn't want the police to be involved and I under-stand that. Can you wait for me? I'll get changed and come back. I don't live far away.'

'Sure. Yes. And I'll pay you, so don't worry about taking holiday.'

She beamed at him and hurried over to a Yamaha scooter.

She started it and drove off, her long black hair blowing in the wind.

'Well, that's a turn up for the books,' said Green.

'Captain Somchai wants to keep an eye on us, that's what's going on,' said Standing. 'She's his spy.'

'You never trust anyone, do you?'

Standing grinned. 'He's an officer and no, I never trust officers.'

CHAPTER 10

Fah was back within twenty minutes. She had changed into faded blue jeans and a red Liverpool football shirt and had tucked her hair into a Liverpool baseball cap. She parked her bike and hurried over to the Fortuner. She had swapped her heels for Converse sneakers and was no longer carrying her gun.

'So you're a Liverpool fan?' asked Green as she climbed into the back.

'My dad was a big fan, so I am too,' she said. 'What about you?'

'Chelsea,' said Green.

'Was your dad a Chelsea fan?'

'I dunno. He left when I was a kid.'

'Oh, I'm sorry. What about you, Matt? Who do you support?'

Standing reversed out of the parking space and headed to the road. 'I've never been a big fan of football,' he said. 'So, we want to go to the hotel where Pete died. Is that okay with you?'

'Of course,' she said. 'I'm just here to help.'

Standing exchanged a knowing look with Green. Was she really there to help, or to spy on them? Green programmed the Best Friends Resort into the GPS as Standing accelerated, heading north.

They drove up to the top of the island, past the ferry terminal, then headed south on the west side of the island. They passed a roadside stall where an old woman was sitting behind a table piled high with the strange fruit they'd seen on the mainland. 'What is that?' Standing asked Fah. 'What is she selling?'

'It's called durian,' she said. 'They call it the king of fruits. Did you try it?'

Standing shook his head. 'It looks strange, with the thorns and all.'

'Yes, you have to be careful when you open it,' she said. 'And it smells bad. Really bad.'

'Seriously?'

She nodded. 'It smells like sewage. Like a toilet that has gone bad. Most airlines won't let you take it on their planes and a lot of hotels ban it.'

'But if it smells so bad, why do people eat it?'

'Because it tastes so good.' She laughed at the look of confusion on his face. 'I know, it sounds crazy. But it really does smell bad. This is a rental car, right?' Standing nodded. 'Well, if you were to eat durian in the car and then take the car back, they would be really angry with you. They might even charge you because the smell will stay for days. But when you eat it . . .' She rubbed her stomach. 'It tastes so good. Like sweet custard. You can eat it raw or you can cook with it. Thai people love it. And they love it in China, too. The Chinese are buying up a lot of land now in Trat and using it to grow durian which they then send to China. The best durian comes from Trat, they say. You should try some. But not in the car. And not in your room.'

'So outside then?'

She nodded. 'And no alcohol while you eat it. It can make your stomach burn if you eat it with alcohol.'

'Good to know,' said Standing.

They reached a busy tourist area with bars, restaurants, resorts and hotels, though everything was at most three storeys high. There were massage shops and tattoo parlours and shops selling clothes, swimwear, and inflatable pool floats. Sunburned Western couples walked hand in hand, others were sitting in the bars and cafes sheltering from the relentless sun.

'This is White Sand Beach,' said Fah. 'Very popular with tourists.'

'Is there much crime here?' asked Standing.

'Not really,' said Fah. 'It's a small island and people can only come in or leave on the ferry, so we tend to know who is here. Theft is the main problem. The people who live here are poor and many of the tourists are rich, so sometimes they are tempted. But usually it's just stealing from hotel rooms. We haven't had a robbery since I moved here and murder is unheard of.'

'What about tourists misbehaving?'

Fah shook her head. 'We don't get those sort of tourists here,' she said. 'They go to Pattaya or Phuket where there is more nightlife. This is a much quieter island. Most of the tourists here are married and lots of families come for a quiet holiday. They do sometimes have full moon parties on the beaches but there are rarely any problems.'

The tourist area ran for a couple of miles and then they were back in the countryside, the towering jungle-covered mountains off to the left. They drove through several small villages which were little more than a line of shops either side of the road, though they passed several signs advertising beach-side resorts.

The farmland gave way to jungle and the road began to twist and turn through trees and vines. It was so steep in some places that they had to slow to almost walking pace and there were signs warning that traffic coming up had the right of way.

'This is one of the most dangerous bits of road on the island,' warned Fah as Standing edged the Fortuner down. 'Motorcycles often crash here and it is even more dangerous when it rains.'

A black Mercedes was coming up towards them and Standing moved the Fortuner as far over as he could and braked. They were on the steepest part of the road and the Mercedes was struggling. Its rear wheels began to spin and the back swung across the road, but then the tyres bit into the tarmac and the car straightened up. As the Mercedes went by, Standing caught a glimpse of the driver, an ashen-faced Thai lady gripping the steering wheel as if her life depended on it.

They reached the bottom of the hill and the road straightened. There was still jungle around them, but it thinned out as they headed south. They went by more resorts, some little more than a collection of wooden huts, though others were beachside luxury villas. There was vegetation both sides of the road, but often on the right they caught glimpses of the sea, off in the distance.

'This is Lonely Beach ahead of us,' said Fah.

'Why do they call it Lonely Beach?' asked Green.

'Because it's so quiet here, I suppose. You can see, it's not busy like White Sand Beach.'

Green looked across at Standing. 'This isn't Pete's style,' he said. 'He hates the quiet. He likes people and music and stuff.'

Standing nodded. 'Yeah, I know. But maybe he just wanted some R&R.'

'He did, but he was never one for sitting on a beach.'

'What was he doing in Vietnam?'

'He said he was out there to see some guy. The father of a Navy SEAL he met when he was embedded with them. The SEAL died and Pete promised to go out and meet the father. I never got the full story.'

'Turn right here,' said Fah.

Standing did as he was told. They drove along a narrow track for about a hundred metres and then it opened out into a clearing about fifty metres across. There was a white SUV and a few pick-up trucks parked in front of a wooden shack with BEST FRIENDS RESORT hand-painted on a sign across the roof.

Standing parked next to a white pick-up truck with a mud-splattered trail bike in the back. They all climbed out and looked around. There was no front wall to the shack, and inside there was a desk and a couple of wicker sofas either side of a wicker coffee table. There was a blackboard on an easel by the entrance offering rooms with aircon for four hundred baht and rooms with a fan for three hundred.

Green pulled a face. 'That was never Pete's style,' he said. 'He could lie in a ditch or a cave in the desert for weeks without complaining, but when he was on holiday he liked his comfort. Marriott or Sheraton, that's what he went for.'

Standing nodded. Green was right. 'So what do you think? He wanted a low profile?'

'Maybe.'

'Fah, what sort of people would stay here?'

'Backpackers, mainly,' she said. 'Or Trat people who want

a cheap beach holiday. The beach here is really pretty and the sea is clean.' She pointed at a red Ford Ranger pick-up truck. 'This one is from Bangkok. Maybe that was Mister Pete's.'

'We can check that easily enough,' said Standing. He opened the back of the Fortuner and unzipped the case they had been given at the Koh Chang police station. He took out the keys and tossed them to Green.

Green caught them and pointed the key fob at the pick-up. He pressed the button and the door locks clicked. 'Bingo!' he said.

As he pulled open the driver's door, a Thai man came running out of the wooden shack, shouting in Thai. He was wearing a dark green polo shirt with BEST FRIENDS RESORT on the pocket and a teak name badge that said DAENG. He had a walkie-talkie in a holster on his hip. 'What are you doing?' he shouted.

He was so intent on shouting at Green that he didn't see Standing and Fah next to the Fortuner.

'That is not your property!'

Green turned around, holding the keys up and smiling. Before he could say anything, the Thai man's face went ashen and he took a couple of steps back as if he had been punched in the chest.

Green opened his mouth to speak, but before he could say a word the man turned and ran back into the shack. 'What's his problem?' asked Green. He climbed into the truck, leaned over and opened the glove box. He pulled out a couple of printed sheets and examined them as Standing and Fah walked over. 'It's the rental agreement,' he said. 'Pete booked it out for a week.'

'Anything else in there?' asked Standing.

Green bent over again and checked. 'Nothing.'

Standing peered in through the open door. There were a couple of empty bottles of water but other than that the cab was empty. There were traces of mud and sand on the carpets but nothing excessive. There was no GPS in the truck, so no easy way of finding out where it had been.

Standing heard voices from the direction of the shack and he turned to see a middle-aged woman with permed hair and sunglasses walking towards them. She was wearing a white high-necked shirt and a long dark blue dress and the man with the walkie-talkie was following her, accompanied by two more Thai men in resort polo shirts. 'What are you doing?' she asked.

'We're just checking the truck,' said Standing. 'My friend rented it.'

He stepped away from the truck and Green climbed out, still holding the rental agreement. The woman gasped when she saw him, and her hand flew up to cover her mouth. The man with the walkie-talkie began talking to her in rapid Thai and she nodded, her eyes wide and fearful.

'What the hell is wrong?' asked Green, and the woman gasped.

'Mister Pete!' she said.

Standing realised what the problem was, they obviously thought that Pete Green was back from the dead.

Fah started talking to the woman in Thai, pointing at Green and then at Standing, then at the truck. The woman relaxed and began to nod, and pretty soon the three men were smiling and shaking their heads.

The woman patted her chest. 'I thought he was a ghost,' she said. 'My heart, I thought I was going to die.'

'No, not a ghost, I'm Billy, Pete's brother,' said Green. He closed the door of the truck.

The woman spoke to Fah and Fah answered. The woman nodded, and then smiled at Green and Standing and waved at the shack. 'Please, let me give you some tea.'

She led them into the shack and over to a table with eight rattan chairs around it. The woman spoke to the man with the walkie-talkie and he nodded and hurried away with the other two men.

'Please, sit down,' she said. 'I am Miss Wassana, and this is my resort.' She smiled at Green. 'I am still shocked to see you,' she said. 'I did not know Mister Pete had a twin.'

They all sat down. 'Miss Wassana, can you tell us what happened to Pete?'

She frowned, then looked at Fah and spoke to her in Thai. Fah nodded and replied, then looked at Standing. 'Miss Wassana was asking if you had spoken to the police and I said you had, but that you wanted more information.'

Standing nodded and smiled at Miss Wassana. 'The police weren't very helpful,' he said. 'They said that Pete killed himself but we don't believe he would do that.'

Miss Wassana looked uncomfortable. 'It was the maid who found him.'

'Can we talk to the maid?'

'She has gone home already,' said Miss Wassana.

'But she will be here tomorrow?'

Miss Wassana nodded. 'Yes.'

'So we can talk to her then?'

'Sure, if you want.'

A girl wearing a company polo shirt and cut-off jeans came over with four glasses of iced tea on a tray and she slowly and carefully placed them on the table.

'Miss Wassana, did you speak to Pete?'

'Many times.' She picked up a glass and sipped her tea, then nodded her approval at the girl, who gave her a small bow and hurried away.

'Did he say why he was on Koh Chang?'

'He said he wanted some peace and quiet.'

Green and Standing exchanged a look. That wasn't Pete's style, but it might well be what he had told her. 'When did he check in?' Standing asked.

'Four days ago,' said Miss Wassana.

Fah and Green sipped their tea, though Green's sips turned into gulps and he drained his glass.

'What did he do every day?' asked Standing.

'He had breakfast,' she said. 'Here in this room. Then he would go out.'

'Go where? The beach?'

She shook her head. 'No, he never went to the beach. He drove his truck.'

'To where?'

'I don't know. He didn't say. But usually he went that way.' She pointed to the right.

'So south. Every day?'

She nodded. 'Every day. And he came back late, after it was dark. Breakfast was the only meal he ate here. I don't know where he had lunch or dinner.'

'And was he alone? Did he have any visitors?'

She shook her head. 'No. No visitors.'

Standing sipped his iced tea. Clearly the resort was just where Pete slept. Whatever he was doing took place elsewhere on the island.

'Can we see the room where it happened?' asked Green.

Miss Wassana frowned. 'Why?' she said.

'I just want to see where my brother died,' said Green.

'Has anyone stayed in the room since you found Pete?' asked Standing.

Miss Wassana shook her head. 'No, the resort is very quiet. Not many guests.' She forced a smile. 'Actually, now we have no guests. People do not want to stay at a resort where someone killed themselves.'

'We would really like to see the room, Miss Wassana.'

Miss Wassana took a sip of iced tea, dabbed her lips with a tissue and stood up. She waved over at the man with the walkie-talkie and spoke to him in Thai. He opened the desk drawer and took out a key and took it over to her. It was on a keyring with a small carved wooden elephant head. She stood up and took it from him. 'This way,' he said.

Standing, Green and Fah followed her through the shack. There was a small kitchen to the left. An old Thai woman in a chef's jacket and hat gasped when she saw Green and took a step back. She was holding a wok and it slipped from her hands and crashed onto the tiled floor. Miss Wassana said something to her in Thai and the old woman bent down and retrieved her wok.

To the right were two toilets, one with a carving of a man doing a wai, the other with a female version. At the rear of the shack was a long flat-roofed concrete building with six doors, with a long washing line in front of it. Standing figured it was where the staff lived.

The land sloped gently down towards a white sandy beach. A path about six feet wide led down to the beach and narrower paths split off it towards a dozen small cabins. The cabins were made of teak planks with sloping roofs, held off the ground by concrete supports. Miss Wassana took them halfway down the main path and then off to the right.

Miss Wassana pointed at a cabin. 'This is where Mister Pete stayed,' she said. She gave the key to Standing. 'I don't want to go inside,' she said.

'I understand. Has it been cleaned?'

Miss Wassana nodded. 'Oh yes. After they took the body away our maid cleaned it from top to bottom. A deep clean, like we did for Covid.'

There was a sign at the bottom of the steps that said PLEASE REMOVE SHOES. Standing and Green took off their shoes and went up the steps. Standing unlocked the door and they went inside. It was a single room with a large window over-looking the terrace and the sea beyond. There was a double bed with a beige quilt, two rattan chairs and a small dressing table with a mirror, and by the bathroom door was a rattan wardrobe. The floor was tiled and there was a large ceiling fan. There was a small air-conditioning unit set into the wall to their right and it was obviously needed as the room was stiflingly hot.

The bathroom was tiny, with a cramped shower, a toilet and a small wash basin. It was clean and there was a strong smell of bleach.

Green looked around the room. 'You'd hear anyone coming, wouldn't you? Footsteps on the path. And the steps creak.'

Standing examined the door. There was a security chain and the door could be locked from the inside. There was a curtain with a palm tree pattern across the window but even if it had been closed it would have been a simple matter to check who was on the terrace.

They both looked down at the bed. The place where Pete

had taken his last breath. 'It doesn't feel real, does it?' said Standing.

'I still can't believe it.'

Standing looked out of the window. 'What was he doing here?'

'I have no idea,' said Green. 'He wasn't a great one for beaches or swimming pools. He liked cities. He'd been to Bangkok a few times. Singapore. Hong Kong. But he'd never sit on a beach, that wasn't his thing. Me, I'm fine with it. Give me a drink and a sea view and I'm as happy as Larry.'

Fah appeared in the doorway. 'Are you okay?' she asked.

'We're fine,' said Green. 'Look, I think we might stay here for a couple of days.'

'On Koh Chang? Of course.'

'No, I mean here,' said Green. 'In fact, I want to stay in this room.'

Standing frowned. 'Are you sure about that?'

'I want to, yeah.'

'Okay, mate. Your call.'

They went out onto the terrace. Miss Wassana was standing on the path, her hands clasped together. 'We'd like to stay for two or three nights, Miss Wassana,' said Green. 'And I'd like to stay in this room.'

'Of course. It is an aircon room, so it is more expensive. Four hundred baht a night.'

'That's fine,' said Green.

'And is that one available?' asked Standing, pointing further down the track. There was another cabin about fifty feet away.

'Yes, that one is empty,' said Miss Wassana. She forced a smile. 'Actually they are all empty.'

'Perfect,' said Standing.

'You are sure about this?' Fah asked Standing.

'Yes, why not?'

Fah shuddered but didn't say anything. She looked away, biting her lower lip. Standing instinctively knew what was going through her mind – ghosts. 'We'll be fine,' he said, but she continued to avoid his gaze.

They walked back to the shack and Miss Wassana checked them in. They gave her their passports and she photocopied the main page before giving them back. Standing paid her for three days in cash and she gave him the key to his cabin. 'Enjoy your stay,' she said automatically.

Fah still looked uneasy. Standing smiled at her. 'It's a nice place,' he said.

She forced a smile but didn't say anything.

'Tomorrow will you be okay to go to the temple with us? The one where Pete was cremated?'

'Of course.'

'Can you come here or shall we pick you up somewhere?'

'You can meet me at the police station, it's on your way.'

'You live near the police station?'

'Not far away, yes.'

'Okay, so we'll run you back now.'

She frowned. 'Run me back?'

'I mean we'll take you home now. We'll give you a lift.'

She shook her head and took out her phone. 'No need,' she said. 'I will phone my uncle and he will collect me.' She was frowning again and she looked around to check that Miss Wassana wasn't within earshot. 'Are you sure you want to stay here?' she whispered. 'There are many other places you can stay.'

'Why? What's wrong?'

'This is where your friend died.' She shook her head. 'Okay, up to you,' she said.

'We'll be fine,' said Standing, but she was already walking away with the phone to her ear.

CHAPTER 11

Standing waved as the motorbike sped off down the road. Fah's uncle was in his forties and had arrived on a battered old Honda Wave 100cc motorcycle. He was wearing black jeans, flip-flops and a Liverpool sweatshirt. The uncle had stayed on the bike as he gave Green and Standing a respectful wai. They had both returned the gesture, then Fah had climbed on the back of the bike and promised to meet them the next day at the police station.

'You like her,' said Green as the bike disappeared into the distance.

'What's not to like?'

'I love the hair.'

Standing laughed. 'It is awesome hair.'

'You know what I'd like to . . .'

Standing put up a hand. 'Please don't finish that sentence, you'll put an image into my head that I'll never be able to get rid of. Anyway. We're not here for romance.'

'Fair enough.' Green sighed. 'What the fuck are we going to do, Matt? The cops aren't going to do anything.'

'Let's see what they say at the temple, tomorrow. If we can find out who wanted Pete cremated, we'll know who covered it up.'

They walked back into the shack. Miss Wassana had gone,

but the girl who had brought the iced tea was sitting at the desk. Standing pointed at the bar and asked her if they were serving drinks.

'Of course,' she said. She went behind the bar and asked them what they wanted. 'I'll have a beer,' said Standing. 'Do you have that Chang beer?'

'We do,' she said, and bent down to open a glass-fronted fridge. She took out a bottle of Chang, opened it and gave it to him with a long glass.

'Have you got Johnnie Walker Black Label?' asked Green.

'Sure,' she said.

'Let me have the bottle.'

She frowned. 'The bottle?'

'I'll pay. And a bottle of soda. And ice.'

'Billy . . .' said Standing.

Green grinned. 'Don't worry. I'll pace myself.'

The girl took a bottle of whisky over to a table, along with a full ice bucket and a bottle of soda water and a glass. The two men sat down on wicker chairs as she opened the whisky and the soda. She started to pour the whisky but Green smiled and took the bottle from her. 'I'll do that, love. Don't you worry yourself.' He opened his wallet and took out a five-hundred-baht note. 'Put the drinks on our bill, but this is for you.'

Her eyes widened and she gave him a very respectful wai before hurrying back to the desk.

Standing sipped his beer. 'They all reacted the same way, you notice that?'

'What do you mean?'

'The whole – what are you doing back? – are you a ghost? – all that stuff. The guy who first saw you, then Miss Wassana. The rest of the staff. They all reacted the same way.'

'Pete and I are twins. People are always getting confused, you know that.' He scowled. 'I've got to stop using the present tense. We were twins. Past tense.'

'The point I'm making is that anyone who knew Pete would be surprised to see you. Back from the dead, right? They were all genuinely shocked. But that police colonel in Trat, he didn't comment on it at all. He accepted that you were Pete's brother but didn't mention that you were his twin. That means that he never saw Pete's body.'

'He didn't seem that interested, truth be told. And like he said, he didn't go to Koh Chang and they never took any pictures of the crime scene.' He scowled again. 'According to them, there was no crime scene.'

'Right, okay, I'll buy that. But the cop here on Koh Chang, the Somchai guy. He was the investigating officer. He didn't bat an eyelid when he saw you. And again, he accepted the fact that you were Pete's brother, but didn't mention that you were his twin. I don't think he ever saw Pete. That means he never went to the crime scene. I never thought of asking him that, I just assumed as he was the investigating officer he would have come here. But he didn't bat an eyelid when he saw you.'

Green frowned. 'That doesn't make sense, does it? He was in charge of the investigation, he should have been here.'

'It would do if Somchai knew the killer, or killers, and it was a cover-up from the start. That's why there are no photographs of the crime scene and no forensics. Somchai was never supposed to investigate the killing, only cover it up. And that's what he did. He's probably the one who rushed through the cremation, to make absolutely sure there was no evidence.'

Green's eyes hardened. 'We should slot the bastard.'

Standing shook his head. 'We're not here to start shooting

cops,' he said. 'And I don't think he's the one who killed Pete. He's a cop, he wouldn't be stupid enough to kill Pete in his own hotel room. No, someone else killed Pete, and Somchai was brought in to cover it up.'

Green gestured at the road with his glass. 'Interesting that Miss Fah wants to meet us at the police station tomorrow,' he said.

'That's where she left the scooter.'

'Yeah, but her uncle is driving her. Why doesn't he bring her back here and we can all go together?'

Standing shrugged. 'The station is on the way to the temple.'

'Or maybe Captain Somchai wants a debrief.'

'You think she's reporting back to him?'

'Well, of course she is,' said Green. 'Don't let the razor-sharp cheekbones and glossy black hair blind you to what's going on.'

'I didn't notice the captain's cheekbones but he did have a good head of hair.'

Green laughed. 'You know what I mean, Matt. She's his spy, he wants to know who we talk to and what we find out.'

'She's also a damn useful interpreter.'

'Yeah, well every cloud. Just watch her, that's all I'm saying.' He frowned. 'There's something else about her that worries me.'

'Her fit, trim body?'

'No, mate. The way she looked at me the first time she saw me in the police station. She looked surprised to see me.'

'I thought it was the fact that there were two of us that threw her. She was maybe expecting one foreigner and two turned up.'

Green shook his head. 'No, I could see something in her eyes when she looked at me. She was surprised to see me.'

'That's impossible, Billy. She never saw Pete. It was that Lance Corporal Chayaphon who went to Pete's room and it was him who put the body in a body bag and took it to the temple.'

Green shrugged. 'I'm just telling you what I saw.' He frowned. 'And remember what she said when she came over? She said that she didn't realise that Pete had a twin. How would she know that I was Pete's twin if she hadn't seen him?'

'Maybe she saw Pete's picture in his passport?'

'Maybe. But then why didn't she mention it?' Green shrugged again. 'Maybe I'm overthinking it.' He rubbed the back of his neck. 'They took Pete's phone for a reason,' he said. 'If it was robbery they'd have taken the wallet, watch and passport. And those binoculars aren't cheap.'

Standing nodded. 'So there was something on the phone they didn't want anyone to see? Either messages or calls, maybe photographs.'

'That's what I was thinking. Is there any way we can find out who he called?'

'That's not in my skill set,' said Standing. 'But I know a man who might be able to help.' He yawned and looked at his watch. 'I'm gonna hit the hay,' he said. 'Jet lag's kicking in.'

Green stood up. 'Can I borrow the car keys for a minute?'

Standing frowned but handed over the keys. Green went over and spoke to the girl at the desk, then headed outside. He went over to the Fortuner, and returned with the box containing Billy's ashes just as the girl arrived at the table with a bottle of vodka. 'That can go on the bill, too,' said Green. She looked confused but he gave her a couple of hundred baht and she smiled and went back to the desk.

Green put the box on the table and tossed the keys to Standing. 'I'm going to have a drink with Pete.'

'You want company?' said Standing, getting to his feet.

'Nah, mate. I'm good. Few things I've got to say to him, that's all. And Matt, thanks for this.'

'For what?'

'For coming out here with me. Above and beyond.'

'Pete was one of us,' said Standing. 'Least I can do.'

Green stepped forward and hugged Standing tightly. 'I'm glad you're here.'

'Just don't try to fucking kiss me,' said Standing.

Green laughed, slapped him on the back, then released his grip. 'See you tomorrow.'

'Not if I see you first.'

Standing walked to his cabin. He locked the door behind him, then kicked off his trainers and lay down on the bed. He pulled out his phone and looked at the screen. He didn't like having to ask for help, but on this occasion he didn't have a choice. He scrolled through his address book and found Dan Shepherd's number. His thumb hesitated over the call button. Spider Shepherd had left the SAS almost twenty years ago, but he was still talked about with reverence, and not just because he had eaten a tarantula in the jungle and had a habit of running around Stirling Lines with a rucksack filled with bricks wrapped in newspaper. He was a living legend who had left the SAS with honours and carved out a new career, first with the cops and now with MI5. If anyone could help him it was Shepherd, but Standing never liked asking for favours. He took a deep breath and exhaled slowly. He had no choice, there was no one else he could ask. He pressed the call button.

Shepherd answered the phone within seconds. 'Yeah?'

Standing had called Shepherd before, so he would have recognised the number. It was impossible to tell from the single word whether Shepherd was unhappy at being contacted or not, hopefully he was just being cagey until he knew for sure that it was Standing on the line.

'Spider, it's Matt Standing, you okay?'

'I'm just fine, Matt. Working my arse off, but that's par for the course these days. You?'

'I've got a problem, Spider, and I need your help. On the QT.'

'What do you need?'

Standing took a deep breath and sighed. 'One of our troopers is dead. Guy called Pete Green. It happened in Thailand and the cops are saying he killed himself.'

'Sorry to hear that, Matt.'

'Yes, but Pete wasn't the type, there's no way that he killed himself. We've been telling them that until we're blue in the face but they won't listen.'

'We?'

'I'm in Thailand with Billy, his brother. An island called Koh Chang. It's about three hundred kilometres east of Bangkok in Trat Province, in the Gulf of Thailand. Close to the Cambodian border.'

'How's Billy taking it?'

'Better than I expected. But he could go mental at any point. I'm keeping him on a tight leash. The thing is, Pete's phone has gone missing and I need to know who he talked to before he died. Can you get his phone records for me?'

'Yeah, I can do that. Give me the number.'

Standing gave him the digits. 'I don't know how long it'll take,' said Shepherd. 'Could be hours, could be a day or two.

But I'll get it done as a priority. What was Pete doing in Thailand?'

'That's what we want to find out. He was supposed to be in Vietnam. But four days after he flew over to Thailand, they found him dead in his room with a plastic bag over his head and his hands tied behind his back.'

'I don't know the guy. How long has he been in the Regiment?'

'Couple of years. He's a good operator. Was, I mean. Past tense.'

'Okay, let me get started on the phone dump. Keep me in the loop, okay?'

'I will do, Spider. But mum's the word. Colonel Davies was happy enough for us to come out here but he made it clear we weren't to go rocking any boats.'

'I hear you,' said Shepherd. 'But be careful out there. It's a few years since I was in Thailand but I doubt it's changed much. There aren't the same checks and balances that we're used to in the UK. It can be a dangerous place.'

'Eyes wide open, Spider.'

Shepherd ended the call and Standing lay back and stared at the ceiling as he tried to process everything that had happened. None of it made any sense. Pete Green shouldn't have been in Thailand and there was no way on God's earth that he would have killed himself. Standing was still running through his options when he finally fell asleep.

CHAPTER 12

S tanding woke just as dawn broke. He shaved and showered and pulled on a polo shirt, a pair of shorts and his trainers. He went outside and headed over to Green's cabin. The curtains were drawn and there was no sign of Green, then he heard his name being called from the beach. Green was standing by the water, wearing only swimming shorts.

Standing walked to the end of the path and stepped onto the sand. The beach was practically deserted. There were a group of Thais off in the distance sitting under a spreading palm tree, but other than that Standing and Green were alone on the beach. Green was dripping wet, his hair slicked back. 'I needed some exercise,' he said.

'Be careful of sharks,' said Standing.

Green's face fell. 'Are you serious?'

Standing laughed. 'No, mate, just winding you up. No sharks here, at least not the sort that will take a bite out of you. You need to watch out for jellyfish, though. They can pack a hell of a sting.'

'You can always piss on my leg,' said Green with a grin. 'I heard that helps.'

'Mate, I'm happy to piss on you, jellyfish sting or no jelly-fish sting.' He turned to look back at the cabins, shading his eyes with his hand. 'You know, anyone could walk into the resort without being seen.' He looked up and down the beach. 'There isn't any security, and there's no CCTV. We asked them if Pete had had any visitors and they said no, but that just means they didn't walk in through reception. If they had come in from the beach, no one would be any the wiser.'

'I don't get why Pete would stay here in the first place,' said Green. 'It'd be far too quiet for him.'

'Maybe he was just looking to stay below the radar,' said Standing. He looked at his watch. 'Why don't you get changed, I'll go and see if I can talk to the maid.'

They walked together off the beach and up the path. Green went to his cabin while Standing walked through to the reception area. Miss Wassana was sitting at the desk in reception, studying her smartphone. She was wearing a canary-yellow dress and there was a walkie-talkie in front of her. She didn't look up as he got to the desk, continuing to tap away with both thumbs. 'Miss Wassana?' said Standing, and she flinched as if she'd been poked. It took her a second or so to process that it was a real person talking to her, but then her smile flicked on. 'Good morning,' she said.

'Do you think it would be possible to talk to the maid who found Mister Pete?' he asked.

Before she could answer, her phone beeped and she looked down to check the screen before looking back at Standing. 'Why do you need to talk to her?'

'Just so that we know exactly what happened,' said Standing.

She frowned. 'Mister Pete killed himself, that's what happened,' she said.

'And we'd like to thank her. And give her a tip, obviously. I'm sure Mister Pete would have wanted us to tip her for him.' He took out his wallet to emphasise the point.

Miss Wassana nodded and smiled. She picked up the walkie-talkie and spoke into it in Thai. There was a crackle and an answer, then Miss Wassana spoke again. She put down the walkie-talkie and smiled at Standing. 'Coming now,' she said.

After a couple of minutes a plump Thai lady appeared on the path. She was wearing pale green overalls, a hair net, and a surgical face mask. She had her name on a small teak badge. NAN.

'Does Nan speak English?' asked Standing.

'A little bit,' said Miss Wassana. 'But you can tell me and I will explain to her.'

'Thank you,' said Standing. He opened his wallet and gave Nan a thousand-baht note. 'Could you tell her that is for looking after Pete's room while he was here?'

Nan took the money and gave him a wai as Miss Wassana spoke to her in Thai.

Nan nodded at Standing. 'Thank you,' she said.

'Miss Wassana, could you ask Nan what happened on the day she found Pete in his room?''

Miss Wassana spoke to Nan again, and Nan spent several minutes replying. When she had finished, Miss Wassana turned to look at Standing. 'There were four rooms to clean that day. She knocked on Mister Pete's room at about nine o'clock but there was no answer, so she cleaned another room and went back to Mister Pete's at about ten thirty. He still didn't answer and the curtains were drawn, so she unlocked the door. The room was dark and when she switched on the light she saw Mister Pete lying on the bed. At first she thought he was asleep, but when she stepped into the room she saw that he had a bag over his head. She left the room and called Daeng.'

Standing nodded. Daeng was the man with the walkie-talkie

who had been on the desk when they had first visited the resort. 'What happened then?' he asked.

'Daeng went to the room. Then he called me. I called the police.'

'Did you go into the room?'

Miss Wassana nodded. 'I went in to check that he was dead, but I could see that he was as soon as I saw him.' She shuddered. 'It was terrible.'

'When you went in, did you or Nan see his phone?'

Miss Wassana frowned, then spoke to Nan. Nan replied and shook her head. 'Neither of us saw a phone. But we only went in to look at Mister Pete and then we went out. We didn't want to stay there with him.' She shuddered.

'And did you phone the police, or did Daeng?'

'I did. They sent an officer and he arrived after about thirty minutes.'

'Did you or Nan go back into the room with the policeman?'

Miss Wassana shook her head vehemently. 'We didn't want to go in.'

'Did you see what the policeman did while he was in the room?"

'I didn't.' Miss Wassana spoke to Nan in Thai. The maid answered and they went back and forth for a minute or so. 'The policeman took the bag off Mister Pete's head and checked to see if he was breathing.'

'What was Pete wearing?'

'Wearing?'

'His clothes?'

Miss Wassana frowned as she tried to remember. 'Jeans,' she said. 'And a T-shirt.'

They heard footsteps and turned to see Green walking

towards them. He had changed into cargo shorts and a green-and-black camouflage-pattern T-shirt. The maid gasped when she saw Green and put her hand up to her face. He couldn't see her mouth but Standing was sure it was wide open.

Miss Wassana saw the maid's discomfort and spoke to her in rapid Thai, obviously explaining that Green was the twin brother of the man she'd found dead. The maid nodded and gave Green a respectful wai but there was still a fearful look in her eyes.

'Nan and Miss Wassana are just telling me about how they found Pete,' said Standing. He looked at Miss Wassana. 'Do you know the name of the police officer?'

'I don't. But I'd seen him before, he's with the Tourist Police. He's tall and quite young.'

'And what did he do? After he had checked that Pete was dead?'

'He took him to the truck. And drove away.'

Standing nodded. 'Okay, but Pete was quite a big man. Did he carry him on his own?'

'No. Daeng and another of our team had to help him. It is quite a long way from the cabin to the car park.'

'Did they put the body on something? Or just carried him?'

'The policeman had a bag. A big black bag.'

'What about his belongings?' asked Green.

Miss Wassana frowned. 'Belongings?' she repeated.

'His things,' explained Standing. 'His clothes, his passport, his shoes.'

'Ah, yes. His things. We put them in a box because we wanted to clean the room.'

'So the policeman didn't tell you to keep the room as it is? He didn't say they were going to look for fingerprints and DNA?'

'No, he said he had finished his investigation. Nan put Mister

Pete's things in a box and gave it to Daeng. I phoned the police station the next day and the policeman came to collect it.'

'The same policeman?'

'Yes. He took the box away. Is there a problem? Is there something missing?'

'We can't find his phone. That's all.'

'I don't think he was robbed because his passport and his wallet were in the room. And thieves know that if they steal a phone they can get caught.'

Standing flashed her an encouraging smile. 'Yes, I think you're right,' he said. 'And again, just to check. When Nan opened the door to Pete's room, it was dark? The lights were off?'

Miss Wassana spoke to Nan, Nan nodded and replied in Thai. 'Yes,' said Miss Wassana. 'It was dark. She couldn't see anything.'

'And was the security chain on?'

Miss Wassana had to translate, then Nan shook her head firmly. 'No,' she said.

Standing thanked her, and thanked Nan, who gave him a respectful wai. He and Green left the shack and headed for the Fortuner.

'Why were you so interested in whether or not the light was on?' asked Green.

'Pete couldn't have killed himself like that in the dark,' said Standing. 'He would have had to have been able to see what he was doing. So if the lights were off when the maid opened the door, somebody must have switched them off.'

Green stopped. 'You're right. That's proof he was murdered.'

'I'm not sure that the cops would see it that way. But yeah, now we know for sure that Pete didn't kill himself. But that doesn't get us any closer to finding out who did it.'

CHAPTER 13

Standing parked the Fortuner outside the police station. Green was munching on a croissant and sipping on a coffee they had picked up from a coffee shop in White Sand Beach. Standing hadn't asked him how much of the whisky he'd drunk but he wasn't showing any signs of a hangover. 'I had a thought,' said Standing.

'Good to know. I guess it was lonely, rattling around in there all on its own.'

Standing ignored the jibe. 'You locked your door last night, right?'

'Of course.'

'Me too. And Pete would have done, as well. But the door wasn't busted in, was it? The maid unlocked it.'

Green raised his eyebrows. 'So Pete must have let them in?'

'Either that, or they had a key. But the doors have security chains and we know it wasn't on because the maid was able to let herself in. She said the chain wasn't on.'

Green nodded. 'He'd open the door on the chain. If it was trouble, he'd have time to react.'

Standing nodded. 'And no one has mentioned any signs of a struggle. So yes, that means Pete had to have let them in.'

'They could have had guns.'

'Pete can handle himself. Men with guns coming through a door, it's no biggie. Bish, bash, bosh.'

'So no bish, bash, bosh means that he knew whoever it was. A girl?'

'I'd say so. He lets a girl in, turns his back, maybe he gets hit on the back of the head.'

'No mention of that in the report,' said Green.

'He wasn't examined by a doctor. Maybe the cop didn't see a head wound, maybe he did and didn't mention it.'

'Which is why they rushed the cremation?' Green nodded. 'That all makes sense. So cherchez la femme?' He grinned. 'Speaking of cherchez la femme, here comes the lovely Miss Fah.' Green nodded over at the entrance to the police station. Fah was wearing a white T-shirt with CHANEL across the chest, and tight faded blue jeans. She had her long hair tied back in a pony tail and was carrying her Liverpool baseball cap. She waved and hurried over to their car.

Green opened the door and climbed out. Fah took his place while he got into the back.

'How did you sleep?' she asked Standing.

'Fine,' he said. 'The bed was really comfortable.'

'Great,' she said. 'So, we need to drive straight on for about fifteen kilometres.'

'Cool,' said Standing. The road was clear but it twisted and turned, so he kept the speed to below thirty miles an hour. They passed a sign pointing to an elephant camp. 'So the island was named after the elephants, right?' he said.

'That's right,' said Fah. 'Koh Chang. Elephant Island.'

'But how did the elephants get here? They can't swim, right?'

Fah laughed and shook her head. 'They came on the ferry,

like everybody else,' she said. 'The elephants were brought over for the tourists, there weren't any here originally.'

Standing frowned. 'So why did they call it Elephant Island?'

'Oh, I see what you mean. It's nothing to do with elephants being here, it's because the island is shaped like the head of an elephant. The bit on the right looks like a trunk and you can see its ears.' She giggled. 'Actually I think you have to be a little drunk to see it.'

'And what about you? Were you born here?'

'I was born in Trat. But my father was born here. He moved to Trat to work and met my mother. I still have family here, though. My uncle, who picked me up last night, and I have two aunts who both work in hotels in White Sand Beach.'

'And you plan to stay here now?'

She shook her head. 'No, eventually I want to move to Bangkok. But I have to prove myself here first.'

'Your English is really good,' said Green from the back seat. 'Did you go to an international school?'

'No, I actually went to a temple school. My parents didn't have much money when I was a kid. But I learned English watching YouTube.'

'Seriously?'

She nodded. 'I love *Only Fools And Horses.*' She laughed. 'Next year we'll be millionaires. You plonker.'

Standing laughed. 'That's brilliant.'

'I watched a lot of British television. And American movies.'

'It paid off,' said Standing. 'Like he said, your English is really good.'

'Have you got a boyfriend, Fah?' asked Green.

'Easy, Billy,' said Standing.

'Hey, I'm just asking.'

'It's okay,' said Fah. 'I think I have a boyfriend.'

'You think?' said Green.

'Well, he was my boyfriend when I was in Trat. But then I moved to Koh Chang and I haven't seen him so much. The only way here is the ferry, and the last ferry is at half past six and it's expensive, so he doesn't come to see me often.'

'Can't he stay with you?' asked Standing.

'Oh no, we're not married, so my uncle wouldn't let him stay. I can stay with him if I go to Trat, but I work long hours, so I don't get to go much.' She shrugged. 'We talk on FaceTime but some days he doesn't call.'

'He's crazy,' said Green. 'You're lovely.'

'What about you, Billy? Do you have a girlfriend?'

'Don't even think about it, Fah,' said Standing.

'What?' she asked. She had an innocent look on her face but Standing was pretty sure she knew that Green was flirting with her.

'We're just chatting, Matt,' said Green. 'No harm in that.'

'I don't want you breaking Fah's heart.'

Fah giggled. 'Does he break hearts?'

'Arms and legs, mainly. But sometimes hearts.'

Fah pointed ahead of them. 'That's the temple there. You can park in front of it.' To the left was a line of shacks that appeared to be a mixture of restaurants and shops, to the right was a Thai temple with white walls and golden windows, topped by a steep red roof with gold trimming. Running around the temple was a wall made from two green snakes or dragons. They turned off the main road, drove alongside the snake wall and parked.

'Is that a snake?' asked Standing.

'They are Naga,' said Fah. 'Serpents. Half human. They are guarding the temple.'

They climbed out of the Fortuner. The sky was cloudless and the sun was relentless. A flight of stone steps led up to the temple, flanked by the heads of the mythical serpents, their red mouths gaping with rows of sharp white teeth. On either side of the serpents were statues of birdlike mythological creatures.

'Do you want to look inside?' asked Fah. 'It is very beautiful.'

Standing and Green exchanged a look. They weren't there for sightseeing, but Fah was so enthusiastic it seemed churlish to turn down her offer. 'Sure,' said Green.

She took them up the steps and they removed their shoes before entering the temple. There was no air conditioning but the inside of the temple was surprisingly cool, helped by three green floor-standing fans. There was a bright red ceiling with a crystal chandelier in the centre, a large seated Buddha on a podium with several smaller gold Buddhas in front of it. There was an ornate multicoloured carpet on the marble floor and garish friezes of Thai scenes around the walls.

Fah knelt down on the carpet and placed her hands together in a wai and sat there for a couple of minutes. Standing and Green stood behind her, their arms folded. Eventually she stood up. 'This temple is very famous,' she said. 'It was built more than a hundred years ago when the King Rama V visited the island.'

'When you pray, what do you pray for?' asked Green.

'For a happy healthy life for me and for my family,' said Fah. 'And I prayed for Mister Pete. I prayed that his next life will be a happy one.'

Green smiled but didn't say anything. Standing knew what he was thinking. In their experience the dead weren't reborn, they stayed dead and all the praying in the world wouldn't change that. But Fah's heart was in the right place, so they just smiled and nodded. She took them out of the temple and they slipped their shoes on.

Opposite the temple was a smaller, far less ornate single-storey building with more buddhas inside, and to the left, on the far side of a grassy area, was a line of what appeared to be accommodation units, two storeys tall and built of weathered teak. A young monk in a saffron robe was sweeping a balcony of one of the upstairs rooms with a long-handled brush.

About a hundred metres to the left of the accommodation block was a simple white building with a blue steepled roof and a tall white chimney. Standing knew without asking that it was the crematorium where Pete had been burned. Fah caught his look and smiled uncomfortably. 'Do you want to see it?' she asked.

Standing shook his head. He looked at Green. 'Billy? Do you want to visit the crematorium?'

Green also shook his head. 'No need. We know what happened. We just need to talk to the top guy.'

'Yes, the abbot,' said Fah. 'His English is not so good, so let me translate for you.'

'Sure,' said Standing.

'Maybe you and Billy can wait here, I'll go and get him.'

Standing nodded.

'What do think that means?' Green asked Standing as she walked towards the accommodation block. 'She doesn't want us to talk directly to him? She's worried what he might say to us?'

'You're a suspicious bugger,' said Standing. 'Maybe the abbot's English is bad and she doesn't want us to embarrass him.'

Fah stood in front of the block and called up to the monk who was sweeping the balcony. He answered and pointed off to the left. Fah disappeared behind the single-storey building.

Green looked over at the crematorium. 'Funny how life works out, right?'

'Hilarious,' said Standing.

'No, I mean, you'd never have thought that Pete would end up here, right, on an island in the Gulf of Thailand, up in smoke, literally.'

'None of us knows where we'll end up, truth be told,' said Standing.

'Assuming we beat the clock,' said Green. Members of the SAS who died in the line of duty had their names inscribed on the plinth of a large clock in the Stirling Lines barracks. 'Beating the clock' meant surviving your time with the Regiment. Pete hadn't survived but he hadn't been on duty when he'd died, so his name wouldn't be added to the list on the plinth. 'What about you?' asked Green.

'What about me?'

'Where do you want to be buried?'

'Me, I'm planning on living forever, mate.'

Green grinned. 'Yeah, well good luck with that.'

Fah returned from behind the building, accompanied by a wizened old man wearing a burnt-orange robe with an orange cloth bag over his left shoulder. His bald head was covered with dark splodges and his face was wrinkled like old parchment. He could have been anywhere between seventy and a hundred years old, but there was a shrewd intelligence behind his eyes and Standing could feel him measuring them up as he walked slowly towards them. Fah was walking one step behind him and slightly to the side and she kept her head down as if trying to make herself smaller.

The abbot stopped and said something to Fah in Thai. His voice was little more than a whisper but there was a strong authority to it. 'The abbot suggests we talk in the shade,' she said, gesturing at the single-storey building.

'Sounds good,' said Standing. They followed the abbot to the building. Fah, Green and Standing slipped off their shoes. Inside was a line of large buddha figures and a plastic table and chairs. The abbot took off his shoulder bag and sat on the floor. Fah knelt down in front of him. The abbot smiled at Standing and gestured at the chairs but Standing guessed that sitting on the floor would be more respectful, so he followed Fah's example and knelt down. Green did the same.

The abbot spoke to Fah in Thai and she replied, then she turned to look at Green. 'He asks if you are a twin. I said yes. He wants me to give you his condolences. He said losing a twin must be like losing a part of yourself.'

'Tell him it is,' said Green. Fah translated.

'So the abbot saw Pete's body?' asked Standing.

Fah and the abbot spoke for a few minutes before she turned back to Standing. 'The abbot says the body was brought here on a police truck the day that Mister Pete was found. The wat has storage facilities for bodies.'

'But the hospital would have that, too, wouldn't it?' said Standing. 'We drove past the hospital on the way here.'

'Yes, that's true,' said Fah. 'I don't know why they brought it here. But they did. The abbot was told to keep the body until it was collected.'

'So it wasn't sent here to be cremated?'

'He says it was sent here to be stored. Until someone came from England to claim it. Sometimes if a foreigner dies on Koh Chang, the relatives decide to have a ceremony here and to have the body cremated. Then they can take the ashes with them. Or sometimes they scatter them in the sea.'

'Do a lot of foreigners die on Koh Chang?' asked Green.

'Not many. Usually motorcycle accidents during the rainy season. Or heart attacks. A lot of old people come here and sometimes they die.' She shrugged.

'So if the body was brought here to be stored, how did it end up being cremated?'

Fah and the abbot spoke in Thai for several minutes back and forth, Fah asking questions and the abbot answering, often with just a word or two and sometimes with a mere shake of the head. Eventually she turned to look at Standing. 'Okay, this is complicated. Mister Pete's body was brought here on a police truck. From the abbot's description it sounds like Lance Corporal Chayaphon. Two of the monks helped him to move the body.'

'Is this cop guy tall and young?'

Fah frowned. 'Yes, he is. How do you know that?'

'He's the one who went to the resort,' said Standing. 'That's how they described him. Tall and young. So where was the body put?'

'In the temple's refrigerated area. It's big enough to store up to a dozen bodies. There were already two there the day that Mister Pete's body was brought here.'

'And when was that?' asked Green.

'On Tuesday. The day he was discovered.'

'What time?'

Fah asked the abbot in Thai and he replied. 'Just after midday.'

Standing looked over at Green. 'They didn't hang about, did they? He must have driven straight here from the resort.'

'They never planned to investigate his death,' said Green. 'They just wanted Pete out of there.'

Standing looked back at Fah. 'And this Lance Corporal Chayaphon said Pete's body was to be stored here?'

Fah nodded. 'Yes. Those were his instructions. The abbot was told that relatives were being contacted and the body was to be kept safe until they came to collect it.'

'Is that normally what happens when someone dies?' asked Green.

'When a foreigner dies yes.' She frowned. 'But usually the body would go to the hospital.'

'They had to drive past the hospital to get here,' said Standing.

'Yes, I know. I will look into this when I get back to the station.'

'Okay, but why was the body cremated? They were told to just store it, so why was it burned?'

'That's where it gets complicated,' said Fah. 'The abbot wasn't here when it happened, he was on the other side of the island visiting another temple. While he was away, the police called and said that the body had to be cremated.'

'You say called?' said Green. 'You mean the police came here or they phoned?'

'Sorry, I meant there was a phone call. But the abbot doesn't know who called. Whoever it was, they spoke to a young monk, a novice. He told the other monks and they cremated the body that morning, before the abbot returned.'

'Can we talk to this novice monk?' asked Standing.

'He left the wat, that afternoon. After the cremation.'

'Where did he go?'

'The abbot says no one knows. He just took his belongings and left. The abbot thinks he was from Chiang Rai in the north of Thailand, but he doesn't know if he went there. It's not unusual for monks to move around, to travel from wat to wat.'

'Is it possible that he went to another wat on the island?' asked Standing.

'Yes, it's possible. I'll ask him to talk to the other abbots and see if anyone knows where he is.'

'That would be great, thank you.'

Fah and the abbot spoke in Thai for a few minutes, then the monk nodded. He picked up his bag and took out a smartphone. Standing smiled as the abbot tapped on the screen. He hadn't expected to see the man using a mobile phone, but of course it made perfect sense and there was absolutely no reason why a man of religion shouldn't embrace new technology. Standing took out his own phone. 'I'll just make a call,' he said, and walked out of the building. He put on his trainers and took the embassy official's business card from his wallet. He tapped the number into the phone and was pleasantly surprised when Butcher answered on the third ring. Standing quickly explained about Pete's body.

'Well, that shouldn't have happened,' said Butcher once Standing had finished. 'The Thai local authorities need the consular letter I gave you before they can release the body for burial, cremation or repatriation.'

'They sent the body to a temple on Koh Chang and they went ahead and cremated it.'

'Again, all I can tell you is that it shouldn't have happened. The authorities should have kept it, which means the body should be in a police station or a hospital. Or with a funeral director's. There's a big hospital on Koh Chang, isn't there?'

'There is. We're planning to ask the local cop why he took the body to the temple and not to the hospital. The temple is all the way at the bottom of the island.'

'I'm not sure what to tell you, Mr Standing. I've never known that to happen before. Even with an accidental death or sickness in a hospital, the rules are quite clear. If the deceased is a foreigner, the body has to be held until they are in receipt of the consular letter.'

'I think they burned the body to get rid of any evidence,' said Standing.

'It could well just be Thai incompetence,' said Butcher. 'There's a lot of that about, especially in the sticks.'

'The cops here are convinced that Pete killed himself, but it looks to me as if he was murdered. Nothing the cops say adds up.'

'Well, as I told you and Mr Green when you came to the embassy, there are a lot of suicides in Thailand.'

'His phone has gone missing. It wasn't theft because his wallet and passport were in his room, but his phone was gone.'

'What do the police say about that?'

'They couldn't care less. They've closed the case and that's that. So I'm calling to ask what my options are.'

'Options?'

'To get the case reopened. Can you get the Bangkok police involved? Can you get them to send a team down here?'

'Unfortunately it doesn't work like that in Thailand,' said Butcher. 'Each force is very territorial. Even Bangkok has different forces for different areas and they rarely share information. It's not unusual for laws to be enforced in one way on one side of a street, and differently across the road if it's in another policing area.'

'What about getting cops out from the UK?'

'Okay, yes, that does happen sometimes, in high-profile murder cases, perhaps. But between you and me, it's usually window dressing to make it look as if the British government is doing something. There isn't much British cops can do out here. They're limited by whatever forensics the Thais carry out, and then there's the language barrier. And in this case, as you said, the Thais are saying it's suicide.'

'The Thais are wrong. Pete was killed, and then whoever it was covered it up by making it look like suicide.'

'I hear you, Mr Standing. And I understand exactly what you're saying. But this is Thailand and I'm afraid things are done differently here. So in answer to your question, no the Bangkok police won't investigate and I think it unlikely in the extreme that the police in Britain would want to get involved. You could, of course, talk to your local MP back in the UK, perhaps they might be able to help.'

'So there's nothing the embassy can do?'

'As I told you in Bangkok, the embassy functions as a conduit between—'

'Yes, you said,' interrupted Standing. He could feel his pulse racing and he had to fight not to give the man a piece of his mind. Butcher was useless and Standing wanted to tell him as much, to shout and rant and call the man every name under the sun. Instead he took deep breaths and began to count to himself.

He had just reached five when Butcher spoke again. 'Are you still there, Mr Standing?'

Standing smiled. The rage had gone. 'Thank you for your time, Mr Butcher,' he said, and ended the call.

Green walked over. Fah was still inside with the abbot, who was talking into his mobile. 'Who did you call?'

'Butcher at the embassy.'

'Any joy?' asked Green.

'None at all,' said Standing. 'We're on our own.'

'Not for the first time,' said Green.

CHAPTER 14

Standing turned off the road and pulled up in front of the police station. It was on the west side of the island, south of White Sand Beach. The building was much smaller than the HQ building where Captain Somchai was based. This station was clearly marked THAI TOURIST POLICE along with its motto – SMART, SMILE, SERVE, SAFE, SECURE. It was in a row of terraced shops including two banks and a tour company, and was opposite a large 7-Eleven convenience store.

Standing twisted around to look at Fah. 'Shall we come in with you to talk to this corporal guy?'

'Do you mind if I go in on my own?' she said. 'He might think he's done something wrong if we all go in.'

'Maybe he has done something wrong,' growled Green, but Standing cut him short with a warning look.

'He'll be nervous if we all go in, and it'll make him look bad in front of his boss,' said Fah. 'If I go in on my own, I can just have a chat with him. He's a nice guy, he's from Trat, too.'

'Okay, Fah, you know best,' said Standing. 'We'll wait here.'

She flashed him a grateful smile and climbed out of the Fortuner. They watched as she walked over to the glass door, pushed it open and disappeared inside. 'Do you think we can trust her?' asked Green.

'Trust her or not, she speaks Thai and we don't, so we don't have any choice.'

'I know we've got to use her, that's not what I'm asking. I'm asking if we can trust what she says.'

'You can see what she's like,' said Standing. 'She's a kid. She smiles when she's happy and she bites her lip when she's nervous. She wears her heart on her sleeve, I don't think she's capable of being devious.' He shrugged. 'She seemed to be up front about what the abbot was saying.'

'Yeah, but how would we know? The abbot could have told her that it was Kit Kat who gave the order for Pete to be cremated, we don't know what he said.'

'Kittisak,' said Standing. 'I hear what you're saying, Billy. And you're right. But all we can do is listen to her and check for ourselves whenever we can.'

Green sighed. 'I guess.' He looked over at the 7-Eleven. 'You want a beer?'

'I'm driving, mate.'

Green laughed. 'The only time we've seen cops is when we were in the cop shop,' he said. 'Haven't you noticed that? There are no cops on the road. We haven't seen a single moving cop car or bike since we got here. Anyway, I've got a thirst.'

'Get me a water,' said Standing.

Green climbed out and crossed over the road to the 7-Eleven. He returned after a couple of minutes with two bottles of water.

'Changed your mind?' asked Standing as Green got into the passenger seat.

'Apparently you can't buy alcohol in Thailand between the hours of 2 p.m. and 5 p.m. I've no idea why, but there are signs up in English and Thai so I guess it's the law.' He handed Standing one of the bottles. 'Anyway, cheers.'

They opened their bottles and drank. Fah came out of the police station. Standing expected her to climb into the back but instead she came up to his window. He wound it down. 'He didn't call the wat and tell them to burn Mister Pete,' she said. 'In fact, he didn't even know that Mister Pete had been cremated.'

'Who told him to take Pete's body to the wat?' asked Green.

'Actually you can ask him yourself,' said Fah. 'He seems okay to talk about it. His shift ends soon so I said we'd go to eat at Jae Eaw Seafood.' She pointed down the road. 'It's a two-minute drive. You can wait for us there. We won't be long.'

Standing nodded. 'Perfect,' he said.

She smiled and stepped back from the car, gave Green a small wave, and went back into the station. Standing closed the window and pulled a tight U-turn. The restaurant was on the right, with a large parking space on the opposite side of the road. They parked and climbed out. A dozen large silvery fish were hanging by their tails from a wooden frame, drying in the hot sun.

They jogged across the road and into the restaurant, which was open to the elements. The restaurant was busy but a waitress showed them to a table overlooking the road and they ordered two beers. The 2 p.m. to 5 p.m. rule clearly didn't apply to restaurants. She left them with two menus and went to get their drinks.

They were halfway through their beers when a black Toyota pick-up truck pulled up outside. It turned into the car park and drew up next to their Fortuner. Fah climbed out of the passenger side. The driver got out and said something to her. He was in his mid-twenties, tall and gangly and wearing dark brown trousers and a long-sleeved beige shirt. He wasn't wearing his uniform but the clothes, his short back and sides and his gleaming black boots marked him out as a police officer.

Fah and the man looked left and right, waited for a couple of cars to pass, then hurried across the road and into the restaurant. They walked over to their table. 'This is Ben,' said Fah.

The man was staring at Green, a look of confusion on his face.

Standing frowned. 'You said his name was Chayaphon?'

Fah smiled. 'That is his official name, yes. But his nickname is Ben. Same as Fah is my nickname.'

'Ben is an English name,' said Standing.

Fah laughed. 'Ben. Like the car.'

'The car?'

The man eventually tore his eyes away from Green and smiled. 'Mercedes Benz. My father always wanted that car. It's Benz but Thai people often say Ben.'

Standing laughed. 'Benz it is, then,' he said. He waved at the seats opposite them. 'Please sit down. We're having beer. Do you want one?'

'Just iced tea for me,' said Fah.

'Water for me,' said Benz.

The waitress came over and Fah spoke to her in Thai.

'Order whatever you want,' said Standing. 'It's on us. The least we can do is to buy you dinner.'

While Fah and Benz spoke to the waitress, Standing tried to get the measure of the man. He was physically fit, with not an ounce of fat on him. He was darker than Fah, with black hair that was already starting to recede. He wasn't wearing a wedding ring and from the way he kept giving Fah sidelong glances, Standing could tell he was attracted to her. He was wearing a stainless-steel Rolex Submariner watch, with a black bezel, the timepiece of choice for many guys in the Regiment. He spoke quietly to the waitress, but there was a firmness to his voice that probably came from the fact that he spent most of the day with a gun on his hip.

As the waitress walked away, Benz sat back in his chair and folded his arms. Standing picked up on the defensive body language so immediately smiled to try to put him at ease. 'Thanks for coming to see us, Benz,' he said. 'I know you must be busy.'

He shrugged. 'My shift has finished.'

'Busy day?'

He shrugged again. 'Always busy,' he said. He looked across at Fah. 'Right?'

She nodded. 'It never stops,' she said.

Benz smiled at her. It was obvious that she was the only reason he had agreed to see them, but Standing would take what he could get. 'Fah has been showing us around the island. We're trying to work out what happened to Pete.'

Benz nodded. 'I am sorry for your loss,' he said to Green. 'It surprised me when I saw you. For a moment I thought you had come back to life.'

'Pete was my twin.'

'I see that. It was a shock.'

Green nodded. 'I'm sure it was.'

'I was surprised that you were there on your own,' said Standing. 'At the resort.'

'We are short-staffed,' said Benz.

'Have you handled many deaths like that?' asked Standing.

'Suicides, you mean?' said Benz.

Standing could see Green tense. His jaw tightened and his eyes had gone hard. Standing flashed him a warning look. Benz was doing them a favour by agreeing to meet them and there was no point in antagonising him. 'It is an unusual way to die,' said Standing. 'Putting a bag over his head and tying his hands behind his back.'

'I haven't seen it before, but I have heard of it. When I found the body I phoned my boss and he said it was common.'

'That would be Captain Somchai?' said Standing.

'No, I am with the Tourist Police. So my boss is Sergeant Wirot.'

'I'm confused,' said Standing. 'I thought Captain Somchai was in charge of the case.'

Fah nodded. 'Captain Somchai is the senior officer on Koh Chang. But because a foreigner died, it was dealt with by the Tourist Police. But informing relatives has to be done through the Trat police station, so the case was sent to them, but that had to be done through Captain Somchai.' She smiled apologetically. 'It is complicated, but we have to follow the procedure.'

'So it was this Sergeant Wirot who said this type of death was common?' said Standing.

Benz nodded. 'He said he had seen it several times. Also . . .' He frowned, obviously struggling to find the right word.

He spoke to Fah in Thai and she nodded. 'Auto asphyxiation,' she said, then smiled, clearly proud at having the phrase in her vocabulary.

Benz nodded in agreement. 'Sergeant Wirot said that sometimes foreigners did that for fun and they died accidentally.'

'I've heard about guys using nooses to strangle themselves, but never plastic bags,' said Green.

'Sergeant Wirot said that sometimes they put their head in a plastic bag to get high, then loosen the bag before they pass out. If they are too slow, they can die accidentally.'

'But Pete's hands were tied behind his back,' said Green.

'Exactly,' said Benz. 'Which is why we knew he wanted to kill himself.'

Green's cheeks reddened and he opened his mouth to retort, but Standing reached over and put his hand on the man's arm. Green shook him away. 'This is bullshit!' Green snapped.

'Billy, keep it down,' said Standing. Several heads had turned to look in their direction, and Fah and Benz were clearly feeling uncomfortable. 'I'm sorry,' said Standing. 'This is very stressful for everybody.'

'I understand,' said Benz. He nodded at Green. 'And I am very sorry for your loss. But all I am doing is telling you what happened.'

Green opened his mouth to speak, but Standing squeezed his arm to silence him.

'We understand that, Benz, and we're grateful,' said Standing. 'But we don't understand how Pete could have tied his own hands like that. Fah showed us the report. It was a zip tie, right?'

'Yes. A big one. As soon as I went into the room I saw it.'

'But his hands were behind his back, weren't they? How could you see his wrists?'

'I mean, as soon as I rolled him over I saw that his wrists were tied with a white zip tie. A thick one, more than half an inch across. Difficult to break.'

'You see that's what confuses us, Benz. How could Pete have bound his hands behind his back?'

Benz nodded. 'Yes, I wondered about that, and I asked

Sergeant Wirot. He said there were two ways. He could have put the zip tie on and pulled it tight with his mouth.' He mimed putting his wrists together and biting on a ziptie. 'Then he could have opened his arms and stepped through so that his hands were behind his back. If you are not too fat you can do that. If you put the bag on your head before you do that, and then lie down, by the time you start to struggle it's too late. Even if you change your mind, you can't get hold of the bag.'

Standing exchanged a look with Green. It sounded plausible, but it just wasn't the sort of thing that Pete would have done.

'Or he could have made the loop first, then put his hands behind his back and put them through the loop. Then if he could reach the zip tie with one of his hands, he would be able to pull it tight. You know how they work, right? You can tighten it but not loosen it. Once they are on, you have to cut them to release them.'

Standing nodded. He'd used them to bind prisoners, many times. Cheap and effective.

'And Sergeant Wirot said he had seen this before, on Koh Chang? This type of suicide?'

'I don't think on Koh Chang. But he said he had heard that it had happened in Bangkok, and Pattaya. You know, a lot of farangs kill themselves in Thailand.'

'Farangs?' said Green.

'Farang means foreigner,' explained Fah.

'And was it Sergeant Wirot who told you to take the body to the temple?' asked Standing.

Benz nodded. 'He said the monks would keep the body until the relatives arranged for it to be taken back to England.'

The waitress returned with two of their dishes on a tray – fried prawns with asparagus and a yellow crab curry that had

Standing's mouth watering. She placed four plates with spoons and forks on the table. Another waitress came over with drinks for Fah and Benz.

Standing waited until the waitresses had walked away before continuing. 'You put the body in a body bag?'

'Of course.'

'So did you know that Pete was dead before you got to the resort?'

'Oh no, we carry the bags in the truck. We always have four. We have a lot of motorcycle accidents on Koh Chang. It can be a dangerous place.'

'What about Pete's phone?' asked Green.

Benz frowned. 'His phone?' he repeated.

'When we got Pete's belongings, we didn't get his phone.'

'I didn't see a phone in the room.'

'He always had it with him,' said Green.

'I didn't see a phone, but I wasn't looking. I checked to see if he was alive and when I saw that he wasn't, I called my boss.'

'So you never searched the room?' asked Standing.

'Why would I search the room?'

'To see if Pete had been robbed. Or if anything had been taken. To check if there had been anyone else in the room with him.'

Benz shook his head. 'But it wasn't a robbery. It was a suicide.'

The waitress returned with two more dishes. Fried rice with what looked like pieces of crab meat in it, and a dozen large grilled prawns. A waiter followed her, holding a large fish in a long metal pan. Under the pan was a black metal box and as he placed it carefully on the table Standing saw that it contained glowing coals. The fish was lying in a bubbling soup containing garlic and chopped red chillies.

'Is that why there was no forensic team?' asked Standing. 'Because you had decided it was a suicide?'

Benz frowned. 'Forensic team?' he said. Fah translated and he nodded. 'Yes. I told Sergeant Wirot what I had found and he said that it was suicide. So there was no need to look for forensics.'

'What about the zip tie on his wrists?' asked Standing.

'What about it?' said Benz, frowning again.

'Well, I'm not a policeman but the obvious thing to do would be to check that Pete's fingerprints were on the zip tie. If they weren't, that would mean that Pete hadn't put it on. And you might have found the fingerprints of whoever did.'

'And the bag on his head,' said Green. 'There might have been fingerprints on that.'

Benz's frown deepened. 'But we know it was suicide. There would be no reason to check for fingerprints.'

Green took a deep breath and Standing could sense that he was close to exploding, so he patted him on the arm. 'Let's just eat,' he said. 'I don't know about you but I'm starving.'

Fah picked up a barbecued prawn and put it on Benz's plate. He smiled at her gratefully.

Standing did the same for Green but Green only scowled at him. 'Eat,' said Standing.

CHAPTER 15

Fah and Benz climbed into the pick-up truck. Standing and Green waved as Benz drove back towards the police station. 'What do you think?' asked Green.

'Awesome food,' said Standing. 'I could eat that crab curry by the bucketful.'

'About Benz.'

Standing shrugged. 'He's not much older than Fah. I get the impression that he just does as he's told and doesn't ask why.'

'The way he tells it, Sergeant Wirot made all the decisions.'

'Yeah, that's how I read it.'

'The whole business of not calling in forensics makes no sense at all.'

'Well, it does if the team has to be brought over on the ferry. Then they'd have to overnight here if they missed the last boat out. Seems to me that they'll always be looking for ways not to call them in.'

'So you think it's about saving money and not a cover-up?'

'I don't know what to think, Billy. But I'm sure of one thing, Pete didn't kill himself. So that means he was murdered, no matter what the cops say.'

'I don't trust that Benz at all. That's an expensive truck for a young guy to be driving. And did you see his watch? It was a Submariner. How much are they now? Eight grand?'

'It could have been a fake. A copy.'

'It didn't look like a copy.'

Standing unlocked the Fortuner and climbed in. Green got into the passenger seat and put on his seat belt. 'So what do we do?' he asked.

'Well, that's the question, isn't it? They've cleaned the room and cremated the body, so there's no evidence left. There's no CCTV at the resort, and as far as we know there were no witnesses.' He grimaced. 'I'm struggling to see a way forward, Billy.'

Green was about to reply when Standing's phone rang. He pulled it out of his pocket and looked at the screen. Either the caller was withholding their number or the fact that he was overseas meant it couldn't be displayed. He took the call. 'It's me,' said a voice he recognised – Spider Shepherd. And the fact that he hadn't used his name suggested it was an off-the-books call, so he was probably using a burner phone or a callbox.

'Hey, how's it going?'

'I'm good. You?'

'Not getting very far, to be honest.'

'Well, maybe this will help. I've got a complete phone dump for the number you gave me. The works. Calls made, texts, and he had his iPhone linked to the Cloud so we have all his photographs. There's hundreds of them. I'll send you a link and you can see everything we've got. It's password protected – use your middle name followed by the day and month of your date of birth.'

Standing smiled. He knew that Spider Shepherd had a near-photographic memory but it was always disconcerting to discover just how much information he had at his disposal. 'That's brilliant, thank you.'

'Any idea when you'll be back?'

'It's open-ended. There's something not right but we're not getting much help from the locals.'

'Anything else you need, you call me.'

'I will. Thank you.' Standing tucked the phone into the pocket of his shorts. 'That was Spider Shepherd. He's managed to get me a data dump from Pete's phone.'

'Spider? He's the guy who went to work for MI5, right? Secret squirrel?'

'That's the guy.'

'I've never met him, but everyone says he's a good guy. A legend.'

'One of the best. He's got all the info on Pete's phone and is going to send it through to us.'

'What is it that he does with MI5?'

'Anti-terrorism mostly, I think. But they use him for action man stuff as well. Most of the sneaky-beaky mob wouldn't say boo to a goose, and they piss themselves if they come face to face with real villains.'

'I thought they carried guns.'

'Nah, that's just on TV. They have to use us or armed cops if they need firepower. But that's where Spider comes in handy, because of his SAS background they can send him in with the armed guys.'

They had just reached Lonely Beach when Standing's phone beeped to let him know he'd received a message. He parked in front of the shack and they walked in. Daeng was sitting at the desk and he smiled when he saw them.

'Do you want a drink?' Standing asked Green.

'Is the Pope Catholic?'

'Last I heard.'

'Hey, Daeng, can I have a bottle of Johnnie Walker Black. And soda. And ice.'

'Yes, Mister Billy,' said Daeng. He stood up and headed for the bar.

'Billy, mate . . .' said Standing.

'I'm not gonna drink the whole bottle,' said Green. 'I'll pace myself.'

Standing shook his head, then waved at Daeng. 'Get me a beer, please,' he said.

They sat down at a table and Daeng carried their drinks over on a tray. As Green paid him in cash, Standing took out his phone and checked the message. It was from Shepherd and was just a link to an anonymous website that required a password. He tapped in the letters and digits, and the screen changed to show three files, one marked CALLS, another marked TEXTS, and the third PHOTOGRAPHS. He clicked on the CALLS file and was presented with a list of phone numbers, with an arrow that showed if the call was incoming or outgoing.

Daeng finished opening their bottles and went back to his desk. Green moved around the table so that he could look over his shoulder. 'Is that from Spider?'

Standing nodded. 'It's everything that was on Pete's phone. He made two calls to Vietnam the day he died. And two calls the previous day. All to the same number. The name is DEAN C.'

'We're going to call it, right?'

'Let me send a text first.'

Standing wrote a text explaining who he was and that he was a friend of Pete's, and was it okay to call him on FaceTime. He sent it and a reply came back almost immediately. GIVE ME TWO MINUTES.

While he waited, Standing checked out the TEXTS file. There were hundreds of texts sent and received. Most of them from the time he had arrived in Thailand were to DEAN C in Vietnam, but there were also texts to several girls. Standing didn't want to pry, but a cursory glance suggested that the SAS trooper was maintaining several long-distance relationships. There were half a dozen texts from DEAN C over the past three days, asking where Pete was. The last one was short and sweet. **ARE YOU OK?**

Green poured himself another slug of whisky and looked at his watch. The seconds ticked by and finally the two minutes were up. Standing made the FaceTime call. It was answered almost immediately by a big man in his seventies, balding with a bushy grey beard. He had watery blue eyes and deep furrows across his forehead as he frowned at the screen.

Standing flashed him a thumbs up. 'Dean, this is Matt Standing, a friend of Pete's. I didn't get your family name.'

'Dean Cooper.'

Standing moved his hand so that Cooper could see Green and immediately the man's face broke into a grin. 'Pete, hey, great to see you. I was starting to think you'd gone AWOL. What's up?' He had an American accent, a deep southern drawl.

'Sorry, Dean, I'm not Pete. I'm his brother, Billy.'

'What?' Cooper shook his head. 'What are you talking about?'

'I'm sorry, Dean,' said Green. 'Pete's dead. I'm here in Koh Chang trying to find out what happened.'

Cooper's frown deepened. 'Are you punking me? Because this ain't funny.'

'I'm serious, Dean,' said Green. 'Pete died on Tuesday. That's why he didn't reply to your messages. I'm Billy. Billy Green. Pete's brother.'

Even on the small screen, Standing could see the colour drain from the American's face.

'Sorry to break it to you like this, out of the blue,' said Standing.

'What happened?' Cooper asked.

'The cops here say that Pete killed himself, but we don't believe it.'

Cooper gritted his teeth and shook his head. 'No way would he kill himself. No fucking way.'

'That's how we feel,' said Green.

'Pete never said he had a twin,' said Cooper. 'Didn't even know he had a brother, but then we didn't talk about his family much.' His eyes narrowed. 'Billy, did you say your name was?'

Green nodded. 'Yeah. Billy.'

'I'm sorry for your loss, Billy. Your brother was something special. I only met him last week, but he was a brother in arms. I'll miss him.'

'Thanks, Dean,' said Green. 'Look, we knew Pete was in Vietnam but we've no idea what he was doing there. Can you fill us in?'

Cooper sighed. 'Sure, but it's a long story. You guys special forces, same as Pete?'

Standing nodded. 'SAS. Both of us.'

'Okay, so I won't be telling tales out of school. Long story short, my son JD was a Navy SEAL. He died out in Syria. Pete was with him.'

'Sorry to hear that,' said Standing.

'It was a bitch. They were on a joint SAS/Navy SEAL capture mission after an al-Qaeda warlord. The shit hit the fan and JD stepped on an IED. Jessie Dean was his name but he was JD ever since he was at school. He always carried my Vietnam War dog tags on him. Said they were his lucky charm. Said that if they got me through my two tours, they'd keep him safe, too.' Cooper forced a smile. 'Didn't work out that way.'

'I'm sorry,' said Green.

'Anyways, Pete was with JD when he died. JD asked him to bring the tags to me along with his own. He wanted me to know that he was thinking about me when he died, and that he loved me.' Cooper blinked away tears, then wiped his eyes with the back of his hand.

'Your boy, how did he end up in the Navy SEALs?'

'Totally his call,' said Cooper. 'His mom was Vietnamese, so he had dual nationality. As a Vietnamese citizen, he had to do his national service. I was trying to find ways of getting him out of it, but he wanted to do it. He loved being a soldier and after his national service was over he wanted to do it as a career. We talked it over and decided he'd be better off in the US Army. I'd applied for his US passport just after he was born and we kept it updated, so he just flew over and enlisted. He wanted to join the SEALs and he did. Loved every minute of it.' Tears were welling up in his eyes again and he blinked them away. 'I am so damn proud of that boy.'

He took a deep breath to steady himself before continuing. 'So, anyway, Pete came over last week. I run a tour company here, just outside Saigon.' He chuckled. 'I still can't bring myself to say Ho Chi Minh City. We take tourists around the old hotspots. Khe Sanh, the Củ Chi tunnels, Huế. We introduce them to former VC, and show them how the country has changed. I gave Pete the tour and we shared a few beers.'

He reached into his shirt and pulled out a set of dog tags. 'And he gave me JD's tags. I'll wear them till the day I die.'

'So what brought Pete to Koh Chang?' asked Green.

'Okay, so JD's mum died when he was born. Hospitals back then weren't great here and she passed away. I brought him up on my own and I remarried when JD was eight years old.' He forced a smile. 'I'm trying to get to the point, it's just that there's a lot to explain.'

'That's okay, we're in no hurry,' said Standing.

'I remarried when he was eight. To another Vietnamese lady, obviously. She'd fallen pregnant and not long after we married, we had a little girl. Kim. Kim's twenty-two now. Or will be next birthday. Two days after Pete arrived, she flew to Bangkok. A friend of hers was marrying some wealthy Thai guy and there was a huge wedding at one of the big hotels. Two days after the wedding she phoned and said she'd met some Chinese guy and she was going to hang out with him at Koh Chang. He had some huge villa there and there was going to be a party. From the way she spoke, I assumed there was a group of them going, so I didn't think anything of it. Then two days after that she called me in the middle of the night and says she was scared and that she wanted to come home, that something was wrong and she'd made a big mistake. Then the phone got cut off and it's been off ever since. I didn't know what to do. I phoned the US embassy in Bangkok and they weren't interested, and I couldn't get anywhere with the Thai cops. That's when Pete said he'd fly over. He called me after he'd got to Koh Chang and said he was looking for the guy, Sammy Lee is his name. He said he thought he'd found the villa but he hadn't found Lee yet. Then he stopped answering my messages and his phone went dead. I didn't know what to do.

I'd run out of options. My wife's going crazy, not knowing what's happened to our daughter.'

'Well, Matt and I are here now,' said Green. 'We'll see what else we can find out. Did Pete have a picture of this guy?'

'Kim had posted several pictures on her Facebook page, so he had those. He's in his thirties. Distinctive dimple in his chin.'

'Do you have any pictures of him?'

'Only what I see on her Facebook page and Instagram.'

'Could you send me what you have? And a decent picture of Kim.'

'Yeah, I'll do that now.'

'And what do you know about this guy?'

'Literally just his name and that he had a place on Koh Chang.'

'Okay, well we have everything that Pete had on his phone, so we'll go through it and see if we can find out how far Pete got,' said Standing.

'What about talking to the local cops?'

'We did that and they've not been much help. They keep saying that Pete killed himself, but that's bollocks.'

'I'll be honest, guys, I'm at the end of my tether here. I've lost my boy and now my daughter is . . . well, I don't know where she is.'

'Leave it with us for a few days, Dean,' said Standing. 'You've got my number now and I'll call you as soon as we get anything.'

'I'm really grateful to you guys. I can't thank you enough.'

'Well, let's see how it plays out before you go thanking us,' said Standing.

Cooper nodded. 'I get that,' he said. 'And I'm sorry about Pete. Truly sorry. I liked him. If he died because he was helping me . . .' He took a deep breath. 'I don't know how I'll be able to live with myself.'

'Pete made his own decisions in life, Dean,' said Green. 'He was a big boy and he played by big boys' rules. If he could he'd tell you that himself.'

Cooper gritted his teeth and nodded. 'Thank you,' he said.

'We'll get back to you as soon as we pick up anything about your daughter.'

Cooper nodded. His eyes were welling with tears again and he ended the call.

'He's in a state,' said Green.

'His son's dead and his daughter's missing,' said Standing. 'Pete was always like that, wasn't he? He'd help anyone.'

Billy smiled thinly and nodded. 'Yeah. He was a soft bastard. So Pete was here to track down this girl Kim? Why would this Chinese guy kill him? To keep the girl with him? Who does that?'

'Plenty of nutters in the world, Billy. People have been killed for less.'

'But then why go to the trouble of making it look like suicide?'

'I don't know. None of this makes any sense to me.'

Green gestured at the phone. 'So all Pete's pictures are on there?'

'In the Cloud, yeah. He had it set up to download everything to the Cloud.'

'Upload.'

'What?'

'You upload to the Cloud. You download from it.'

'Now you're correcting my grammar?'

Green laughed as he added whisky to his glass and topped it up with soda. Standing tapped on the screen and went to the folder of photographs. He clicked on the most recent. It was a shot of what looked like an island with a few large villas close to the beach. There were several more shots of the villas, and then a few concentrating on one of them – a large villa with a terrace on the upper floor and a private jetty jutting out into the water.

'Think that's where the guy is?' asked Green, leaning over to get a better look.

'Maybe.'

'Any of the guy? Dean must have given him a picture, right?'

Standing flicked back through the pictures. Most were views of buildings and boats. In one of the pictures there were men on the jetty, close to a large speedboat, but even when he zoomed in it wasn't possible to get a good look at their faces.

There were more pictures of the villa, then of another speedboat, bigger than the first. 'So they're delivering stuff, do you think?' said Green.

'Delivering or exporting, it's difficult to know which,' said Standing.

'When was that one taken?'

Standing clicked on the photo and called up the date and time details. 'The day before he died.'

Standing flicked through more photographs. There were several taken on the same day. Then there were more boats the previous day. Always speedboats, small ones with single outboard motors, bigger ones with two or even three motors. The resolution was never good enough to get a clear look at the faces of the men on the jetty or of the men who from time to time appeared on the upstairs terrace. 'The iPhone takes good pictures but there's a limit to the zoom facility,' said Standing. 'Maybe that's why he had the binoculars.'

'I wondered about the bird book,' said Green. 'I mean, he liked birds all right but never the sort with wings.'

'So he was using the binoculars for surveillance but had the book with him in case anyone asked him what he was doing? That makes sense.'

The phone vibrated to show that he had an incoming message. It was from Dean Cooper. There were two photographs, both of a young Eurasian girl with an older Chinese man. The girl had long hair, dyed blonde. The man had a dimple in his chin. Sammy Lee. In one photograph they were in a rooftop bar, holding champagne flutes. In the other they were in a Japanese restaurant with plates of sushi in front of them.

In both pictures Lee was wearing a suit, black in the first, dark blue in the second. He wasn't smiling, but the girl – presumably Kim – was beaming in both. In the bar photograph she was wearing a low-cut white top and tight black trousers, in the restaurant she had on a tight purple dress.

'So that's Kim?' said Green, looking over his shoulder.

'I suppose Sammy Lee brought her to Koh Chang and Pete wanted to play white knight?' said Standing.

'Yeah, he was always one for rescuing damsels in distress. So what do we do, Matt?'

'What do you want to do?'

'You know what I want to do. We find this Sammy Lee and if he killed Pete, then we do what needs to be done.'

'And by that you don't mean go to the cops, obviously.'

'For all we know, this Lee is paying the cops off,' said Green. 'You need to ask Spider for help. He can fill you in on this Sammy Lee.'

'I don't like asking him for favours. Once is enough, I don't want to piss him off.'

'Fuck that. He's former Sass. And his mob aren't shy when it comes to asking us to drag their nuts out of the fire. You were out with him in Kabul last year rescuing that MI6 officer who got trapped, weren't you? From the way you talked about it, he owes you, big time.'

'I hear you, Billy. And yeah, you're right.' He used his phone to capture a head-and-shoulders shot of the man with Kim, then sent it to Shepherd's number along with a short message. SAMMY LEE. CHINESE. MIGHT BE BEHIND PETE'S DEATH. ANY INTEL GRATEFULLY RECEIVED. He grinned at Green. 'Done and dusted.'

He went back to the PHOTOGRAPHS file and flicked through them quickly. Most of the more recent photographs were views of the villa and the jetty. Then he found a video file and played it, holding the phone out so that Green could see. 'This was two days before he died,' said Standing. The video was taken through the side window of a vehicle. From the look of it, Pete was driving with the phone in his left hand. There was a villa behind a barred gate. Then trees and bushes. Then a high wall. The vehicle slowed. There was a large black barred gate. There were several expensive cars parked on the far side of the gate, and beyond them a huge villa with a double-height entrance. The vehicle – probably the Ford Ranger that Pete had rented in Bangkok – picked up speed as it passed the house and then the video ended. There was another video, filmed a few minutes later. This time he was driving in the opposite direction and the camera was pointing through the window on the driver's side. Again he slowed as he passed the mansion.

'So Pete drove by the house,' said Green. 'That's the view from the opposite side to the jetty, right?'

'I guess so,' said Standing. He replayed the second video, paused it, and then zoomed in on the gate. He studied it for several seconds, then froze the video and showed it to Green. 'Take a look at this.'

Green squinted at the screen. There was an Asian man standing behind the gates, staring directly at the phone. He was holding something in his right hand and Green's eyes hardened as he realised what it was. A Kalashnikov assault rifle. 'He was spotted,' said Green quietly.

'It looks like it,' said Standing. 'And two days later he was dead.' He took the phone away and flicked through the photographs. There were no clear faces in any of them.

He stopped when he saw a group of people at a circular table filled with plates of food. Pete was there, sitting between Dean Cooper and a Vietnamese lady who Standing assumed was Cooper's wife. Kim was at the table, along with a couple of other large Western men, the same age and build as Cooper, probably friends of his. There were several photographs of the group, and dozens of other photographs of Vietnam tourist spots, including one of Pete and Cooper and two other Westerners standing in front of a sign that said CU CHI TUNNELS. They were all wearing black and white VC scarves and holding AK-47s. Standing showed it to Green and they both chuckled. 'Tourist shots,' said Standing. 'I wonder if they'll ever do anything like that in Afghanistan? Or Syria?'

'I bet they will in Ukraine at some point,' said Green. 'Selfies in front of burned-out Russian tanks. And look at Auschwitz. People are always posting selfies from there. It's a sick world, mate, and getting sicker by the minute.'

Standing flicked back to the photographs that Pete had taken of the villas.

'This villa, the one he drove by, where do you think it is?' asked Green.

'No idea,' said Standing. 'There's nothing in any of the pictures that shows where it is. Except the jetty means that it's next to the water.'

He flicked back through to the photographs of the boats moored to the jetty. 'It looks like an island, right?'

'Yeah. But you've been to the beach here, there's no islands you can see.'

Standing launched his Maps app and tapped in Koh Chang. There were several small islands to the south of Koh Chang, but nothing to the west.

He went back to the pictures of the jetty and the villa and looked at them closely. There was nothing but mountainous jungle behind the villa, no landmarks that might provide a clue as to where they were.

There were other photographs of a pier, hundreds of metres long, sticking out into the sea. The line of villas was in the far distance, beyond the long pier. There was an orange-roofed pagoda at the end of it. Some of the photographs of the long pier appeared to have been taken from a terrace that had been painted in red, yellow and green stripes. In another picture he could see the island beyond the pier, and in another the villas were visible off in the distance. One of the photographs had been taken inside a building and there were concrete chairs and tables that had been painted in the same red, yellow and green colour scheme. Green peered over Standing's shoulder. 'What's that?'

'That's where Pete was when he had the house under surveillance, I think. What are those colours?'

'It's a Rasta place, man,' said Green. 'They're the colours

of the Ethiopian flag. The red is for bloodshed. The yellow is for gold. The green is the jungle. You not a fan of the old reggae music, man?'

Standing flicked through to another photograph. There was a conch shell full of stubbed-out hand-rolled cigarettes, also painted in red, yellow and green stripes. 'This can't be on Koh Chang, surely?'

'We could ask Miss Fah, she might know.'

'If we tell her, she'll tell Captain Somchai and I'm not sure that I trust him. Maybe the staff here might know.' He looked around. Daeng was sitting at the desk, his head bent over his smartphone.

Standing and Green went over to him and Standing showed him a photograph that included the red, green and yellow painted terrace. 'Do you know where this is?' he asked.

Daeng squinted at the screen and then smiled and nodded. 'Rasta View,' he said. 'Famous bar.'

'Where is it?'

'You go out, turn right and drive for about six kilometres. Before you get to Bang Bao Pier you turn left and it's before Golden Beach. You will see it, it's very colourful.'

Standing thanked him and took five hundred baht from his wallet. 'This is for you, Daeng.' He handed him the money and Daeng gave him a wai and thanked him. Standing flicked through the photographs of Sammy Lee and Kim and showed one to Daeng. 'Did this man ever come to see Pete?'

Daeng shook his head. 'Mister Pete had no visitors.'

'Did you ever see him here on his own? Or with someone else?'

Daeng studied the screen again and shook his head. 'No, never.'

'What about the girl? Did you ever see her?'

Daeng shook his head again.

Standing thanked him and looked over at Green. 'Fancy a drive?'

'You read my mind,' said Green. He pointed at the bottle of whisky on the table. 'I'll be back for that later, Daeng,' he said.

CHAPTER 16

Standing and Green drove south through woodland and farmland until they saw signs for Bang Bao Pier and then they headed east. There were no hotels or resorts, just a few roadside shacks. They drove alongside a rubber plantation, the Fortuner's beams illuminating lines of evenly spaced trees with white latex sap dripping from cuts in the bark into collecting cups.

'There it is,' said Green, pointing to the right.

Standing slowed. There was a building on the side of the road, what looked like a collection of shacks pushed up against each other with a corrugated iron roof. The walls had been painted with red, yellow and green stripes, and next to a line of half a dozen motorbikes and scooters there was a sign saying RASTA VIEW.

There was a dusty parking space on the other side of the road and Standing pulled up. Facing them was a large portrait of Bob Marley and a poster with four pictures of the man. As they climbed out of the Fortuner they heard 'No Woman, No Cry' coming from the building.

There was no door, and not much in the way of walls, and it took Standing a few seconds to work out how to get inside. There was a small bar to the left, and a Thai girl was making a blue cocktail. There was a line of stools overlooking the water, and to their right a collection of concrete tables and chairs, most of which had been painted in the Rastafarian colours. There was a group of three Western girls in tie-dyed dresses sitting at one of the tables, passing around a large joint. Two young Western men were at another table with beers in front of them, also smoking.

'There you go,' said Green, nodding towards the sea. Directly opposite was the line of villas, each with its own jetty. Lights were on in most of them. And sticking out ahead of them was the long pier with the pagoda at the end. There were lights at regular intervals casting shadows on the sea below. Further to the right, maybe half a mile away, was an even longer, wider pier with a white lighthouse at the end. This pier was lined with what looked like fishing boats and there were people walking along it.

Standing realised that they weren't looking at an island ahead of them, it was a peninsula. That must have been how Pete had managed to do a drive-by.

They walked to the edge of the bar. It was on a steep slope that led to a beach far below. The track finished and then Bob Marley began to sing 'Get Up Stand Up'. 'This is where he was doing his surveillance from,' said Standing. He pointed over at one of the villas. 'And that's the house he was looking at.'

'Can't see much without binoculars,' said Green.

'Pete?' said a voice behind them. 'For fuck's sake, Pete.'

They turned to see that one of the women had come up behind them. She was in her late twenties with curly ginger hair and a sprinkling of freckles over her nose and cheeks. Her eyes were a brilliant green and they sparkled when she smiled at him. 'They fucking told me you were dead.' She had a South

African accent, Standing realised. She stepped towards Green, threw her arms around his neck and kissed him full on the mouth.

Green put his hands on her hips and tried to push her away but she had him in too tight a grip. Eventually she broke away, panting. 'Was it some sort of sick joke?' she said. 'What's going on?'

Her lipstick was smeared across his lips and Green wiped it away with the back of his hand. 'I'm sorry,' he said. 'I'm not Pete.'

Her eyes narrowed as she stared at him, then she looked at Standing. 'It's true,' he said.

She looked back at Green. 'This isn't funny,' she said. She looked over her shoulder at her companions. 'He says it isn't him,' she said.

The two girls laughed. 'He just wanted to dump you, Kayla!' one shouted.

'Told you he was ghosting you!' shouted the other.

Kayla turned to glare at Green. 'Is that it, you bastard? You wanted out so you got everyone to tell me you were dead? You're one sick fuck.' She lashed out with her foot and kicked him just below the left knee.

'Hey, whoah, no,' said Green, holding up his hands in an attempt to placate her. 'I'm not Pete, I'm his brother, Billy!'

'You bastard!' she shouted, and tried to kick him again. This time Standing moved quickly behind her and picked her up. 'Get the fuck off me!' she shouted as her feet left the ground.

'Listen to me, Kayla,' he hissed into her ear. 'Pete's dead. This is Billy, his brother. His twin brother. Now stop making a fool of yourself.'

She stopped struggling. 'Really?' she said.

'Really,' said Green.

Standing lowered her to the ground.

'So Pete is dead?' she said.

Green nodded. 'I'm afraid so.'

'Fuck.'

Standing released his grip on her. 'Sorry about that. But the days of slapping hysterical women are long gone.'

'I was not hysterical,' she snapped.

Green laughed. 'You damn near took my leg off.'

'Sorry about that,' Kayla said. 'It's just it was a real shock, you walking in here like that. Everyone said you'd killed yourself, they found your body in your hotel room.'

'Yeah, that's what the cops are saying.'

Kayla looked at Green and smiled sympathetically. 'I'm sorry for your loss,' she said.

'You were a friend of Pete's?' asked Green.

'I don't think she kisses strangers like that,' said Standing. 'Though I could be wrong.'

He stepped back and put his hands up as Kayla whirled around to glare at him, but her face broke into a smile and she laughed. 'You got me,' she said. 'How about I get you guys a drink, by way of apologising?'

'One each, or do we have to share?' asked Green.

'I can run to one each,' she said.

'I'll have a Johnnie Walker Black Label with soda. And ice.'

Kayla laughed. 'Yeah, you're definitely not Pete,' she said. 'Vodka was his drink.' She looked at Standing. 'What about you?'

'Just a beer's fine.'

'Why don't you join my friends while I get your drinks?' she said, gesturing at the table. 'Don't worry, they won't bite.'

She leaned towards them and whispered conspiratorially. 'Actually I think Zuri might, so be careful.' She was chuckling as she walked to the bar.

Standing and Green looked over at the two girls sitting at the table. They were both Kayla's age, one was black with long dreadlocks, the other was petite with short blonde hair and pixie-like ears. The blonde girl waved for them to come over.

'What the hell just happened?' she asked Standing. 'Did you just pick up Kayla? Literally, I mean. Feet off the ground?'

'Only after she assaulted my friend,' said Standing. The remains of the joint they had been smoking were in a large conch shell that had been painted red, green and yellow.

'She knows Pete, she just got upset because you were ignoring her.'

'And because she thought you were dead,' added the black girl. 'You're not dead, obviously.' She had a London accent and a chrome stud in her nose.

'I'm Pete's brother,' said Green. He and Standing sat down. There were no cushions on the seats, so they were sitting on bare concrete.

'He never said he had a twin,' said the blonde girl. Her accent was American, Californian maybe. 'But then he never really told us much about himself.' She forced a smile. 'I'm sorry about your brother,' she said. 'We only hung out with him for a few days, but he was a nice guy.' She held out her hand. 'I'm Sarah. This is Zuri.'

'Matt,' said Standing, shaking her hand and then Zuri's.

'Billy,' said Green, and he shook their hands.

'I'm sorry for your loss, Billy,' said Zuri.

'Thank you,' said Green.

'Did you come over to arrange a funeral?' asked Zuri.

Green snorted. 'That was the plan, but the plan changed,' he said.

Zuri frowned. 'What happened?'

'They cremated Pete and gave me his ashes in a cardboard box.'

Zuri's hand flew up to cover her mouth. 'That's awful,' she said.

'Tell me about it. The plan was to bury him back in the UK.'

'I guess you could bury the ashes in the UK,' said Sarah. 'They do that, right?'

'I suppose so,' said Green. 'I suppose I should look on the bright side, it'll be a lot cheaper to get him back now.'

'You can probably take him in your hand luggage,' said Zuri, then her jaw dropped. 'Oh my God, I can't believe I just said that,' she said. 'I'm so sorry.'

Green grinned and shook his head. 'The same thought had occurred to me already,' he said. 'And don't worry, Pete would be pissing himself laughing at that.'

'Sometimes I speak without thinking,' said Zuri. 'I need to remember to engage my brain.'

Kayla returned with Green's whisky and soda and Standing's beer. 'So did you guys introduce yourselves? To be honest, we almost keeled over when you walked in, Billy. I really didn't know what to think. Pete never mentioned the fact that he had a twin.'

Sarah nodded. 'That's what I said. You'd think he would have said something.'

'No, I'm the same,' said Green. 'Obviously if we're together it comes up, but if we're on our own I tend not to mention it. But then I'm the good-looking one.'

'And Pete was the one with the brains?' said Zuri. 'She put her hand over her mouth. 'Oh my God, I'm doing it again.'

'Earth to Zuri, engage brain before speaking,' laughed Sarah.

'So we've got a Yank, a South African and a Brit in a bar,' said Standing. 'Sounds like the start of a bad joke. How did you girls get together?'

'We met at a full moon party on Koh Phangan,' said Kayla. 'It was amazing but after twenty-four hours partying non-stop I really had to find somewhere to chill and I'd been told about Koh Chang. Sarah and Zuri had the same idea. It's everything they said it was. Pure relaxation. But they have full moon parties, too.'

'Where are you staying?' asked Standing.

'Here. They have cabins close to the beach. It's not four-star but you wake up to the sound of the waves, what could be better? What about you? Where are you staying?'

'Up the road, Lonely Beach.'

'Oh, that's where Pete stayed . . .' she began, but then cut herself short. 'I'm sorry, of course that's why you're there.'

'Yeah,' said Standing. 'The Best Friends Resort. We came to find out what had happened, and to take Pete's body back to England. The cops keep saying that Pete killed himself, which is bollocks.'

'I said the same when I heard that Pete had killed himself,' said Kayla. 'He wasn't the type. He wasn't depressed at all, he'd sit up there with his binoculars, twitching away.' She pointed at a mezzanine level above their heads.

'Twitching?' repeated Standing.

'Yeah, bird-watching. He'd be up there all day and only came down when it was dark.'

'Did you ever visit him at the Best Friends Resort?' asked Green.

Kayla shook her head. 'I didn't know where he was staying. It was only after we heard that he'd died that we found out he was staying at Lonely Beach.'

'So who told you?' asked Green.

Kayla frowned. 'I'm not sure.' She looked at her friends. 'Who was it told us about Pete?'

'It was a couple of guys who were staying up there, remember?' said Sarah. 'The guys with the Harleys. The bikers.'

'Like Hell's Angels?' said Green.

'No, they were old guys, playing at being bikers,' said Sarah. 'They were in their sixties. Probably having a mid-life crisis.'

'Foreigners?'

She shook her head. 'Thais. They had on leather vests, which is just weird in this weather, and cowboy boots, which is equally weird. But they spoke really posh English. They had been staying at the resort and were there when they took the body away.'

'How did he kill himself?' asked Kayla.

'They didn't tell you?' asked Green.

'I don't think they knew. They had just been told it was suicide.'

'The cops are saying that Pete put a plastic bag over his head,' said Green.

'He did what?' said Kayla.

'A bag. Over his head.'

'Like a sex thing?' said Zuri. 'I had a boyfriend who was into that. He wanted me to put a plastic bag over his head while we were, you know . . .' She shuddered.

'No, Pete was fully dressed,' said Green. 'And he was never into weird stuff like that.'

'True,' said Kayla. 'He was plain vanilla when it came to sex.' She put up her hands when Standing and Green looked at her. 'Guys, we made out a couple of times, okay? No biggie. But he definitely wasn't into weird stuff.'

'You said you didn't go to his room?' said Standing.

'He came to my room here,' said Kayla. 'It was just casual.' She grinned. 'But energetic, let's leave it at that.'

'You are such a slut,' said Zuri.

'Come on, you were tempted, it was just that I got in first,' said Kayla. She bit down on her lower lip. 'Sorry, Billy, that's a bit insensitive, I know.'

'Nah,' said Green. 'It's good to know that he was having fun.'

'Oh yes, we had fun.' She sighed. 'I can't believe it, you know? That's why I went a bit crazy when I saw you. I keep thinking he's going to walk back in here with his bird book and his big floppy hat.'

'Floppy hat?'

'Sometimes he'd sit in the sun while he was bird-watching. So he had the hat and lots of sun cream.'

Standing looked at Green and pointed at the mezzanine floor. 'Want to check it out?'

'Sure,' said Green. He stood up. 'Back in a minute, ladies.'

There were stairs at the side of the bar, behind a bright yellow American convertible that looked as if it had been reversed in years ago and never left. They headed up the stairs, taking their drinks with them.

The stairs opened onto a large wooden platform overlooking the sea. There were two hammocks hanging from the roof, and a couple of sofas and coffee tables, all painted with red, yellow and green stripes. There were large black-and-white photographs of Bob Marley on the wall. There was a low balustrade at the far end and they walked over to it and peered over. They could see the bar underneath them, and the hillside sloping away to the beach. Green turned to look at the hammocks. 'Great place for an LUP,' he said. 'Beer on tap, toilets nearby and a nice sea breeze.' He gestured at the lights of villas across the water. 'And a perfect view of the villa and its jetty.'

Standing nodded. An LUP – Lying Up Position – was more often a hole in the ground or a hide under a bush, often with no toilet facilities other than a plastic bag. Lying in a hammock with a beer at hand would have been a pleasant change. But that might have been Pete's undoing. If he could see the men in the villa, they would have been able to see him. 'They spotted him driving past, then they must have tracked him here,' said Standing.

'Yeah, but they didn't kill him here, did they?' said Green. He sipped his drink. 'How did they know where he was staying?'

'They must have followed him back,' said Standing. 'Either from here or when he did the drive-by.' He drank his beer as he looked over at the villa. It looked as if there were two men standing on the terrace, but it was impossible to make out any detail, all he could see were shadows. 'We're going to have to be careful what we say to the girls,' he said. 'I know we've already said that we didn't think Pete killed himself, but best we not talk about murder. Or Sammy Lee. Just leave it that we're confused.'

Green nodded. 'Makes sense.' He grinned. 'Do you think Kayla would be up for it, for old time's sake?'

'Please tell me you're joking.'

'You saw the way she shoved her tongue in my mouth.'

Standing shook his head. 'I can't believe I'm hearing this.'

Green's grin widened. 'I'm only messing with you. Though I have to say, it wouldn't be the first time we've shared.'

'I really don't want to hear any more of this,' said Standing. He went back down the stairs and Green followed him. Zuri was heading to the table with more drinks, blue cocktails with salt on the rims.

'That looks interesting,' said Standing as he sat down at their table.

'Blue Margaritas,' said Sarah. 'Always reminds me of the sea. Blue and salty.'

'Bit like giving Papa Smurf a blow job,' said Zuri. Her eyes widened. 'Did I just say that? What is wrong with me?'

'It's probably due to the fact that we've been drinking since eleven o'clock this morning,' said Kayla. She picked up her glass and held it aloft. 'To Pete,' she said. 'Like a bird singing in the rain, let grateful memories survive in time of sorrow.' She drank and the others followed.

'Did you just make that up?' asked Green.

Kayla smiled and shook her head. 'Robert Louis Stevenson.'

'Nice words. Thank you.' Green raised his glass. 'He fought the good fight, he finished the race, he kept the faith.' They all drank.

'I'll get a round in,' said Standing. He was about to stand up when a waitress came over, so he ordered a round of drinks. 'And a double vodka. With ice.'

'For Pete?' asked Green as the waitress went over to the bar.

'Sure. Why not?'

'Good idea.'

'So, did Pete have any other friends here?' asked Standing.

'He kept himself to himself, most of the time,' said Kayla.

'It's only because we wouldn't take no for an answer that he agreed to have a drink with us.'

'We can be persuasive,' said Sarah.

'Basically we wore him down,' said Zuri.

The three girls sipped their cocktails.

'Are you soldiers, same as Pete?' asked Kayla.

Standing nodded. 'Yeah, we served together.'

'Pete said he spent most of his time sitting behind a desk. He said lots of guys spend their whole Army careers without shooting at anybody. Is that right?'

Standing smiled. It was protocol to never admit to being in the SAS, and Standing preferred not to even talk about being in the Army. But it was often easier to say that you served in the Paras. 'Being a soldier isn't as exciting as they make it seem in the adverts,' he said.

'Be All That You Can Be,' said Sarah. 'Isn't that the slogan?'

'For the Yanks, yeah,' said Green. 'For the Brits, it's Be The Best. Says it all really. British soldiers aspire to be the best, Yanks try to do the best they can. That's why they fuck it up so often. Because their best often just isn't good enough.'

The waitress returned with their drinks on a tray and the girls all finished the ones they had. They were clearly serious drinkers.

'So what are your plans?' asked Zuri. 'Are you going to stay on Koh Chang for a while?'

'Probably for a few days,' said Green. 'I mean, we literally only just arrived. I'm still jet-lagged.'

'And then what? Will you take Pete's ashes back to England?'

'That's the plan,' said Green. 'Well, the plan was to take his body back and arrange a funeral in the UK. That's what our mum wants, anyway. She wants him buried in the local church so that he'll be close by. She probably wants to go around each day to nag him.'

Kayla smiled. 'She nags, does she?'

'She could nag for England, our mum,' said Green. 'That's why we did so well in the Army. Getting a slagging off from the sergeant major was nothing compared to an earful from our mum.'

'How is she taking it?' asked Sarah.

'I haven't really had much time to talk to her,' said Green. 'She got the phone call from the British embassy and she called me and I came straight out. But she'll be in bits. It's not right, is it? A kid dying before the parent.'

'You don't have kids?' asked Kayla.

Green shook his head. 'Never married. Pete was the same.' He gestured at Standing. 'Matt's never married, either. There's no rules against it but it takes a particular type of woman to want to be an Army wife. I don't know how they put up with it.' He drained his glass and waved at the waitress for another.

'I'm not sure I want to be buried,' said Standing. 'I mean, my plan is to live forever, but if I do die, I don't think I want to be buried in the ground. The idea of rotting . . .' He shuddered.

'You're dead, you don't know that you're rotting,' said Zuri.

'I just think cremation is faster and cleaner, I suppose,' said Standing. 'The idea is to get your atoms and stuff back into the universe as quickly as possible and cremation does that efficiently because you go up in smoke. They say that every breath you take, you inhale an atom or two of Jesus.'

'And Hitler,' said Zuri.

Green laughed. 'Now there's a thought. 'The waitress brought him over a fresh whisky and soda. 'But I'm with Matt.

I'd prefer to be cremated and have my ashes scattered, rather than rotting in the ground.'

'Where would you want your ashes scattered?' asked Zuri.

Green sipped his whisky. 'That's a good question.'

'I think I'd like my ashes to be thrown out of a plane,' said Standing. 'One last jump.'

'Nice one,' said Green. 'Maybe I'll have mine scattered on Pen y Fan.'

Kayla frowned. 'What's that?'

'A mountain in Wales.'

'Is it pretty?' asked Zuri.

Green chuckled. 'It's challenging rather than pretty.' He looked over at Standing. 'What do you think?'

'I can see the attraction,' said Standing. Pen y Fan was the highest peak in the Brecon Beacons and formed the centrepiece of the SAS's endurance phase of the selection process. At the end of the first week, recruits had to march up and down the mountain with a full Bergen, a total of 40kg, and then go back again, in under four hours and ten minutes. The Fan Dance, as it was called, was in technical terms a load-bearing, non-navigational TAB (tactical assault to battle) test, which meant that it was an endurance event, against the clock, but navigation wasn't an issue. Meeting the deadline meant clocking up an average speed of six kilometres an hour, so jogging was necessary for most of the way. The mountain was also used in the final test of the endurance phase – The Long Drag. The Long Drag was a forty-mile march with a 25kg Bergen and rifle, with recruits having to complete the course in twenty-four hours with just a map, compass and memorised grid references. Every single member of the SAS had memories of Pen y Fan, fond or otherwise. Standing could see the attraction of ashes being scattered at the summit of a place that had played such a big part of their lives.

'To be honest, I think that's what Pete would want, too,' said Green. 'He was never a fan of graveyards.'

'I don't think anyone is,' said Standing.

'I had a boyfriend once who had a thing about graveyards,' said Sarah. 'He used to like making out on gravestones.'

'Oh, that is disgusting,' said Zuri.

'He was a Goth.'

Zuri laughed. 'That's even more disgusting.'

The three girls laughed and drank their cocktails. Standing looked at his watch. It was just after eight. 'You got somewhere to go, Matt?' asked Green.

'I guess not. You wanna stay here for a while?'

'Sure. Why not? I'll be the designated driver.'

'No need,' said Green. 'We haven't seen a single cop on the streets since we got here.'

'It's true,' said Sarah. 'The cops here don't come unless you call them. There's no speed cameras, no breathalysers, no beat cops. But they'll come right away if you call 911.'

'Or 191,' said Zuri. 'Or 1155 for the Tourist Police. Or 1584 for a taxi driver who refuses a fare. Or if you're in a road accident, 1146.'

Standing laughed. 'How do you know all of them?'

Zuri shrugged. 'I've always been good with numbers.'

'What she's saying, Matt, is that you can carry on drinking.'

Standing sighed. 'Fine,' he said. 'You've talked me into it.'

CHAPTER 17

Standing and Green arrived back at the Best Frien...
just before midnight. The girls were still drinki...
Rasta View and had shared another three joints betw...
They had offered the joints to Standing and Green...
had declined. Drug use was grounds for instant dism...
the Special Air Service, with no exceptions and n...
Military compulsory drug testing teams visited...
barracks at Stirling Lines an average of twice a ye...
rare for anyone to test positive for cocaine, heroin,
methamphetamines or steroids, but if they did...
returned to their unit and likely to be thrown out of...
Standing's drug of choice had always been alcohol,
that was usually in moderation. He figured that noth...
ever equal the adrenaline rush that came with being...
so why bother trying to recreate it?

Daeng was sitting at the desk when they walke...
shack and he smiled and nodded. Electric lights...
switched on to illuminate the walkways and they...
shadows as the two men walked towards their cabins...
the plan tomorrow?' asked Green.

'Let's go to the Rasta View at eleven. We can eat...
hang out all day. We should take the binoculars a...
book.'

'We're going to pretend to be bird-watchers?'

'We can just say we found the book and were curious. We'll be out of the way up on the mezzanine.'

Green nodded and headed towards his cabin. Standing watched him go inside and then walked along to his room. He let himself in and switched on the light. He wasn't tired so he lay on the bed, plugged his phone into its charger and logged onto Netflix.

He drifted off to sleep while he was watching a lacklustre comedy but was woken when his phone vibrated. He took it out and saw that he had a message. His phone didn't recognise the number but it was clear from the message – **CALL THIS NUMBER ON WHATSAPP** – that it was from Shepherd.

He left his cabin and hurried over to Green's. He knocked on the door and Green opened it with the chain on. He nodded when he saw it was Standing, took the chain off and opened the door. 'Spider wants a chat,' said Standing.

'Cool,' said Green. The bottle of Johnnie Walker was on his bedside table, along with a half-filled glass. The box containing Pete's ashes was on the dressing table, next to the bottle of vodka. Standing could see that Green had continued drinking in his room, but was far from drunk.

'You want a dram?' asked Green.

'Yeah, go for it,' said Standing.

Green grinned. He picked up a fresh glass and poured in a large measure of whisky. Standing took it, toasted the box of ashes and drank.

'What does Spider want?'

'It'll be about Sammy Lee. He wants us to call him on WhatsApp, probably because WhatsApp is encrypted.' He added the burner phone number to his contacts list.

'Covering his arse.'

'Covering his tracks. That means something's up.' He placed his phone against a pillow on the bed and pulled up a chair. Green took the other chair and sat down next to him as Standing opened WhatsApp. 'Ready?'

'Sure,' said Green. He leaned over and picked up his glass of whisky.

Standing pressed the button to call Shepherd's burner phone. It rang out for thirty seconds before Shepherd answered. He was wearing a suit and tie, which probably meant he was in the office, but the picture was close in on his face so it was impossible to make out the background. 'Hey guys,' he said. 'You okay?'

'We're good,' said Standing. Green nodded.

'So where are you guys?'

'Koh Chang,' said Standing.

'I mean right now? No one can overhear us, right?'

'We're in Billy's room. Place called Best Friends Resort. Actually it's the room where Pete died.'

'Got it,' said Shepherd.

'We checked out the numbers you gave us and spoke to the guy he was with in Vietnam. He's a vet, and Pete knew his son who was a Navy SEAL. Long story short, the vet has a daughter who went missing in Koh Chang. Pete came over to see if he could find her. From the pictures you sent it looks as if he was on the trail of the guy she was last seen with, guy called Sammy Lee.'

'That's why I need to talk to you, Matt. Sammy Lee is a dangerous bastard, you're going to have to watch yourself.'

'What is he, some sort of triad?'

'That and more,' said Shepherd. 'Sammy Lee AKA Lee

Yat-fung started off as an enforcer for the 14K triad in Hong Kong but went independent a few years ago. For some reason no one understands we gave him a British passport long before we started resettling people from Hong Kong, and he has Cambodian citizenship. He's a major dealer in illegal wildlife products, shipping ivory and animal parts into China and using the same network to ship heroin and amphetamines all around Asia.'

'Are you guys interested in him?' asked Green.

'Interested yes, pursuing no,' said Shepherd. 'He doesn't supply drugs to Europe, or to the States. So we keep tabs on him, as do the DEA, but that's as far as it goes. He's also a big-time human trafficker, and there he does operate in the UK and the US, but he keeps the actual trafficking at arm's length. Remember those Vietnamese immigrants who suffocated in that truck on the way to the UK? We're fairly sure that several of the young girls who died were smuggled in by Lee's people, but we could never prove it. He also takes girls to Mexico and across the border into the States. But again, he uses Mexican smuggling gangs so it's near impossible to prove that he's involved.'

'You think he might have trafficked this girl?' said Green.

'Unlikely,' said Shepherd. 'You saw the social media pictures, right? I had a look at the pictures when you sent me Lee's name. Sammy Lee doesn't drink champagne with the girls he traffics. I'd say he was involved with her and then something happened, maybe she saw something she wasn't supposed to see.'

'That's what her father said. She made a call from Koh Chang saying that something was wrong and then the phone went dead.'

'That's not good, is it?'

'So you think she's dead?' said Green. 'You think he killed her?'

'That'd be supposition, Billy,' said Shepherd. 'No way of knowing. But the reason I wanted to talk to you both is to warn you that this guy is big trouble. He's worth billions and has his fingers in a lot of very dirty pies. He wouldn't think twice about killing anyone who threatened his organisation. And he has politicians, cops and who knows who else on his payroll out there. He can operate pretty much with impunity. The Hong Kong cops tried to get undercover agents into his organisation three times and each time it ended badly.'

'Do you think he's in Thailand now?' asked Standing. 'Billy was looking at a house here on Koh Chang.'

'No way of knowing unless you get eyes on him,' said Shepherd. 'But what if you do find him? What's your plan?'

'No plan as yet,' said Standing.

'Just finding him isn't going to get you anywhere,' said Shepherd. 'The DEA aren't after him and we've got no warrants out for him. Europol have no interest, either.'

'By "we" you mean Five, right?' asked Standing. 'What about the cops? The National Crime Agency?'

'I checked. Nothing. He hasn't broken any UK laws. The Vietnamese girls that died, we had intel connecting him but nothing conclusive. Certainly not enough to put him in a court. What I'm saying is that even if you find him, you won't be able to call in the cavalry and have him picked up.'

'No one there cares?'

'He hasn't broken any UK laws, Matt. I guess you could see if the Thais were interested in arresting him, but my gut feeling is that he wouldn't be living there openly if he didn't have protection. Even more so in Cambodia.'

'I hear you,' said Standing.

'So if the police aren't an option, I guess I have to ask you how you're going to move forward, if you do find him?'

'That's not your problem, Spider.'

'Well, it sort of is, now that I'm involved.'

'You're not involved,' said Standing. 'We just had a chat, that's all, and nobody is ever going to know what the chat is about.'

'He's right, Spider,' said Green. 'It's all down to us. We'll handle it.'

Shepherd shook his head. 'You need to think long and hard about where that road leads, guys. There'll be repercussions. I've been down that road myself, and so have you, Matt. You have to be aware of the consequences, and you have to be prepared to live with those consequences.'

Standing put up his hand. 'Message received and understood,' he said.

'Okay, I can see you're not going to change your mind. But think on this. Lee is very unlikely to have done this himself. His heavies would do it for him. And they're not likely to tell on their boss. So you'll never know for sure.'

'We hear what you're saying, Spider,' said Green. 'But we can take it from here.'

Shepherd forced a smile. 'No problem, guys. It's obviously totally up to you. Stay safe.'

Standing flashed him a thumbs up and ended the call.

'What did he mean, about you going down this road before?' asked Green.

'It doesn't matter.'

'You've done something like this before?'

Standing grimaced. 'A few years back my sister died. And I held some people accountable. That's all.'

'Accountable?' Green nodded. 'Yeah, that's a good word. If more people were held accountable for their actions, maybe they'd behave better.' He sipped his whisky. 'What did he mean about living with the consequences? Does he mean guilt? Because fuck that, I wouldn't feel the least bit guilty.'

'No, I didn't feel guilty about what I did. I didn't take any pleasure in doing what I did. But it had to be done. It's like combat. Somebody tries to kill you but you kill them first. You don't feel guilt afterwards. You were doing what had to be done. That doesn't mean you take pleasure in it, but I don't wake up in the middle of the night thinking that I did a bad thing.'

'We both know guys who do enjoy it, though.'

Standing nodded. 'Yeah, we do, and they're not right in the head. They never make it into the Regiment, they get weeded out in Selection. You can't do what we do because you get a buzz out of killing. That only ever ends one way.'

Green took another sip of his whisky. 'So what did he mean by consequences?'

Standing sighed. 'I guess that when you take the law into your hands, there's always someone who knows what you did. And they can hold it over you.'

'So Spider knows what you did?'

'Yeah, he knows. But he's not the only one, and therein lies the problem.' He shrugged. 'It doesn't matter, Billy. He was just warning us that we need to be sure of what we're doing. Like he said, he's been down this road, so he knows where it leads.'

'So he killed someone for revenge?'

'Billy, mate, Spider and I have worked together, but we're not bosom buddies. He doesn't tell me everything. And this isn't about him or me or what we might or might not have done. This is about you. And Pete. What do you want to do? Whatever you want is fine by me. I'll do whatever needs to be done.'

'Let's take a good look at this Sammy Lee,' said Green. 'See if he's still on Koh Chang, for a start. And we need to know who's working for him. Then we can decide what we're going to do.'

CHAPTER 18

According to the bar's website the Rasta View opened at nine o'clock in the morning, so Standing and Green met in the Best Friends reception shack at ten to. They were both dressed casually in T-shirts, shorts and training shoes. Green had found his brother's floppy hat in his luggage and was wearing it with the binoculars around his neck. He was carrying the bird book. Standing laughed when he saw him. 'That's what the best-dressed birdwatcher is wearing these days, is it?'

'Twitchers, mate. That's what they call us. That's what Kayla called it.'

'Yeah, I didn't get that. Why are they called twitchers?'

Green grinned. 'I Googled it. It's because a famous bird-watcher from the Fifties had a nervous twitch. Can you believe it? If the guy had a farting problem, they'd all be called farters now.'

They climbed into the Fortuner and ten minutes later they were parked outside the Rasta View. There were already two tourists sitting at the bar overlooking the sea, eating plates of fried rice.

They ordered breakfast from a waitress. Standing wanted to try the fried rice and Green asked for scrambled eggs and toast. They both wanted coffee and Standing suggested that they order iced water. It was already hot and clearly going to get much hotter and they needed to stay hydrated. Standing pointed up at the mezzanine. 'Okay if we sit upstairs?' he asked.

'Of course,' said the waitress.

They went up the stairs and looked out over the sea. There was a long thin yellow speedboat with Thai writing on the side moored at the villa's jetty. Two men were carrying cardboard boxes from the villa towards the boat. Green put the binoculars to his eyes. Another man was watching the speedboat from the terrace.

'Be nice to know what's in the boxes,' said Green.

'Doesn't look too heavy,' said Standing. 'So maybe not drugs or cash. The guy on the terrace, is he armed?'

Green checked him out with the binoculars. 'I don't see anything. But he's got a jacket on, so he could be carrying. So this is what Pete did, right? Sat here and watched.'

'I guess so.'

'And the fact that he kept watching presumably meant that he didn't see Kim.'

'If he had seen her, there'd be no need for the drive-by,' said Standing. 'So, yes, I'd agree with that.' He sat down on one of the sofas.

'So what are we going to do? How long do we wait?'

'Let's just get the lie of the land,' said Standing. 'No matter what happens down the line, we need to know what we're up against.'

'What if we see this Sammy Lee but don't see Kim?' He lowered the binoculars and turned to look at Standing.

'Mate, it's all hypothetical at the moment,' said Standing. 'We're still at the intel gathering phase. No point in making plans until we know what's what.'

Green straddled one of the hammocks and lowered himself into it, then chuckled as he realised that it gave him a perfect view of the villa. 'Now this is the sort of surveillance I could get used to,' he said.

'Just make sure you don't fall asleep.'

They watched as the two men continued to load boxes onto the boat. There were a dozen in all. Then they climbed in and drove off, heading south towards the islands in the distance. Eventually they disappeared from sight.

The man on the terrace went inside, and a few minutes later another man appeared, this one wearing a T-shirt, shorts and a baseball cap. Even without binoculars, Standing could see that he had a carbine on a sling. 'Is that an AR-15?' he asked.

'That or an M16,' said Green. 'Whatever they've got in there, it's valuable.'

'Could just be Lee's bodyguards,' said Standing. 'But that's pretty heavy fire power for personal protection.'

The man walked back inside. Green leaned over and picked up the bird book. He had tucked a ballpoint pen inside and he used it to scribble a note on the inside cover.

They heard footsteps on the stairs and turned to look at the waitress carefully carrying a tray with their food. She placed the plates on the table in front of Standing, flashed him a beaming smile, and went back downstairs.

'Breakfast is served,' said Standing.

Green swung his legs off the hammock and went over to the table. He sat down and began to devour his eggs and toast, keeping a watchful eye on the terrace.

Standing's rice was packed with chunks of prawn, chicken and pork, and came with a small dish of pungent fish sauce and chopped red chillies on the side to give it a kick if he wanted. He sprinkled some over the rice and tucked in. They both drank their coffee and water. The roof overhead provided shade from the burning sun and there was a soft breeze blowing in from the sea, but it was still as hot as a sauna and their shirts were damp with sweat.

Just as Green was finishing his last piece of toast, a man in a black Adidas tracksuit appeared on the terrace of the villa. Green grabbed the binoculars but the man had already turned his back and was doing some stretching exercises. Another man appeared, holding pads in either hand. He was in his sixties with a slight stoop and he held the pads up so that the man in the tracksuit could punch and kick them.

'Is that him?' asked Standing. 'Is that Lee?'

'Can't see his face,' said Green, walking towards the balustrade.

Standing stood up and joined him, and they watched the man spar for ten minutes or so but at no point did he turn towards them. Eventually he stopped sparring and went inside, followed by the older man. 'You have got to be kidding me,' said Standing.

'I think that was him,' said Green, lowering his binoculars.

'Yeah, but we can't be sure. We need to be sure.'

Green gave him the binoculars. 'You can have a go,' he said. 'My eyes are starting to hurt.'

'No problem,' said Standing.

'Do you want the hammock?'

'Nah, I need to walk around. My back's starting to ache.' He stood by the balustrade, squinting his eyes against the sun. Off in the distance, a white speedboat was heading towards the jetty. There were two men in the bow and something covered with a tarpaulin in the stern. Standing used the binoculars but the boat was too far away to make out much detail.

Green climbed into the hammock, put his floppy hat over his face, and was soon snoring softly.

Standing watched as the white speedboat tied up at the jetty. Two men came out of the villa and approached the boat.

The two men on the boat pulled off the tarpaulin and Standing's jaw dropped. 'Hey, Billy, you gotta see this.'

Green was instantly awake. He took the hat away from his face and sat up. He put a hand up to shield his eyes from the sun. 'Are you kidding me? He swung his legs over the side of the hammock and went over to join Standing.

Two more men came out of the villa, pushing a trolley between them.

The men on the boat had removed the tarpaulin, revealing two small tiger cubs in separate cages. Standing handed the binoculars to Green. 'They can't be more than a few months old.'

Between them, the six men lifted the two cages onto the trolley. Standing took out his iPhone and videoed them as they covered the cages with the tarpaulin and pushed them along the jetty to the villa.

'What do think they'll do with them?' asked Green.

'There's a huge market for tiger cubs,' said Standing. 'They fetch thousands of dollars.'

'As pets?'

'As pets. Or as parts. A couple of our guys went on to work for an anti-animal-trafficking company after they left the Regiment. They were back in Hereford last year, recruiting. It's a huge business, worth billions. Ivory, rhino horn, tiger parts. All of it illegal.'

'What do you mean, tiger parts?'

'Parts and products. Having a tiger skin on your wall and floor is a status symbol in parts of Asia. They make tiger-bone wine in Vietnam and they use a medicinal paste made from the bones. They use tiger teeth in jewellery. The Chinese use tiger penises in medicine. If those cubs are lucky, they'll be kept as some rich man's pet; if they're not, they'll get ground up into paste. It's a sick business.'

'Where do you think they've come from?'

'Poachers catch them in India. But they breed them all over the world. I'd guess that those two were bred in Thailand and he's getting ready to move them through Cambodia to Vietnam.'

The speedboat pulled away from the jetty and headed back to the open sea as the two tiger cubs disappeared into the villa.

'Bastards,' hissed Green.

'Yeah.'

'We need to put a stop to this.'

'We will,' said Standing. 'But one step at a time. We're still not even sure if Lee is there. And we need to find Kim Cooper. If we go off half-cock and they know we're onto them, we might never find her.'

Green nodded. 'I know. I just wish I had that bastard Lee in my sights right now.'

'Assuming you had a gun, you mean?'

Green grinned ruefully. 'Yeah. Assuming that.'

CHAPTER 19

Standing and Green went downstairs at just after one o'clock to order lunch. Green wanted a burger and chips and a whisky and soda. He grinned when he saw Standing raise an eyebrow. 'It's just one drink. Come on, how often do we get to enjoy ourselves on a surveillance op?'

'It's going to be a long day,' said Standing.

There were three young Thai men sitting at one of the tables with fresh coconuts in front of them, passing around a thick joint. 'Buffalo Soldier' was playing on the sound system.

'Can I have one of the coconuts?' Standing asked the waitress.

'Of course,' she said.

'And what Thai food is good? I had the fried rice this morning, what else is there?'

'People like our kao pad gaprao gai kai dao,' she said.

Standing laughed. 'Say what now?'

She repeated it slowly but he was none the wiser. She grabbed a menu and pointed at a picture of a fried egg with what looked like meat and chillies on top of boiled rice. 'Rice with chicken holy basil stir-fry and a fried egg,' she said.

Standing grinned. 'Sounds perfect,' he said.

The waitress made Green his whisky and soda, then took a prepared coconut from the fridge and expertly hacked a hole in the top. She popped in a straw and gave it to Standing. 'Enjoy,' she said.

The two young tourists had gone from the bar overlooking the sea, so Standing and Green went over and sat down there to wait for their food. They could see the jetty and villa from where they were sitting. Green scanned the area through his binoculars. 'So what do you think? This is some sort of staging post?'

'It would make sense. The only way on and off the island by regular means is the ferry, and that only operates during daylight hours. His place is on the far south of the island and we know that there's little in the way of a police presence here. We haven't seen any sort of coastguard, so it looks as if small boats can come and go as they want. The Cambodian coastline isn't far away and from there it's overland to Vietnam and then on to China. He could be sending animals and animal parts to China and bringing drugs back the same route. Down from China through Vietnam to Cambodia, and then by small boat to his villa. Then bigger ships can sail into the Gulf of Thailand and he can send the speedboats out to them. From there the drugs can go anywhere in the region.'

'I still can't get my head around there being a trade in animal parts,' said Green. 'I mean, how many buyers of tiger penises can there be?'

'According to the guys I met, the illegal wildlife trade is worth more than 120 billion dollars a year. Billion.'

Green raised his eyebrows. 'No shit.'

'No shit,' said Standing. 'They were saying that African rhino horn sells for twenty thousand dollars a kilo, about the same as heroin or cocaine. But Asian rhino horn sells for twenty times that. Four hundred thousand dollars a kilo. Mainly to the Chinese.'

'And don't tell me, they buy it to make themselves horny – ha ha.'

'Nah, it's used in all sorts of medicines. To treat fever, rheumatism, gout, even cancer. But the point is, there's serious money to be made.'

Green sighed as he looked over at the villa. 'So what do we think? Kim meets Sammy Lee and he invites her down to his villa. She finds out what's going on and threatens to expose him and he does what? Locks her in a room somewhere? Or tops her?'

'Unfortunately the latter is more likely, isn't it? He's going to kill to protect his interests, isn't he? Our only hope is that he might have decided to traffic her instead.' He shrugged. 'I've got a bad feeling about it, but we've got to try. Maybe he just locked her up.'

The waitress came out of the kitchen with their food. She put the plates down in front of them and Green immediately grabbed his burger and bit into it.

'Enjoy your food,' said the waitress, but Green was already swallowing his first mouthful.

Standing's food was delicious, the meat stir-fry was spicy and full of flavour and the egg was just as he liked it, crispy on the bottom and the yolk soft. It came with the same fish sauce and chillies that he'd been given with his fried rice earlier that morning and he used some sparingly. It had a fierce kick, and several times he had to stop and drink some coconut water.

When they had finished, they bought bottles of water and went back upstairs. It was Green's turn with the binoculars, so he climbed into one of the hammocks and trained them on the villa.

Standing picked up his phone and clicked through to the website that contained the dump from Pete Green's phone. He began going through the photographs in reverse order to see if there were any men who matched the ones that he had seen through the binoculars. There were lots of shots of men loading and unloading boxes onto various speedboats, but the resolution wasn't good enough to make out their faces. They didn't seem to be armed, but again it was difficult to make out the detail. In a perfect world Pete would have used a camera with a telephoto lens, but that would probably have been too conspicuous. The binoculars did the job but they didn't provide a lasting record.

Interspersed with the speedboat photographs were pictures of various men on the terrace overlooking the jetty. Again, the faces weren't clear but from the body types and clothing there seemed to be at least eight different men. One of the men, tall and thin and wearing a white suit, was holding an assault rifle, an AR-15 or an M16. In one picture two stocky men with black hair seemed to be comparing handguns. None of the men in the photographs appeared to be Sammy Lee.

'New face on the terrace,' said Green.

Standing went over and took the binoculars. There was a dark-skinned Asian man wearing a white jacket and blue jeans standing at the edge of the terrace, looking out to sea. His hair was short and spiky and he was holding a mobile phone. As he talked on the phone, the wind tugged at his jacket to reveal a handgun stuck into his belt.

Standing gave the binoculars to Green and went back to his table. He took a sip from his water bottle before opening the folder that contained the calls that Pete had made from his mobile. There were two calls on the day that he had died, both to Dean Cooper in Vietnam.

There were two more calls to Cooper on the previous day, a call to a number in Hereford, and a call to 1155. Standing frowned as he looked at the number. 'Hey, what number did Kayla say was for the Tourist Police?' he asked Green.

'1155,' said Green. 'Why?'

'Because Pete called that number the day before he died.'

Green twisted around in his hammock. 'No way.'

'He was on the call for eleven minutes. They might have put him on hold but it's more likely that he spoke to someone.'

Green frowned. 'That doesn't make any sense.' He rolled out of the hammock. Shepherd held out the phone and Green squinted at it. 'If he called the cops, why didn't they mention it?'

'I'm going to call Fah.' He pulled Fah's card from his wallet and tapped out her mobile phone number. She answered after half a dozen rings. 'Hello, Fah, it's Matt.'

'Good afternoon, Matt. How are you today?'

'I'm good. We're good. I'm here with Billy.'

'Where are you?'

'A place called Rasta View. On the south of the island. Have you heard of it?'

'Of course. It's a well-known tourist place. Why are you there?'

'Just hanging out,' said Standing. 'Relaxing.'

'Okay,' she said. 'Do you know when you'll be going back to the UK?'

'We're not sure,' said Standing.

'But there is no reason to stay, now that you have Mister Pete's ashes.'

'We'd still like to know what happened, Fah. We know that Pete didn't kill himself. Look, Fah, I have a question for you.'

'Sure. Go ahead.'

'Did Pete ever speak to anyone at your station?'

'No, of course not. Why do you ask?'

'We know that Pete phoned the Tourist Police number the day before he died. 1155.'

There was a pause of a few seconds before she spoke. 'How do you know that?'

'We have his phone records.'

'But you said his phone was missing.'

'It was. It is. But we have his records, so we know what numbers he called. And he called 1155. Do you know if he spoke to Benz or to Captain Somchai?'

'If he had spoken to them, they would have mentioned it to me. How did you get the phone records, Mister Matt?'

'That doesn't matter, Fah. What matters is that he spoke to someone at the Tourist Police the day before he died. And it would be very helpful if you could find out who that was. Can you do that for me?'

'Maybe,' she said. 'That number is the national number, so the call will have gone through to a central switchboard. They might have been able to answer his question straight away. Or they might have transferred him to one of the stations. Not necessarily on Koh Chang.'

'Okay, but they might have put him through to one of the Koh Chang stations, right? That would have made more sense. Can you check for me?'

'Of course. Can you give me the number he used, and the date and time of the call?'

Standing gave her the details and she repeated them back to him.

'I'll call you if I find out anything,' she said. 'How is Billy?'

'He's okay.'

'I would have thought he would have been more comfortable in England with his family.'

'He just wants to know what happened, Fah. And so do I.'

He ended the call and looked over at Green. 'She okay?' Green asked.

'She seemed a bit put out, to be honest.'

'Probably thinks you're accusing her of not doing her job properly.' He sipped his drink. 'Why do you think Pete called the cops?'

'Maybe he spotted Lee. Or Kim. If he saw her in the villa, that would be reason enough for the cops to go in. Maybe he called them and they weren't interested, so he did a drive-by.' He grimaced. 'I dunno, Billy, it's all supposition, isn't it? But the same thing applies to us, right? The moment we see Kim in that house we can get Captain Somchai on the case. Assuming that she's being held against her will, they can get her out.'

'I don't want the cops to deal with Lee,' said Green. 'I want to do that myself.'

'One step at a time, Billy,' said Standing. 'We're not even sure that he's in there.'

'That many heavies, I'd say he's there.'

'Then we'll keep eyes on the villa until we're sure.'

'And once we know that he's here, we go in, right?'

'We're going to have to talk about that, Billy.'

Green's eyes hardened. 'Are you having second thoughts, Matt?'

Standing shook his head. 'Pete was one of us, I'll do what needs to be done. But the guys at the villa have got guns and we haven't. And I'm not sure where we go about getting tooled up, are you?'

'We can get to the villa at night, take out one of the guards, take his weapon. We're up and running.'

Standing grinned. 'That's the plan? Even John Wick gets his guns together before he goes charging in.'

'So do you have a better idea?'

'I don't have any ideas, Billy. That's the problem. We've seen how many guys today? Eight? Nine? Plus there'll be guys at the front gate. That video Pete took showed at least one guy and he had a Kalashnikov. Bound to be more. And we don't know for sure that Sammy Lee is there. Plus let's not forget about Kim Cooper. That's what started all this, remember? I don't see that Pete got any pictures of her and we haven't seen her. If we go charging in and do manage to get Sammy Lee, what do we do if Kim's not there? Think we'll ever find her?'

Green shrugged. 'I hear you.'

'I know you want revenge for what they did to Pete, and I'm with you one hundred per cent. But as things stand, here and now, we don't know if Sammy Lee is in that villa and we don't know where Kim is. We go in half-cock, we could blow everything.'

'Suppose we see that Kim's there? Then what do we do?'

Standing frowned. 'What do you mean?'

'There's no point in getting the Thai cops involved.'

'It's an option.'

'It's a shit option. We can't trust the cops here and you know it. They've been trying to pass Pete's murder off as a suicide from day one.'

'Kim Cooper's an American citizen. We could ask the US embassy to get involved.'

Green laughed. 'What makes you think they'll be any better than that Butcher arsehole from the British embassy?'

'Fair point.'

'Look, Matt, this is down to us doing what needs to be done.'

'I'm not arguing with you, Billy, I'm just pointing out that we're under-equipped for any mission at the moment.'

'I had a thought about that. When we were on the other side of the island, driving to the temple, I saw a shooting range. Well, the signs for it, anyway.'

'Yeah. I saw that. For tourists.'

'Then you saw the posters. Glocks, Uzis, Kalashnikovs, they've got all sorts of guns.'

'So we just break in?'

'How well protected can they be?' said Green. 'We can take a run out tomorrow, fire off a few guns and take a look at their security arrangements. I doubt it'll run to more than a few padlocks. But we won't know until we've had a look. Are you up for it?'

'Sure. We can do it first thing. Before we come here.'

'See, now we've got a plan.' Green walked back to look at the villa through his binoculars, then he scanned the sea. 'There's another boat coming,' he said.

Standing joined him and they watched as a long thin red speedboat with a white flash on the side moored alongside the jetty. Four heavies emerged from the villa, two with assault rifles hanging from slings. Standing took out his phone and videoed the heavies as they walked to the boat. Four young Asian girls climbed out of the boat and onto the jetty. The girls kept their heads down and huddled together, before the heavies grabbed them and marched them towards the villa.

'They don't look like they're on holiday, do they?' said Green.

Standing continued to video until the men had taken the girls inside the villa. 'No, mate. They're being trafficked. One thousand per cent.' He put his phone in his pocket.

Green made a note in his book. They heard the sound of scooter engines outside. Standing walked to the other end of the terrace and looked over the road. Kayla, Zuri and Sarah had parked next to the Fortuner across the road. They waved when they saw Standing looking down at them and he waved back. They were all wearing brightly coloured dresses and carrying knitted cloth bags. Zuri had tied her dreadlocks back and was wearing huge sunglasses, Kayla and Sarah both had large floppy hats to protect themselves against the sun. They hurried across the road and into the bar.

'The girls are here,' said Standing.

'What do we do?'

'We stay here. If they come up, you can just say you're a farter.'

'Twitcher.'

'I know. It was a joke.'

Two men walked out onto the terrace of the villa. Green studied them through the binoculars. 'One of them is a fresh face,' said Green. He scribbled a note in the bird book. Standing went over to the hammock and took the binoculars from him. 'The one on the left,' said Green.

He was right. Standing hadn't seen the man before. He had the look of a weightlifter, with bulging forearms accentuated by a tight tank top and baggy shorts that stopped just above huge curved calves. His head was shaved and he had a large diamond stud in his left ear.

The red speedboat was still moored at the jetty and two men were pulling large wheeled holdalls towards it. The man leaned over the railings and shouted something at them. Whatever it was that he said, it made them hurry up.

'How many is that?' asked Standing, taking the binoculars away from his eyes.

Green scanned the notes he'd made in the book. 'Twelve so far,' he said. 'Four came on the boats, two seem to just move stuff on the jetty and six different guys on the terrace. The four who came out to collect the girls, I'd seen them before.'

'Pete took pictures of eight guys on the terrace over three days. It's hard to know if they're the same guys we're looking at, the resolution just isn't good enough.' Standing gave the binoculars to Green and went back to the balustrade.

They heard footsteps on the stairs and Kayla appeared, holding a red cocktail with a cherry and a chunk of pineapple sticking out of it. 'Hello, boys,' she said. Her mouth opened wide when she saw Green. 'Oh my God, that's Pete's hat. And his binoculars. You really are the spitting image.'

'That tends to be the case with twins,' said Green.

'I know, I know. But in that hat . . . it's uncanny.' She frowned. 'So you are a twitcher?'

'Not really,' said Green. 'I just . . .' He shrugged. 'I dunno, I just felt like I had to, you know?'

'I guess it makes you feel closer to him?'

Green nodded. 'Yeah, I think that's probably it. So what were you girls up to today?'

'We did a trip to see one of the waterfalls, but frankly it wasn't impressive. Just a dribble through a few rocks.' She held up her glass. 'Now it's cocktail time. Why don't you come down and join us?'

'We will,' said Standing.

'We've got some pot, too.'

'I thought cannabis was illegal in Thailand,' said Standing.

'It's a grey area,' said Kayla. 'You can grow it, and you can smoke or eat it for medicinal reasons. No one seems sure what the rules are for tourists.' She grinned. 'But the great thing about Koh Chang is that you never see a cop, right? So illegal or not, it's not a problem.' She went over to Standing. 'What ya looking at?'

Standing pointed at the piers off to their left, the long thin one with the pagoda at the end, and the larger one further up the coast, with the lighthouse. 'I was just checking out the two piers over there. Any idea what they are?'

She looked over at where he was pointing. 'Sure. That thin one belongs to the resort down the beach. The water is quite shallow here so most boats can't get too close to the shore. They moor at the pier there and people go out to them. Fishing trips or trips to the islands. Or sometimes people just go and sit in the pagoda and have a picnic.'

'And the bigger one?'

'That's Bang Bao fishing village. It used to be a real fishing place but now it's more of a tourist trap. You should go and have a look – it's full of dive shops and shops selling tacky Chinese-made souvenirs, but the views from the pier itself are fantastic. There are a couple of decent seafood restaurants there.' She pointed at the brightly coloured boats that lined both sides of the pier. 'Back in the day they would be fishing boats, but these days they're mainly for tourists – day trips to the islands, or diving or snorkelling. You know what's funny?

The guys we met yesterday were telling us that there are still a few fishing boats that go out, but all the seafood they catch gets shipped to Bangkok. Apparently it's of such good quality that they can get a better price selling it to five-star hotels in Bangkok. So the restaurants on Koh Chang have to bring their seafood in from wholesalers on the mainland – it's cheaper but the quality isn't so good.'

'That's capitalism for you,' said Standing.

'It's madness,' said Kayla. 'So, are you guys ready for a drink? We can watch the sun go down.'

'Okay, maybe later.'

'Cool.' She turned to look at Green. 'How's the twitching going? See anything interesting?'

'We saw a black-headed bulbul earlier.'

'Did you, now? And does it really have a black head?'

'Of course,' said Green. 'Why do you ask?'

'Well, back in South Africa we have a white rhino, but it isn't white.'

Green frowned. 'Why's that?'

'I heard it was because the early Dutch settlers said it had a wide lip and the English thought they were saying white,' said Standing.

'That's what they say,' said Kayla. 'But it's not true. Do you speak Dutch, or Afrikaans, Matt?'

'Sadly not.'

'Well, the thing is, the Dutch word "wijde" is what would have been used at the time, but it would only ever be used to describe a distance between places, not a body part. So it's a good story and you'll hear guides all over the country telling it to tourists, but it's almost certainly not true.'

'Well, you live and learn,' said Standing.

She raised her glass in salute. 'Yes, you do,' she said.

'Hang on, I'm confused,' said Green. 'So the white rhino isn't white?'

'No. And the black rhino isn't black. They're both grey.'

'So how do you tell them apart?' asked Green.

'Oh, they're chalk and cheese,' said Kayla. 'The black rhino has a pointed lip so that it can pull leaves off trees and bushes. The white rhino has a square lip so that it can graze. And they're easy to tell apart at a distance because the black rhino's horns are the same length but the white rhino's front horn is much longer than the second horn behind it.'

'But they're both grey?' Green shook his head. 'None of that makes sense.'

'I agree, it's confusing.'

'Matt and I were just talking about rhinos,' said Green. 'He was saying that rhino horn is more expensive than heroin.'

'That'll be right,' said Kayla. 'My uncle owns a game farm up by the Kruger National Park and poaching is a huge problem. Poachers will kill a three-ton rhino just for its horns.' She frowned. 'Why were two twitcher-soldiers so interested in rhinos all of a sudden?'

Standing laughed. 'I met a couple of guys who investigate animal trafficking, that's all,' he said. 'I couldn't believe the prices people will pay for dead animals.'

'It's mainly the Chinese,' said Kayla. 'The market is huge. Something needs to be done, but, you know, money talks.' She shrugged. 'Capitalism.' She drained her glass. 'I need a refill.' She winked at Standing. 'Catch you later, Matt.' She turned and headed back down the stairs.

Standing looked over at the villa. The jetty was empty and there was no one on the terrace.

'I could do with a drink,' said Green.

'Go on, then,' said Standing. 'I'll stay up here on my own.'

'You're sure?'

'Yeah, go on, it doesn't need two of us.'

Green walked over and gave him the binoculars, the bird book and the pen. 'You're a star.' He headed for the stairs.

Standing settled back on the sofa and stretched out his legs. He opened the back of the bird book and looked at the notes that Green had made. He had listed his sightings with the time and a description using what looked like code. There were letter combinations such as AK, BF, SH, TT, TS. He looked at the last man they had seen. Green had written the time along with TT, BS, SH, DS. Standing pictured the man they'd seen and then smiled. Tank Top, Baggy Shorts, Shaved Head, Diamond Stud. Standing wasn't sure how useful the code system was but at least anyone sneaking a look wouldn't be any the wiser.

He put the binoculars to his eyes and scanned the villas on the island, then the jetties, then looked out to sea. Another speedboat was heading towards Lee's villa. Whatever he was up to, there was a lot of coming and going. But until they spotted the man himself – or the missing girl – all they could do was watch and wait.

CHAPTER 20

Standing stayed on the mezzanine level until darkness fell and all he could see of the villa were its lights. The boats had stopped coming about an hour before dusk. The men on the boats came and left, sometimes helping to unload or load whatever the cargo was. Sometimes the boats were delivering, sometimes they were collecting, and occasionally they did both. The men who appeared on the terrace stayed on the terrace, they never went down to the jetty or interacted with the men who arrived on the boats. Everyone had their job to do – transport, logistics, security. But where was the man supposedly running the show?

Standing went down the steps. Green was sitting around a table with the three girls and the three young Thai men who had been smoking a joint when he had ordered lunch. Green grinned when he saw Standing and raised his glass in salute.

The group had pulled two tables together and added more concrete chairs. There was an empty one next to Kayla and she waved him over. 'What have you been doing?' she asked, holding the binoculars that were hanging around his neck.

'Just relaxing,' he said.

'So you're not really a twitcher?'

'He's a farter,' said Green. He giggled and raised his glass, clearly slightly worse for wear.

'A what?' said Kayla.

'It's a joke,' said Standing. 'Sort of.'

Kayla waved at the three Thai men. 'This is Bank, New and Ball.' They all put down their glasses and waied him in unison. Standing couldn't help but smile and he gave them a wai back. A waitress came over and he ordered a beer.

'Are those your real names?' Standing asked, and the three men laughed.

'Of course,' said Bank.

'We met a guy called Benz,' said Standing. 'His dad was a fan of Mercedes.'

Ball laughed. 'My dad loves golf. So my older brother is called Golf. And I'm Ball.'

'And I bet you have a sister called Tee,' said Green.

Ball's jaw dropped. 'You know my sister?'

'I was joking,' said Green. 'Are you serious? You have a sister called Tee?'

'I do,' said Ball.

'But they can't be real names, surely,' said Standing.

'It's what we call a *chue len*,' said Ball. 'A play name.'

'A nickname,' said Standing.

'Yes, exactly,' said Ball. 'So I call my brother Golf and he calls me Ball and my teachers would call me Ball and I'm Ball at work. It's my name. But I have an official name that is on my ID card and my passport and my driving licence. But most people wouldn't know it and no one would really use it.'

The waitress reappeared with Standing's beer. He raised it to the Thai guys. 'Good to meet you,' he said. 'My name's Matt.'

'Is that a nickname?' asked New.

'No, that's my real name,' said Standing.

'His nickname is Lastman,' said Green.

The three Thais frowned. 'Lastman?' repeated Bank.

'Lastman Standing,' said Green. 'It means the last one to be on his feet in a fight. But really it's because he's the last man you want to be in an argument with.'

'What are the binoculars for?' asked Bank.

'They're birdwatchers,' said Kayla. 'At least Billy is.'

'Is Koh Chang a good place to look for birds?' asked Ball.

'Oh yes,' said Green. 'It's a stopping-off place for birds on their way to Siberia. It's a great place for kingfishers and swifts. I saw a family of Asian palm swifts this morning. That was something. But it was my brother who was the real birdwatcher.'

Standing nodded at Green, impressed at the man's suddenly acquired bird knowledge. He had obviously done his research. Probably on Google.

'But you don't take photographs?' asked Kayla.

'Well, like I said, Pete was the really keen one. I just used to keep him company sometimes.'

'But Pete didn't have a camera, did he?'

'True. He preferred to see something with his own eyes rather than a picture.'

Standing sipped his beer and looked over at Billy. 'Do you want to eat here or go back to the resort?'

'Oh no, come with us, there's a party on the beach at White Sand,' said Kayla. 'They've got these awesome fire jugglers.'

'Not my sort of thing,' said Standing.

Kayla turned to look at Green. 'You'll come, won't you, Billy?'

'Fire jugglers, huh?'

'The best in Thailand, they say.'

'I'm up for that,' said Green. He looked over at Standing. 'What about you?'

'Not really,' said Standing.

'Come on, how often do we get to see fire jugglers?'

'You go, mate. I'll head back to the hotel. Early night.'

'I'll run him back on the bike,' said Kayla. 'Does he have a curfew?'

Standing laughed. 'Providing you bring him back in one piece, he'll be fine.' He looked over at Green. 'Are you okay?'

'I just need to blow off some steam.'

'I get it.' Standing drained his beer and got to his feet. 'I'll head off,' he said, looking around the group. He picked up the bird book and binoculars. 'You all have a great evening.'

He headed out of the bar, crossed the road and climbed into the Fortuner. He didn't like leaving Green but he was in good company and Standing understood what the man was going through. He'd just lost his twin brother and maybe a night out drinking with three pretty girls might take his mind off things for a while.

He started the engine and drove back to Lonely Beach. Daeng was sitting at the desk and he smiled when he saw Standing. 'Did you lose Mister Billy?'

'He's out watching some fire jugglers,' said Standing. 'Is the chef here? Can I have food?'

'Of course. What would you like?'

'I had fried rice this morning. And I had some chicken with rice and egg for lunch. So maybe something different for dinner?'

'The chef does a very good Pad Thai,' said Daeng.

'What is it?'

'Fried noodles. With chicken, pork or prawn. Or all three.'

'Prawn sounds good. And a beer?'

'Of course, Mister Matt.'

As Daeng hurried off to the kitchen, Standing sat down and looked through the photographs that Pete Green had taken, reassuring himself that there were none of Sammy Lee. Maybe the man wasn't even on Koh Chang. Maybe he had done something to Kim Cooper and left. Or maybe he had taken her with him. It was frustrating not knowing, but there was nothing he could do to speed up the intelligence gathering phase of the operation. All they could do was sit, watch and wait.

CHAPTER 21

Standing went to bed just after midnight. He fell asleep quickly but woke when he heard footsteps on the path outside. As he sat up he heard a motorcycle driving off down the road. He went over to the door, slipped the security chain and opened it. He grinned when he saw Green heading towards his cabin. 'Walk of shame?' he said.

Green laughed. 'No shame,' he said. 'Bit of tongue-on-tongue action, that's as far as it went.'

'Are you serious?'

'She instigated it,' said Green. 'And she made it very clear she'd do more.'

'Seriously?'

'She's lovely, I can see why Pete hung out with her. Smart, too. And funny. Pete and I hardly ever went for the same girl, but she's different.'

'So why isn't she staying the night with you?'

Green shrugged. 'You'll think I'm crazy.'

'That ship has sailed, Billy.'

Green forced a smile. 'It's Pete.'

'Pete?'

'He's in the room, isn't he? I can't very well do anything while he's there, can I? And even if I could, Kayla would freak out.'

Standing couldn't help but smile. 'Maybe she'd be up for a threesome.'

'Oh, you are one sick puppy.'

'Nah, I'm just saying I agree with you. It'd be pretty hard to perform with Pete's ashes there on the table.'

'Sick, right?'

'Uncomfortable, yeah.'

'So you see my problem. Even though she was well up for it. So do you want a nightcap?'

'I was asleep.'

'It's early yet.'

'I guess the jet lag kicked in.' He looked at his watch. It was just after one o'clock and now he felt wide awake. 'Yeah, okay, I'll have a drink with you. Just let me get some shoes on.'

'Cool,' said Green. 'See you over there.'

Green headed up the steps to his cabin while Standing went back inside and put on his trainers. He had been sleeping in an old Oasis T-shirt and baggy shorts, but he doubted that there was a dress code in Green's cabin so he didn't bother changing. He switched off the light, locked the door and headed down the steps.

Green had a beer waiting for him when Standing arrived at his cabin, and he was pouring himself a whisky and soda. Standing clinked his bottle against Green's glass and they both drank.

Standing sat down on the bed. 'Did you eat?'

'Yeah, had chicken wings at Rasta View. That's a hell of a bar, isn't it? If it was any more laid back, it'd be horizontal.'

'That's why people come here, to chill.'

'I dunno about that. Kayla said there are some pretty wild

parties on the beach here. DJs come from all around the world to play.'

'Yeah, it's a far cry from Hereford, that's for sure. A fun night out for the locals there is trawling the pubs looking to take a swing at an SAS trooper. Not sure I could stay here forever, though.'

'Sure, you need action. You're like a bloody shark, you die if you stop moving.'

Standing raised his beer bottle. 'I can chill with the best of them, Billy.'

'But can you, though? Seems to me that you're never really happy outside a war zone. In combat you're totally calm. Like the eye of a tornado. That's why guys like to stick close to you when the bullets are flying.'

'What, now you're saying I'm a lucky charm?'

'It's not that, so much as the fact that you know exactly where to be and you work that out quicker than anyone else. Remember when we were in Iraq last year? That kill mission, the guy from Kilburn who was making a name for himself beheading journalists?'

Standing nodded. Kamran Amin, beloved son of a GP father and a primary-school teacher mother who decided that hacking heads off infidels was preferable to following the medical career that his parents were hoping for. MI6 had drawn up a list of almost two hundred British citizens who had joined Islamic State and tasked the SAS with killing or capturing them. On paper, any of the terrorists who were captured were to be handed over to Iraqi security services, but in practice it was much simpler to double tap them in the desert. In Amin's case, because he was so well guarded, MI6 hadn't even bothered with the capture option. Amin had been traced to an Islamic

State training camp outside the city of Hawija, some three hundred kilometres north of Baghdad. The training camp had become a centre for holding hostages before they were beheaded live on social media, often by Amin, who favoured a yellow-handled bread knife for the task. He always had a black-and-white keffiyeh scarf across his face, but his North London accent was easily identifiable on the videos.

According to MI6's intel, Amin was being taken from the training camp to an IS safe house midway between Hawija and Baghdad, where an American newspaper photographer was being held captive. The plan was for Amin to decapitate the photographer live on a Facebook stream, so he – and his breadknife – were taken by convoy late at night to the safe house.

Standing was put in charge of a four-man team who took up position close to the road that led to the safe house. Their mission was to identify Amin and then call in a drone attack, painting the target with a laser that a Hellfire missile would home in on.

The drone had run into technical problems and had been pulled out at the last minute. Standing had been given the opportunity to cancel the operation, but knowing that the hostage's life was in the balance he had decided to press ahead with an assault on the safe house.

They had rushed the safe house and killed the IS members inside, shooting them all dead and releasing the grateful hostage. Then they had waited for Amin and his bodyguards to arrive. Within half an hour three pick-up trucks, two armed with M2 Browning machine guns, had turned up.

One of the men in the lead pick-up trucks had been on a walkie-talkie, and Standing had realised he was trying to contact someone inside the safe house. Knowing that if they didn't make contact there was every chance they would start shooting at the house, Standing rushed out and opened fire. He was so quick and so accurate that within seconds he had taken out the two IS fighters manning the machine guns and the driver of the front pick-up truck. He was then joined by the rest of his team and it was all over within seconds.

The mission had been a runaway success – Standing had personally double tapped Amin, the hostage had been freed, and the SAS team had killed sixteen IS fighters without a single injury between them. But Green was right – it would have been a very different story if the first few seconds had gone differently, and that had all been down to the way Standing had reacted.

'You saved a lot of lives that night, Matt. And on other nights, too.' He drained his glass and stood up to get a refill. 'Shit,' he said, as he looked out of the window. 'Lights.'

He hurried over to the door and hit the light switch. Standing rolled over the bed and switched off the bedside lamp. 'What is it?' he hissed.

'Two guys coming up the path from the beach, both with guns with suppressors. Two more guys on the beach with M16s.'

Standing looked around the room. There was pretty much nothing to hand that could be used as a weapon. A thrown lamp wouldn't be much good against a handgun, and no use at all against an M16 assault rifle. The only way out of the cabin was through the front door, and that would take them straight into the path of the gunmen. The wooden cabin might be sturdy enough to withstand 9mm rounds from a handgun, but the M16s' more powerful 5.56 NATO rounds would probably go straight through. Sitting tight and trusting in a locked door wasn't going to cut it.

'Bathroom,' said Standing. They kept low as they rushed over to the bathroom. The wall behind the washbasin faced away from the cabin's window and it was simply planks of wood nailed to a frame. The planks were thick but the nails were old and rusting. Standing kicked to the left of the washbasin, Green kicked to the right. Green wasn't wearing shoes but his kicks still had considerable force and after a few blows the planks started to loosen.

'Come on,' grunted Standing. He put all his weight behind his next kick and two planks splintered and pushed outwards.

Green's next kick pushed the planks even further back.

Standing nodded at Green. 'Together,' he said.

They both kicked out at the same time and the combined force sent the two planks tumbling to the ground outside.

'Go!' said Standing.

Green dropped down onto his knees and crawled through the opening. There was a loud bang from the cabin door, a kick rather than a knock. Then there was a loud pop and the window exploded in a shower of glass. Standing slammed the bathroom door and flicked the lock shut. It would only take a second or two to kick it open, but even a single second could be a life-saver.

Green's bare feet disappeared through the gap. The sound of a kick was followed by the tearing of wood as the cabin door crashed open. Standing leapt through the gap, wriggling as his shirt caught on the rough wood. Green got to his feet and he turned and helped to pull Standing through. As they started to run up the slope towards reception they heard the bathroom door being kicked in. Standing had to fight the urge to look over his shoulder, because all that mattered at that point was to put as much distance between themselves and the guns as they could.

He heard the loud pop of a silenced gun being fired but he figured the shooter was wasting his time firing uphill through a gap in the cabin wall.

There was a cabin ahead of them and as soon as they ran by it they swerved to the side to use it as cover. They peered over at the reception shack.

The air was shattered by the sound of an M16 being fired on fully automatic, and rounds ripped through the leaves of the trees above their heads. Leaf fragments fell around them like rain as they scrambled up the slope. The shots were a waste of time and ammunition, so long as the cabin was between them and the shooters.

The slope evened out and they ran towards the shack. Daeng was standing up and looking in their direction, obviously wondering what was going on.

'Daeng, run!' shouted Green.

Daeng frowned in confusion, then he flinched as the M16 fired again and rounds thudded into the roof of the shack above his head. The shooter was obviously firing as he ran and his aim was way off. They were clearly amateurs, but even amateurs could get lucky.

Standing and Green reached Daeng, who still hadn't moved. He stood transfixed with fear, his mouth and eyes wide open. Green threw his arm around Daeng. 'Come on!' he shouted. He pulled him around and pushed him towards the road.

Standing finally took a quick look over his shoulder. There was no sign of the two men with handguns, but he saw two heavies with M16s coming up the slope. He recognised one of them from the terrace – it was the guy wearing the black Adidas tracksuit, the one who had been practising kickboxing moves. The other man was shorter and wearing a sweatshirt and cut-off jeans, dressed more for the beach than a night-time assassination. Both men stopped and raised their guns, so Standing started running again.

They ran through the shack, past the desk and the dining area. Standing cursed as he spotted a black BMW SUV parked by their Fortuner.

There were two men standing by the SUV, and another sitting behind the wheel.

'Get down!' shouted Green, pushing Daeng to the side. The man on the right of the SUV had an M16 up against his shoulder and he fired on fully automatic.

Green threw himself to the ground and Standing followed him. They rolled behind the table as rounds thwacked into the roof above their heads.

Standing looked over at Daeng. 'Stay down!' he shouted, but Daeng was confused and shocked and stayed where he was. The M16 fired again and bullets raked across his chest. He staggered back, his shirt wet with blood, and fell to the floor.

Standing looked around. There was nothing close by that they could use as a weapon. And staying put meant certain death. He looked at Green, and Green nodded and grimaced. They were in deep shit.

The M16 fired again and rounds thudded into the ground near their feet. Then the firing stopped. Standing nodded at Green. 'Now.' Hopefully the magazine had emptied and the shooter would have to slap in a fresh one. A professional could change magazines in less than two seconds but an amateur could take up to five. Hopefully the guy wasn't a pro.

They jumped up and headed towards the parked SUVs. Self defence experts would always say you should charge a gun and run from a knife, but most of those experts had never been in combat. In the real world charging a gun rarely ended well, especially when the gun was a carbine set on fully automatic and in the hands of a professional. But beggars couldn't be choosers and just then Standing and Green had zero choice, all they could do was to cover the distance in as short a time as possible.

The shooter on the right was fumbling with his magazine. Not a professional. The other shooter seemed to have been taken by surprise by their run and his M16 was pointing at the ground.

Standing and Green were about twenty feet from the men now, their feet pounding on the wooden floor. They hurtled out of the shack and into the parking area, running at full pelt, their feet kicking up plumes of red dust.

The guy on the left began to swing his carbine up, but his finger wasn't on the trigger so there was no immediate threat. The guy on the right was still fumbling with the new magazine. It fell from his fingers and he screamed in frustration as it fell to the ground.

The shooter on the left had his gun up at waist height, but Standing could see the look of confusion on the man's face and his finger was still outside the trigger guard. Standing pushed the gun to the side with his left hand and punched him in the throat with his right.

Green went for the guy on the right, punching him in the face, then twisting the M16 from his grasp and slamming the stock into his stomach.

The shooter that Standing had hit was choking and he

released his grip on his weapon. Standing pulled it away from him, stepped back and shot him. The selector had been set to fully automatic and five rounds had smacked into the man's chest before Standing released the pressure on the trigger.

As the man started to fall, Standing turned his gun on the other shooter and fired a short burst into his chest.

Green bent down, picked up the full magazine and inserted it into his M16. Rounds from the shooters who had been at the cabin were whizzing around them now and they both turned and dropped down on one knee and fired.

The shooters ducked back behind the cabin.

'You head for the track and I'll cover you,' said Green.

Standing nodded.

'Go,' said Green. A round smacked into the floor by his foot and he looked over to see one of the gunmen pointing a silenced automatic at him from the side of the cabin. Green swung the M16 up and pulled the trigger for a fraction of a second, long enough to send four rounds thudding into the cabin close to the man's face. 'Go!' he shouted.

Standing turned and ran towards the track as Green continued to lay down covering fire. He reached the track, turned and went down on one knee to take aim at the cabin. Standing flicked the selector lever to single shot. The magazine held thirty rounds but if he fired on automatic he would soon be out of ammunition. 'Go!' he shouted at Green.

Green fired a final burst, then turned and ran towards Standing. Standing fired single shots at the cabin, forcing the shooters there to take cover.

As Standing fired, he saw movement off to his right – two more men were heading up from the beach.

He fired two more shots, one at each side of the cabin. Then he turned his attention to the two men coming from the beach, forcing them to drop to the sand.

Green reached him and knelt down. 'I don't suppose you've got the Fortuner keys?'

Standing shook his head. 'They're in the cabin. Best bet is to get into the jungle on the other side of the road.'

'That works,' said Green.

They both fired at the cabin, and Standing sent two rounds towards the men on the beach, then they ran down the track towards the road.

Two rounds screeched above their heads. Their pursuers had obviously realised they were falling back and were giving chase.

They ran down the track to the road. Another black SUV was heading towards them to their left. A BMW. Almost certainly one of Lee's vehicles. Other than the SUV, the road was empty. The SUV braked hard and the tyres squealed on the tarmac. Standing stopped, turned and fired at the windshield. It shattered, and the SUV ran off the road and crashed into a palm tree.

There were three wooden shacks on the far side of the road, restaurants that had closed for the night. Standing and Green ran towards them.

An M16 burst into life down the track and Green gasped. Three rounds had smacked into his back. He dropped his gun and fell to his knees. Standing fired at the shooter – one of the men who had been taking cover behind the cabin. His first shot missed but the second blew his head apart and he fell to the ground.

Green fell forward and rolled onto his back, bloody foam dribbling from between his lips. Standing knelt down beside him. 'Billy, mate . . .'

Green almost managed a smile, but then the life faded from his eyes and he went still. Standing cursed. There was nothing he could do for him. He turned and ran across the road and between the shacks. He heard shouts behind him and the SUV's doors opened and closed. He pushed his way through the undergrowth and felt thorns scratching at his bare legs. He had barely gone twenty feet into the jungle when he was almost in complete darkness. The tree canopy overhead blocked out most of what little moonlight there was and he figured that Lee's men would be reluctant to pursue him too far. He stopped and listened. There were more shouts off in the distance. Presumably they were deciding what to do. They outnumbered him and had more firepower, but the jungle was a great leveller. He doubted that they had much experience in hunting and killing in the jungle, but it had formed a big part of Standing's SAS training.

After he had passed the endurance phase of SAS Selection he had been shipped out to the British Army Training Support Unit in Belize, and it had truly been six weeks of hell. The theory was that if you could fight in the jungle you could fight anywhere. Basic survival was tough enough in the jungle, but SAS troopers were put through exhausting training programmes while living on rations or what little wildlife they could catch. It was the jungle phase of Selection that really did separate the men from the boys. Standing lost almost six kilograms of bodyweight during his six weeks in the jungle, but the experience he had gained was priceless. He doubted that Lee's soldiers would have a fraction of that experience, so he had no qualms about taking them on.

He heard a rustling ahead of him and he crouched down, his finger on the trigger. The rustling stopped for a few seconds, then started again. He saw a figure emerge from behind a tree. It stopped, then moved again, a dark patch against the grey undergrowth. Standing sighted on the chest and pulled the trigger once. The man fell back without a sound. Standing didn't bother with a double tap, he was almost certain it had been a killing shot and his priority now was to conserve ammunition.

Standing stood stock still, his breathing slow and even, listening intently for any sound other than the insects moving along the forest floor or clicking away up in the tree canopy. He heard more shouts off in the distance. Then the sound of car doors opening and closing and the engine starting. The engine noise stopped abruptly after a few seconds. Standing figured they had driven off the road and stopped on the track leading to the resort. They clearly hadn't bothered to retrieve the body of their colleague. Maybe they were too scared to enter the jungle. Standing smiled to himself. Good. He wanted them scared.

He needed a plan of action, but as things stood he didn't have many options. He had no food or water, but that wouldn't be an issue for a day or so. He had enough ammunition to take out a dozen or so bad guys and he wasn't in immediate danger, but as soon as he left the jungle he would be a target. His phone was in his cabin, along with his passport, though his wallet was in the pocket of his shorts. He was going to need both to get out of the country. At some point he was going to have to go back to his cabin to retrieve his belongings, but he was sure that Lee's men would be waiting for him. They'd be checking the road, too. And probably watching his car, though the keys to the Fortuner were in the cabin.

His best course of action was to wait until dawn, and then at least he'd be able to see what sort of opposition he was up against. He looked back at the hill behind him. He needed to get up high so that if they did work up the courage to come into the jungle, he'd be ready and waiting for them.

CHAPTER 22

Standing rubbed his eyes, then stretched. He looked up at the tree canopy above his head. The first streaks of light were appearing in the sky. The M16 was in his lap. He had struggled to stay awake throughout the night but a combination of stretching and mental gymnastics had stopped him from falling asleep. The men with the guns hadn't entered the jungle so far as he could tell, and he was too far from the road to hear any vehicles. He held the carbine in his right hand as he stood up. He had to get to his cabin to retrieve his phone and passport, but he wasn't sure which was the best route. There was a good chance they would be watching his car, so heading down the track to the resort wouldn't be a smart move. Coming in from the beach would be the better option. It would mean cutting around the resort, but there weren't any other buildings close by so he could probably do it without being spotted.

The gun was an issue. The M16 wasn't concealable, not by any means. But going in without the weapon wasn't an option, not while there was a risk of Lee's men being at the resort. Hopefully it would be too early for a passer-by to spot him.

He started down the hill, cradling the gun across his chest. He moved slowly, trying to keep any noise down to a minimum, his eyes scanning the foliage ahead of him. Once the ground levelled out he changed direction, heading to the left, parallel to the road. He went about a hundred metres and then worked his way through the undergrowth to the road. He listened for a while but heard nothing, so he emerged slowly from the bushes, looking left and right.

The track that led to the resort was to his right. The road was empty in both directions and there was no sign of any black SUVs parked up. He held the gun down at his side and jogged across the road, making his way through a cluster of small coconut palms to the beach. There was enough light to make out the crests of the waves but the sun was still below the mountain behind him.

The nearest of the Best Friends cabins was about fifty metres away. Standing stopped by a coconut palm, the M16 at his side, and he looked up and down the beach. He was alone. He padded along the shore, bringing his gun up to his chest. He stopped again and listened, but all he could hear was the sea lapping on the beach.

He reached the path that led from the beach up to the resort and he sought cover behind another palm, slowly checking out the terrain. When he was convinced there was no threat, he stepped off the path and cut across the grass towards his cabin. The lights were off and the cabin was in darkness. The lights were also off in Green's cabin and he didn't see any movement there.

He reached the bottom of the steps leading up to his cabin and he crouched low, his finger on the trigger of his M16. He listened again, then slowly made his way up the steps. He used his key to unlock the door, then he pushed it open slowly. The cabin was empty and just as he had left it. He slipped inside, closed the door and then peered out through the window.

There didn't seem to be anyone around. Standing was starting to wonder if Lee's men had packed up and gone.

His phone was on the bedside table and he cursed himself for not charging it. His battery was down to about twenty-five per cent. His passport was in his hand luggage and he slipped it into the pocket of his shorts, then had second thoughts and quickly changed into a pair of black jeans and a clean black denim shirt. He would have preferred camouflage gear, but when he'd packed his case he didn't know that he was going to be running for his life in the jungle.

He looked out of the window again and the beach was still clear. If Lee's men had actually gone, he could take his bag to the Fortuner and drive away. That was a better option than going back into the jungle.

He slipped out of the door and stood for a full minute listening and looking. There was still no sign of anyone on the beach and the only sound was the waves breaking on the shore.

He walked down the steps and along the path, his finger curled around the trigger of the M16. He stared at the cabin that Green had been using but couldn't see anybody, so he began moving up the path towards the shack. The sky was getting lighter and he could see inside. It was deserted. He stepped onto the wooden floor and looked over to where he had last seen Daeng. The body had been moved. From the look of the blood smeared across the floorboards, he had been dragged behind the desk.

Standing heard a muffled voice from the parking area and he stiffened. He heard a cough and someone clearing their throat and spitting. He went down in a crouch and moved forward, his gun at the ready, but stopped when he saw a man standing next to the Fortuner. There wasn't enough light to see the man's features but Standing could make out the gun he was carrying. An Uzi or possibly a MAC-10. The MAC-10 was chambered for the powerful .45 ACP cartridge while the Uzi fired the smaller 9mm rounds, but at close range the difference was minimal especially when fired on fully automatic.

Standing slowly backed away. He was almost at the path when he heard a scraping sound behind him. He whirled around to see a man about twenty metres away, taking aim with a handgun and silencer. It was one of the men he'd seen firing from behind Green's cabin the previous night. The man fired but he did it one-handed and the shot went wide. As the round whizzed by Standing's shoulder he was already pulling the trigger of his M16 and he hit the man in the chest. As the man began to fall, Standing turned and ran back towards the beach. He didn't want to risk a firefight with an Uzi or a MAC-10, not when he was in a shack with no obvious cover. He ran onto the path and then headed left, back the way he'd come.

A second heavy appeared from the beach, this one carrying an M16. He fired a short burst at Standing and rounds thudded into a palm tree behind him. Standing fired on the run but the shot went wide. He fired again but that went wide too, though it made the shooter dive for cover.

Standing turned left around the final cabin and sprinted up towards the road. As he reached it, he saw a black SUV driving towards him. He fired at the nearside front tyre, blowing it apart and sending the SUV into a spin. Standing fired on the run and the windscreen shattered.

The SUV was still spinning as Standing ran across the road

and into the undergrowth, keeping his head down and concentrating on the ground in front of him.

He heard shouts from behind him and then the *brrrrrrrrrrrt* of an Uzi being fired on fully automatic. Standing threw himself to the ground as the vegetation around him was ripped and shredded. The Uzi emptied itself in three seconds. The big question was whether the shooter was going to reload or not, so Standing lay where he was. The question was answered almost immediately when a second burst of fire tore into the undergrowth to his left.

It came to an end as quickly as the first and, as soon as it did, Standing jumped to his feet and began running, zig-zagging through the trees. Once he had covered about thirty metres, he hid behind a large palm and pointed his M16 towards the road.

The Uzi fired a third burst and Standing ducked back behind the tree. Once the third magazine had emptied, Standing brought his M16 up again and peered around the palm tree. He saw movement off to his left, the blur of something passing behind a bush. He tracked the movement. The figure went behind a tree, paused and came into view again. It was a man in a white T-shirt, holding an Uzi. Standing smiled to himself. White wasn't the best colour to wear if you were going on a manhunt in the jungle. He aimed at the patch, and as the man moved around a bush he pulled the trigger. A red flower blossomed on the white shirt and the man pitched forward.

A round smacked into the palm, just above his head. Standing knew instinctively where the shot had come from and he swung the barrel of his M16 to the right, dropping into a crouch because there was every chance the shooter would be pulling the trigger a second time. He knew he had made the right call when a round hit the tree again, this time at the exact spot where his head had been.

The shooter had an M16 and was handling it like a pro. Standing aimed at the man's chest and pulled the trigger, but the man ducked back behind a tree and the round missed. Standing kept his gun pointed at the spot where he had last seen the man. He was breathing steadily and evenly. The man's head appeared from behind the tree and Standing squeezed the trigger. The man jerked his head back and the round whizzed by harmlessly. 'Lucky,' whispered Standing. He kept his finger on the trigger and waited. The seconds ticked by. Standing stayed focused, knowing it was only a matter of time before the man peeped around the tree again, but his concentration was broken by movement to his left, at the periphery of his vision. He turned to see another heavy heading towards him, an M16 at his shoulder.

Standing turned his weapon towards the new target, but the man had already started to fire and Standing was forced to duck as rounds whizzed over his head.

He knelt and aimed and fired twice at the man, who was now just forty metres from him. The first round went to the left but the second caught him in the chest. The man didn't go down and Standing realised he must be wearing a vest. Standing raised his aim and fired again, this time blasting the man in the face.

As the man fell back Standing turned to aim at the figure behind the tree. The man was already there, his weapon pointing at Standing. Standing threw himself to the side and rolled on the ground as rounds rat-tat-tatted around him. He came up onto his knees and fired, but his aim was off and the round missed its target by more than a metre. Standing felt the M16's bolt lock back. He was out of ammo.

He jumped up, bent at the waist and began running up the hill, zig-zagging as he went. He heard several rounds thudding into the ground by his feet, but then he swerved around a large tree and the firing stopped. He kept moving in a straight line as best he could for ten metres or so, then began zig-zagging again. His legs began to burn but he kept running at full speed, knowing that each metre he put between himself and his pursuers increased his safety margin.

They didn't fire again, which he assumed was because they had lost sight of him. Visibility was down to less than fifty metres in the jungle, so providing he kept moving they shouldn't be able to get him in their sights. He continued to sprint up the hill for another minute or so, then cut across the hill at an angle to the right. That was slightly less effort but it was still exhausting and he was already panting and sweating. He still had the M16 clasped to his chest, even though its magazine was empty. A soldier never gave up his weapon.

He ran for another minute, then stopped and listened. He could hear movement, and then shouts, but they were down below and some distance away. He started running along the contour of the hill, heading south, determined to put as much distance between himself and his pursuers as he could.

CHAPTER 23

Standing's face was bathed in sweat and he wiped his fore-head with the back of his arm. He had kept up a blistering pace as he headed south and he now had a raging thirst. He turned and stared back the way he had come. So far as he could judge he was about halfway up the mountain, but the thick jungle meant that he couldn't see more than fifty metres or so. He had been moving for the best part of twenty minutes and reckoned that he had covered more than a kilometre as the crow flew. He moved his head from side to side and listened intently but couldn't hear any pursuers.

He took out his mobile phone and gritted his teeth when he saw that he had no signal. He was going to have to get closer to the road. That meant putting himself in harm's way but he didn't have any choice. He was going to need help to get out of the mess he'd gotten himself into.

Something rustled off to his left and he narrowed his eyes as he scrutinised the vegetation, then he smiled as he saw a small brown monkey emerge from a bush. The monkey sat down and looked up at Standing. A second, larger monkey, maybe the mother, appeared, with a tiny monkey clinging to her back. The mother put a protective hand on the smaller monkey's shoulder and chattered at Standing. Standing grinned. 'I get it, you're out for a walk,' he said. 'I won't bother you, I'm just passing through.'

The monkey chattered again, then tugged at the smaller monkey and pulled it back into the bush. There was more rustling as they moved away, and eventually silence again.

Standing headed down the mountain, moving slowly and carefully and trying to keep any noise to a minimum. He stopped every ten or twenty metres to listen for a few seconds, knowing that with an empty gun his options were limited if he did make contact with his pursuers.

Eventually the slope began to level out and he knew that the road was close by. He stood behind a large tree and took out his phone again. He had one bar of signal, but his battery was low, down to below twenty per cent. He'd given a lot of thought about who he should call, but at the end of the day there was only one person who would be able to get his nuts out of the fire. Standing made the call and said a silent prayer that he didn't go through to voicemail. His prayer worked and Shepherd answered within seconds. 'Spider, it's me,' said Standing. 'I'm in deep shit.'

'What's happened?' asked Shepherd.

'Billy's dead. I'm in the jungle and they're after me.'

'Who? Who's after you?'

'Lee's heavies. I recognised two of them.'

'What do you need, Matt?'

'Shit, Spider, I don't know. A helicopter would be nice.'

'Where are you exactly?'

'I'm in the middle of Koh Chang. It's all jungle here. I'm a mile or so from a place called Lonely Beach where we were staying. The heavies turned up, killed Billy and chased me.' He heard a noise off to his right and he turned towards it. 'Hang on,' he said, then took the phone away from his ear as he listened intently. There was a rustling sound but it sounded too small to be human. He put the phone to his ear. 'Okay, I'm back. We're going to have to keep this short, I don't have much battery left and there are no chargers in the jungle.'

'Can you call the cops?'

'I think the cops might be in on it. The bad guys were shooting up our resort last night and killed Billy and the night man. The cops didn't turn up and the killers hadn't put much of an effort into covering their tracks.'

'You went back?'

'I needed my phone. The point is, if the cops haven't turned up after all that's happened, there has to be a reason. The bad guys are still at the resort so I can't get my car, and even if I could I'd be a sitting duck. They're just going to wait me out.'

'Okay. Got it. How are you fixed weapon-wise?'

'An empty M16, that's it. Figured I could use it as a club if necessary, but that's all I've got.'

'No wounds?'

'I'm good.'

'Okay, look, I know a guy who lives not far from Koh Chang. Guy by the name of Lex Harper. Former Para. He's a freelance contractor these days but if he's in country he'll be able to help. I'll reach out to him. Let's stick to text messages. What's the cell phone coverage like where you are?'

'It's fine so long as I'm near the road. It gets patchy when I move away.'

'Well, keep it on but don't call, and configure it to use as little power as possible. I'll get Lex to contact you when he's there. If he's not available I'll text you with a Plan B.'

'What's Plan B?' asked Standing.

'I don't actually have one yet,' said Shepherd. 'So keep your fingers crossed.'

CHAPTER 24

Lex Harper headed down Beach Road at a steady pace, the grey Pattaya sea off to his right. The sun had been out for less than an hour so it was still cool, and there were few tourists around. The beach vendors were setting up their umbrellas and the speedboat operators were getting ready for the exodus of tourists heading for the beaches of the outlying islands. He had started his run at the Dusit Thani Hotel and headed west, the orange PATTAYA sign on the hill ahead of him. It was almost three kilometres to Walking Street, the start of the main nightlife area, and he usually ran there, did some stretching, press-ups and sit-ups on the beach, and then ran back to the hotel. The run out was at a steady jog, but he always tried to do the return leg at full speed.

He passed two elderly expats sitting on the wall overlooking the beach, their skin the colour and texture of old leather. One had an aluminium wheeled walker in front of him, the other was gripping a walking stick with both hands as if he feared it was trying to get away from him. They turned to watch Harper run by.

A middle-aged Thai lady in denim hotpants, glossy black high heels and a low-cut top smiled and gave him a wave from the shade of a spreading palm.

'Good morning, Noy,' he said.

Noy had been a regular on Beach Road for longer than Harper could remember, looking for short-time customers or perhaps even a foreign husband who would be prepared to support her and her three children, presently in the care of her aged mother up in Udon Thani. In her heyday Noy had been a top go-go dancer in several of Walking Street's busier bars, but that was years ago and now she eked out a living as a freelancer on Beach Road. It was getting to the end of the month, which meant her rent was due, so she had obviously made an early start. Either that or she had been there all night without finding a customer.

'You look good, Lek,' she called, and blew him a kiss. Thais seemed to have trouble saying Lex and most ended up calling him Lek, which was a common Thai nickname. It meant small, which Lex definitely wasn't, but he was happy enough to answer to it.

'You too!'

Harper reached the Hilton Hotel, part of a huge shopping centre that marked the halfway point of Beach Road. Pattaya had once been a sleepy fishing village but those days had long gone, now it was a buzzing holiday town that welcomed more than four million tourists a year, attracted by its nightlife, cheap food and booze, year-round sunshine, and an estimated thirty thousand hookers. As attractive as those traits were, Harper's main reason for living in Pattaya was that the Thai authorities had zero interest in him and he could come and go as he pleased. The police were happy to leave him alone providing he greased their palms and didn't overtly break the country's laws, and the Thai taxman never bothered to ask him how he was funding his fairly lavish lifestyle. Harper was happy to stay in the Land of Smiles for as long as he could, but he still had a bugout bag in the false ceiling of his apartment with several passports, wads of dollars, pounds and euros, and enough gold chains to buy him passage across any border with Thailand if he had to get out in a hurry.

His phone buzzed in his bumbag and he slowed to a jog as he fished it out. It was Dan 'Spider' Shepherd and he rarely called just to chat, so Harper jogged over to the shade of a palm tree and took the call.

'Can you talk?' asked Shepherd.

'I'm a bit out of breath,' said Harper. 'But, yeah, go for it.'

Shepherd chuckled. 'Please don't tell me you were having sex.'

'I'm out for my morning run. But sex is on the cards later this afternoon, thanks for asking.'

'Other than that, do you have much on?'

'Nothing I can tell you about,' said Harper. 'What's up?'

'A couple of SAS lads have been killed in your neck of the woods. Billy and Pete Green. Pete died a few days ago, Billy was killed yesterday. Place called Koh Chang. You know it?'

'Sure, it's an island a few hours' drive from Pattaya. What the hell happened?'

'Pete was on a surveillance operation. For a friend, not official business. He was killed and whoever did it tried to make it look like suicide. Billy went out there to find out what happened and he was gunned down last night. We think a Chinese gangster by the name of Sammy Lee is responsible.'

'Lee Yat-fung? Yeah, he's an evil bastard. Was that who Pete was looking at?'

'Seems that way, yeah.'

'Then he was playing with fire. You don't fuck around with Sammy Lee.'

'You know him?'

'I know of him. Haven't crossed his path and wouldn't want to. I'm sorry to hear about Pete and Billy. But how can I help?'

'Billy was out there with a friend of mine. Serving SAS sergeant by the name of Matt Standing. He's stuck on the island and needs help. He's in the jungle and Lee's enforcers are after him. I need you to do an extraction.'

Harper ran his hand through his hair. 'Bloody hell, Spider, you're not asking for much.'

'Can you get there and get him out?'

'Is he armed?'

'He is, but he's out of ammo.'

'So not armed, then. Hell's bells, Spider. I can get there but it's going to take me four or five hours. The only way onto the island is by ferry, and that shuts at dusk.'

'You can get there, though? Today?'

'Sure. Yes. And I can pick him up, that shouldn't be a problem, providing he isn't injured. Not sure if I'll be able to extract him before the last ferry, though. Are you coming out?'

'I can't, Lex, I'm up to my eyes in something here that I can't get out of. But I'll cover any expenses.'

'Nah, mate, you've done me enough favours over the years. This is on me.' He sighed.

'Are you okay?' asked Shepherd.

'I'm just thinking that I'm going to need guns,' said Harper. 'A lot of guns.'

CHAPTER 25

Standing stopped and squinted at the track ahead of him. It was definitely a track, more than a metre wide, the reddish soil flattened by thousands of feet over the years. It went to the right, down to the road, and to the left it wound its way around the side of the mountain, in a roughly south-easterly direction. Standing listened but heard nothing. He stepped onto the track and looked up. There was a small wooden sign nailed to a tree, an arrow pointing up the track and four wavy lines. He frowned at the sign, and then reali-sation dawned. The island was dotted with waterfalls and the trail must lead to one of the more popular ones. He looked at his watch. It wasn't eight o'clock yet, hopefully too early for there to be any tourists about.

He started walking up the track, his M16 on his shoulder. The track curved to the right and after a hundred metres or so there was another wooden sign. He stopped and listened and this time he heard babbling water. He increased his pace and after a couple of minutes the track opened into a clearing. Facing him was a large pool of water dotted with massive rocks, and behind it a wall of rock down which water was trickling with about the same force as an overflowing bath. Waterfall seemed too generous a term, but while Standing would have regarded it as a waste of a trip if he was sightseeing, the fact that he was thirsty and had spent the night in the jungle meant that the pool of water was exactly what he needed.

He stripped off his trainers and clothes and put them on a rock with his M16, then slid into the ice-cold water. He waded over to the waterfall and drank his fill before standing under the flow and letting the water run over him.

He only allowed himself a couple of minutes to drink and wash because even the trickle of water was loud enough to cover the sound of anyone approaching. He climbed out of the pool, shook himself as dry as he could, then pulled on his clothes and trainers, picked up his M16 and left the track, heading through the jungle towards the road.

CHAPTER 26

Harper braked sharply to avoiding hitting the family piled onto the 125cc Yamaha motorbike. Dad was driving, Mum was riding pillion with their two-year-old son sitting between them. A young girl was sitting on the father's lap, holding onto the handlebars. The father had switched lanes without indicating, checking his mirror or looking over his shoulder. He had just changed lines blindly, trusting that Buddha would take care of him. Harper didn't bother banging on his horn. There was no point. A blaring horn wasn't going to correct twenty-odd years of bad driving. And maybe Buddha would indeed take care of the man and his family.

Harper was driving down Second Road, parallel to Beach Road and the sea. It was a hot day and he'd changed into a blue linen shirt and baggy shorts and was wearing his Ray-Ban Wayfarers. He had plenty of time before the last ferry left the mainland for Koh Chang, but Matt Standing was in big trouble, so the sooner he got there, the better.

Harper was behind the wheel of a battered four-door Isuzu pick-up truck. It wasn't the most elegant of vehicles but it was sturdy, reliable and didn't stick out. The windows were darkened so that most people wouldn't realise it was being driven by a farang – a foreigner – and meant he was less likely to be pulled over by the cops looking for a shake-down.

He made a left turn, smiling to himself as he checked his mirrors and indicated. Unlike most Thai motorists, he was a firm believer in defensive driving.

He'd had the storage locker for almost five years, under the name of a Thai company. His was in the middle of a line of twelve lockers, each big enough to hold a car, with roll-up metal doors. He'd looked at a dozen self-storage facilities before he'd chosen Wonderful Storage. It was professionally managed with full-time onsite security, but the main attraction was that while there were lots of CCTV cameras covering the site, there were none pointed at the unit he used.

He swiped his keycard and tapped in a six-digit pin number to access the site, and waved at a uniformed guard who was sitting on a stool under a massive umbrella. The four-storey main building to the right contained the smaller units, but Harper drove to the left where there were four narrow roads each with a dozen single-storey units either side. There was no one else in the road as he pulled up outside his unit.

He climbed out of the pick-up truck, took out his key and used it to unlock both sides of the door, then pulled it up halfway. He'd parked so that no one could see into the unit, but he still looked both ways before slipping under the door.

There was a light switch to his left and he flicked it on. The single overhead LED tube cast a clinical cold light over the contents of the locker, a dozen or so large plastic tubs on metal shelving on one side, and an equal number of black nylon kitbags on the other.

Harper had put together his wish list on the drive over to the storage facility and he moved quickly and efficiently. He pulled out an empty kitbag and unzipped it, then took down one of the plastic tubs. He peeled off the lid. Inside were six handguns, each individually wrapped in an oiled cloth. He took two Glock 17s and put them in the holdall. He closed the lid and put the tub back on its shelf. Another tub contained a range of silencers and he added two to the holdall. From another tub he took a first-aid kit, then decided better safe than sorry so took two. He had a number of assault weapons in the locker including several AK-47s, but he figured that Standing would be more familiar with the Heckler & Koch 417, so he put one of those in the kitbag. He had thought long and hard about what he'd choose for himself, and had decided on a weapon that he'd only recently purchased from an Israeli gun dealer who had been passing through Bangkok. He'd shown Harper the latest twin-barrel machine gun that fired a thousand shots per minute, two rounds at a time. It was effectively a double-barrelled AR-15 which dealt a double tap with one pull of its double triggers. It was called the Gilboa Snake, was manufactured by the Israeli company Silver Shadow and was already being used by special forces units around the world. One of the selling points was that if one side jammed the other would continue to fire. It had two sixteen-inch barrels, took two M16-style magazines, and the only downside was that it burned through its ammunition too quickly if you were trigger-happy. He took the gun, encased in bubble wrap, and put it into the holdall.

The ammunition was stored separately, so he pulled out filled magazines for all the weapons and put them in the kitbag. He added two large hunting knives in scabbards, and two Tasers.

He packed two sets of night vision headsets and two Kevlar vests, then took half a dozen flashbangs from one of the tubs and added them to the holdall. He zipped it up and carried it outside to the pick-up truck and put it in the back of the cab. The road was still deserted.

He locked the door, pocketed the key and climbed into the Isuzu. He sat for a few seconds running through his mental checklist then, when he was satisfied he had everything he needed, he headed for the exit.

CHAPTER 27

Standing's phone buzzed to let him know that he had received a message. He checked the screen. His phone didn't recognise the number. THIS IS LEX. OK TO CALL? He was sitting with his back to a large tree, shielded by bushes to his left and right. The road was about fifty metres ahead of him, close enough for him to hear the occasional vehicle drive by. He had a strong mobile signal though his battery level was down to just fifteen per cent.

Standing replied. YES. The phone vibrated within thirty seconds and Standing accepted the call. 'This is Matt.'

'Hi, Matt. This is Lex. Spider said you needed an extraction.'

'As soon as,' said Standing. 'Where are you?'

'I'm parked up about half an hour from the ferry terminal at Trat. Assuming there's no delay, I should be on Koh Chang in just over an hour. Even if the ferry's busy, it'll be two hours, max. Where are you, exactly?'

'I'm in the jungle, about a hundred metres from Lonely Beach. I was staying at a resort there. If I go any further into the jungle I lose my signal. I went to the resort to get my phone and they were waiting for me. I'm assuming they have the road staked out.'

'Give me a second to check my map.' Harper went quiet for a minute or so. 'Okay. I see Lonely Beach. There's just the one road there running north-south, so it'll be easy for them to keep an eye out for you. How are you energy-wise?'

'I'm okay.'

'Up for a hike?'

'What do you have in mind?'

'I think you're right, they're going to have people on the road, so there's a chance they'll see me picking you up. But if you can head east, over the mountain, I can pick you up on the east side of the island.'

'How far?'

'Four, maybe five kilometres. The peak is about seven hundred and fifty metres. No worse than the Fan Dance. It's jungle, so it'll slow you down and you'll have to watch out for snakes and stuff, but I reckon you could do it in three hours. It's not all jungle, there are farms and rubber plantations. If you head due east you come to a temple. A big one.'

'Wat Salak Phet?'

'That's right.'

'I've been there. Okay, that works for me. But I'll be out of contact while I'm in the jungle. And I only have about fifteen percent of my battery left.'

'Okay, so leave your phone off. Switch it on again once you've crossed the island. Fall-back position, I'll wait for you outside the temple.'

'Thanks.

'Thank me when it's done,' said Harper. He ended the call.

Standing switched off his phone and put it into the pocket of his jeans. He picked up his gun and looked up the mountain. Harper was right, a seven-hundred-and-fifty-metre climb was nothing. Pen y Fan was close to nine hundred metres, though the Welsh peak wasn't covered in jungle. On the other hand he didn't have a 40kg Bergen on his back, so swings and roundabouts, really. He grunted and began heading up the hill.

CHAPTER 28

Harper had been one of the first to drive onto the ferry in Trat and so was one of the first off. He drove away from the ferry terminal, turned left and headed east. He hoped that Standing had made good time over the peak, but he didn't want to drain the man's phone by texting or calling.

There had been no checks on the ferry and no police presence, but as he left the terminal he had seen two black SUVs parked near the entrance. It could have been a coincidence or it could have been Sammy Lee's soldiers keeping an eye out for Standing. All the windows had been tinted, so Harper wasn't able to get a look at the occupants.

The road curved to the right and he was soon driving south, the sea off to his left. He had never been to Koh Chang before but it appeared no different to any other province out in the sticks, shabby buildings, overhead power cables, people working in fields with large hats to protect themselves from the burning sun. It wasn't much fun living in rural Thailand, though the people always seemed happy enough. They called it the Land of Smiles and people genuinely did smile a lot, though out in the countryside often it revealed a worrying lack of dental care.

Most tourists who visited Thailand didn't see the rural poor – they visited Bangkok or Pattaya, or the island of Phuket, with Michelin-star restaurants and five-star hotels. But you didn't have to drive far from the gleaming skyscrapers and mass-transit systems of Bangkok to find people who were literally dirt poor, who slept on the floor and cooked with charcoal and who ate what they could find in the fields and forests around them.

Thailand was consistently rated as the worst country in the world in terms of wealth inequality. The rich were obscenely wealthy and the poor were poor almost beyond belief, getting by on just a few dollars a day, often earned by carrying out backbreaking farm work under the unrelenting sun. Economic power was concentrated in the hands of a few billionaire families who lorded it over a corrupt political and financial system that was designed to keep their families rich at the expense of the poor. Every year the gulf between the rich and the poor widened and there were no plans to change the status quo that Harper could see.

That was why men like Sammy Lee AKA Lee Yat-fung were able to thrive in Thailand. His money brought him protection and even respect. The Thais didn't care where a person's money came from, a drug lord's money was the same as a business-man's or a doctor's. In Thailand money talked and the more money you had, the louder your voice. If Sammy Lee had decided that Matt Standing should die, the police and the courts wouldn't stand in his way. But Harper would. Harper might not have anywhere near as much money as Sammy Lee, but he had guns and he wasn't afraid to use them.

CHAPTER 29

Standing peered through the undergrowth. Ahead of him was farmland and a couple of wooden shacks, and beyond it he could see the top of the tower of the temple's crematorium. He had been watching for more than half an hour, but other than the monks going about their duties he hadn't seen anyone. He had switched on his phone and grimaced when he saw that he was down to his last ten per cent of battery power.

His phone buzzed and he looked at the screen. It was Harper. A message. OK?

Standing pressed the call button and Harper answered almost immediately. 'Yeah, I'm okay,' Standing said. 'I'm about two hundred metres away from the temple.'

'I'm here now,' said Harper. 'I don't see anyone around.'

'Me neither,' said Standing. 'How do we do this?'

'I'm as far west as I can go with the vehicle, you'll have to get to me on foot.'

'I'm carrying an M16,' said Standing.

'You need to dump it where it can't be found,' said Harper. 'What sort of state are you in?'

'I'm good, but I look like I've spent the night in the jungle.'

'Okay, get rid of the gun and send me a text when you walk out into the open. I'll walk out to meet you. If you see me scratch my head, drop to the ground, it means I've seen something. If you see anyone other than a monk, or any vehicle, hit the ground.'

'Got it,' said Standing. He ended the call and went over to a large spreading bush. He knelt down and hacked away at the reddish ground with the butt of the carbine but it didn't make much of an impression, so he ejected the magazine and used the open end to dig a hole large enough to take the weapon. He dropped it in and used his hands to cover it with soil, then patted it down and pulled vegetation over it. He wiped his hands on his jeans and took out his phone. He sent a message to Harper – ON WAY – and started walking towards the temple. His head swivelled from side to side, alert for any possible threat, all too well aware that he was unarmed. He kept away from the two wooden shacks and followed a track between two fields that had been planted with a green vegetable that he didn't recognise.

As he got closer to the crematorium he saw the wooden building where the monks lived, and then finally the temple itself came into view. As he walked around the monks' quarters he saw Harper for the first time. He had a runner's build, but with wide shoulders as if he lifted weights. He was wearing a blue linen shirt and baggy shorts and had a dark blue baseball cap pulled low over impenetrable sunglasses. He raised a hand in greeting and Standing waved back.

Harper stopped walking and looked around at the road and the temple. He tensed when he saw a white Honda saloon coming towards them but quickly realised that there was an old woman at the wheel and he flashed Standing a thumbs up.

Standing held out his hand as he reached Harper, and the two men shook. 'Thanks for this,' said Standing.

'No problem,' said Harper. They headed towards the pick-up truck, eyes watchful. The old lady had parked behind Harper's truck. She climbed out and took a basket of flowers into the temple.

'Best you stay on the floor in the back of the cab,' said Harper. 'The windows are tinted but you should keep your head down just in case we get stopped. What vehicles were they using?'

'I just saw black SUVs. BMWs maybe.'

Harper nodded. 'There were two black BMW SUVs at the ferry terminal,' he said. 'That's obviously their vehicle of choice. Gangsters can be so stupid sometimes.'

'I don't want to go to the ferry, Lex,' said Standing. 'There's something I need to do.'

'I don't think it's an option,' said Harper. 'If they've got the terminal covered they might be sending people over on the ferries and we'd be sitting ducks. While I was waiting, I booked a cabin in a resort close by. I can park right next to it and we should be able to sneak you inside. We can discuss our options there.'

'You're a star, thanks.'

Harper opened the rear passenger door. There was a large black holdall across the rear two seats but there was enough space on the floor for Standing to curl up. Harper tossed a blanket on him and shut the door. He got into the driver's seat. 'You hungry now or can you wait? I've got biscuits and fruit if you want some.'

'I'm okay. I can wait. And I found water, so I'm good.'

'Okay, just stay down until we reach the resort.'

CHAPTER 30

Harper parked the truck next to the cabin and switched off the engine. 'Stay where you are until I'm sure that the coast is clear,' he said. He climbed out and looked around and then opened the rear passenger door. 'I'll take the bag in. You stay put.'

'Got you,' said Standing. Harper pulled the large black nylon holdall off the back seat and closed the door. Standing heard his shoes crunch on the path and then pad upstairs. A door opened and closed, and then there was just silence broken only by the sound of Standing's breathing. After a couple of minutes the door opened and closed again and he heard Harper walk back towards the truck. The rear passenger door opened. 'Okay, I don't see anyone around. Straight out, up the steps and through the door.'

'Got you,' said Standing. He lifted himself up onto his knees and stepped out, grunting as he straightened up. He kept his head down as he walked quickly to the steps and hurried up. The door was open. Harper followed him and closed the door.

The room was similar to the one Standing had stayed in at the Best Friends Resort, just a little bigger and with two single beds instead of a king size. Harper had closed the blinds and the lights were on. Standing sat down on one of the beds. 'Home, sweet home,' he said.

'I chose it for the privacy rather than the amenities,' said Harper.

'Hey, I wasn't complaining, I spent last night in the jungle, remember?'

Harper tossed him a carrier bag containing new clothes. 'Maybe grab a shower, you smell a bit ripe,' he said. 'I took a guess at your size, you SAS guys are all pretty much the same.'

Standing thanked him. Harper had taken off his baseball cap and sunglasses. He had unruly sandy hair, blue-grey eyes and a nose that looked as if it had taken a punch or two. 'You were never in the Regiment?' asked Standing.

'I was attached for a while, that's how I first met Spider. I was a Para but I realised early on that I didn't want to be a soldier forever.' He grinned. 'I never liked following orders.'

'No one does,' said Standing. 'At least in the Sass they tend to let us do our own thing. How much did Spider tell you?'

'The basics,' said Harper. 'But jump in the shower before you bring me up to speed. I wasn't joking about the smell.'

'Sorry,' said Standing. He had bathed in the waterfall, but that was before he had hiked over the mountain. It had been tough going and he had worked up a sweat as the sun had risen higher in the sky. He grabbed the bag of clothes and popped into the bathroom. It was double the size of the one at Best Friends and had a proper tub with a shower at one end. There were toiletries on a shelf above the washbasin and he shaved and brushed his teeth while he filled the tub.

After he'd bathed and changed into the clothes that Harper had given him, he went back into the bedroom. Harper was sitting on one of the beds, drinking a can of beer. He grinned when he saw that the T-shirt and cargo shorts fitted perfectly. 'Told you, all you guys are the same build.' He waved his can at the fridge. 'Help yourself to a beer. And there's a bag of food there.' He pointed to a 7-Eleven carrier bag on the bed. 'Sandwiches and some fruit, there wasn't much choice, I'm afraid.'

'Cheers,' said Standing. He bent down, opened the fridge and took out a can of Singha beer. He popped the tab, sat on the bed and drank.

'So Spider says that Sammy Lee killed Pete Green, and when you and his brother came to find out what had happened, his men killed the brother and chased you into the jungle.'

Standing nodded. 'That's pretty much it.' He reached into the carrier bag and took out a plastic-wrapped cheese sandwich.

'Did you know how dangerous this Sammy Lee is?'

'Not until Spider told me. We just knew he was a rich Chinese guy who'd met the daughter of a friend of Pete Green's. She vanished when she was on Koh Chang, so Pete came out to see if he could find her.'

'I guess if he'd known who Lee was, he might have taken more precautions.'

'You know him?'

'Like I told Spider, I know of him. There's a lot of guys like him in Thailand but he's one of the worst. I really wouldn't want to be on his radar.'

'Yeah, well hindsight is a wonderful thing.' Standing wolfed down the cheese sandwich, then took a banana from the bag and began eating that. He hadn't realised how hungry he was.

'You said that they killed Pete but made it look like suicide?'

Standing nodded. 'The guy at the embassy said that a lot of Westerners kill themselves out here,' said Standing. 'Is that true?'

'It's true enough,' said Harper. 'A lot of guys come out here, fall in love with the place, and before you know it they've burned through all their money. Some of them just go back with their tail between their legs, but others can't face that and they top themselves. It happens pretty much every week in Pattaya.'

'The Pattaya Flying Club?'

Harper grinned. 'You heard about that? Yeah, we do get a lot of people falling off balconies. But there are quite a few reasons for that. I'm sure some of them are suicides, guys with a broken heart or a broken bank balance who decide to take a flyer. Thailand can be a paradise if you've got money, but if you're flat broke it can be hell on earth. Especially when it's all in your face. They can see what they're missing every time they set foot out of the door. And Thai girls can generally wrap Westerners around their little fingers. They can be real heartbreakers. A guy gets upset, has a few drinks, and over he goes. But there are health and safety issues, too.'

'Say what now?'

'Well, lack of health and safety is an issue, I suppose. The average male in Thailand is maybe five feet eight, five feet nine. The women as I'm sure you've noticed are very petite, usually under five two. So when a developer builds a tower block, he generally puts the balcony railing at a Thai height. And a railing that comes up to the waist of a Thai man might only reach the thigh of a six-foot-two-inch farang. So if he's a drinker or he's high on drugs and he goes out on the balcony for a smoke or a breath of fresh air and he stumbles, well he's straight over, isn't he?'

'So, accidental, you mean?' Standing finished the banana and took another sandwich from the bag.

'Well, one man's accident is another man's stupidity, right?

But yes, I think a lot of members of the Pattaya Flying Club just made a bad call and probably regretted it all the way down.' He sipped his drink. 'Then we have the not-so-accidental falls. There are so many deaths off balconies in Thailand that it's become the perfect way to kill someone. You get into their apartment with a couple of heavies, grab him and drop him over. Job done.'

'That happens?'

'Happens a lot. No question. Sometimes over money, sometimes a jealous wife or girlfriend. Or boyfriend.'

'And the cops don't do anything?'

'If it looks like a suicide and the guy was a bit of a low-life, they won't bother taking a closer look.'

'What's the story with the Thai cops?' asked Standing. 'If we tell them about Lee, will they do anything?'

'Depends on what protection he has,' said Harper. 'But trust me, he'll have a lot. He'll have some very senior cops on his payroll. Probably a few government officials and judges as well.'

'So a lot of corruption, yeah?'

'It's pretty much built into the system,' said Harper. 'A cop starts on about forty thousand baht a month. That's about ten grand a year. Maybe double that after he's been in the job eight or ten years. That's not enough to take care of a family, not in Bangkok. You'd struggle, even in the sticks. Plus they have to buy their own uniforms and gear, including their own gun. That's two months' salary right there. The only way to get their earnings up is to take bribes. And a big chunk of that has to be sent up the food chain, to the bosses. And if you want a promotion, you have to pay for that on the basis of how much the job gets in bribes. So with the best will in the world, an honest cop just isn't going to be able to stay in the job.'

'And you pay them off?'

Harper grinned and held up his hands. 'Me? I'm as pure as the driven snow.'

'No offence intended.'

Harper laughed. 'I'm messing with you, Matt. I have to pay hand over fist to do what I do back in Pattaya where I'm based. I couldn't survive without police protection. There's three high-ranking officers who get paid every month, and every Thai New Year I drop off cases of Thai whisky at all the substations. If I see a cop in a bar or a nightclub I'll send over a bottle of brandy or whisky. It all helps.'

'And that keeps you out of trouble?'

Harper chuckled. 'Let's just say that it keeps lines of communication open, so that if I do have a problem they'll take my call and tell me what I need to do to resolve the problem. But, yes, with the right protection, every problem can be solved. Unfortunately Lee will have better protection than I have, so he's pretty much untouchable.' He sipped his drink. 'What do you want to do, Matt?'

'I want to take out Sammy Lee and the bastards that killed Billy. And Pete.'

'Not for dinner, presumably.' He winced as Standing flashed him an angry look, and he raised his hands in surrender. 'Just trying to lighten the moment.'

Standing forced a smile. 'Sorry. I'm still a bit raw.'

'Whatever you need, I'm here for you.'

'It's not your fight, Lex. And this is some serious shit.'

'I specialise in serious shit,' said Harper. 'And this guy is a nasty piece of work. He deserves his comeuppance.'

'What have you heard?'

'The drugs and the animal stuff is common knowledge,' said Harper. 'But he's been buying up land around Trat and anyone who tries to stand up to him gets hurt. Very hurt. Only Thais can buy land. That's the law. If you're a foreigner you can buy a flat, that's fine. Or you can take out a long lease on a house or a factory. But only Thais can own the land. You can try doing it through the back door by setting up a Thai company and having the company own the land, but the Thais are onto that and if they realise it's a front company they'll shut it down and confiscate the land. So, what the Chinese have been doing is buying land through nominees, usually Thai women. Sometimes they marry them, sometimes they don't, but the end result is that the Chinese control the land and the women have to do as they're told. If they don't, they're never heard from again.'

'But what do they want with the land?'

'You've seen that weird-looking fruit? Durian?'

'Yeah. Smells like shit, I'm told.'

'It does,' said Harper. 'But the Chinese love it. They ship tons to China every day. They used to come down here and buy the fruit from Thai farmers, then pay a Thai shipping company to ship the fruit to China. It didn't take them long to realise that if they owned the land and grew the fruit themselves and ran their own freight firms, then they'd boost their profits no end. So that's what they've been doing. They've been buying up acres and acres of land, and they've built their own processing factories and warehouses, all of it on land owned by these Thai women. Sammy Lee is one of the biggest operators out here. And the word is that the trucks that go to China with durians often take illegal animals and animal parts and when they come back, they bring drugs. Lots of drugs.'

'Yeah, we saw him take delivery of two tiger cubs. And what about people trafficking? We saw four young Asian girls being taken into the villa and they didn't seem happy.'

'There's a lot of that. He trafficks women from all over South East Asia into the United Arab Emirates, Europe and the US.'

'I heard that he doesn't send drugs to Europe or the US?'

Harper nodded. 'He knows that if he does that, he'll have Interpol and the DEA on his case. Out in Asia he can buy protection, which is what he does, in spades.' He raised his can. 'So whatever you want to do is fine by me. But you'll need a plan.'

'I figure he's in the villa that Pete was looking at.'

'Where is that?'

'It's on a peninsula, not far from a tourist fishing village on the south of the island. There's the one road in and out, and there's nothing there other than a few homes, a hotel and a few resorts. All Lee has to do is put a man on the road and they'll be able to see everyone who arrives. And if we do get onto the peninsula and there's a shoot-out, two men with guns can seal it off. And Lee has a lot more than two men. We saw almost a dozen while we were there, and a lot of them are armed.'

Harper took his phone out of his pocket and used the Google Maps app to get a bird's-eye view of the peninsula. 'You could maybe drive by and say you were going to the resorts, but red flags will be raised if you so much as look at the house. Strangers will be spotted a mile off, especially farang strangers.'

He handed the phone to Standing and he looked at the screen. 'Pete did just that, and we think he was spotted.'

The entrance to the peninsula was about fifty metres across with no buildings. Then the peninsula widened. To the left of the road were the houses and resorts, most with jetties sticking out into the sea. To the right of the road was dense jungle. He gave the phone back to Harper. 'How good a swimmer are you?'

'I can swim. I'd probably need fins and a wetsuit, but yeah, it's doable.'

'But we've still got the same problem that Billy and I had,' said Standing.

'What's that?'

'Guns. Or rather the lack of them.'

Harper grinned. 'Oh, we've got lots of guns,' he said. He swung the black holdall onto the bed and unzipped it. He reached in and took out two night vision headsets and two Kevlar vests, and put them by the pillow. Standing whistled when Harper took out six flashbangs.

Standing picked one up and looked at it. 'Where did you get these from?'

'Friend of a friend,' said Harper. He took two hunting knives and two Tasers out of the bag. 'Just in case you want to go easy on them.'

'I don't see that happening,' said Standing.

Harper reached into the bag and brought out two Glock 17s and put them on the bed, then took out the silencers. 'Oh, that's perfect,' said Standing.

'There's more,' said Harper.

He took out a Heckler & Koch 417 and handed it to Standing. Standing grinned as he checked the action. 'Oh, come to Papa,' he said.

'Thought you'd appreciate a Heckler,' said Harper.

Standing's eyes widened when Harper took out the next weapon and pulled off the bubble wrap it was encased in. 'Is that a Gilboa Snake? I've heard about those. I think they had some at Stirling Lines for testing but I never got my hands on one.'

Standing put down the HK417 and Harper gave him the twin-barrelled weapon. 'This is one awesome gun,' said Standing. 'You've fired it?'

'A few times, but never in anger,' said Harper. 'It's a beaut. You point it at the target, pull the triggers and get an instant double tap. It kicks like a mule and is noisy as hell, but at close range against multiple hostiles, I can't see it can be beat.'

'And ammunition?'

Harper tilted the holdall so that Standing could see inside. 'Loads of it,' he said. 'So we're good to go?'

'Bit more gear and we will be,' said Standing.

CHAPTER 31

Standing spent almost an hour stripping the guns and cleaning them. They were the tools of his trade and everything depended on them working flawlessly when needed. When he'd finished he lay down on one of the beds and catnapped. It was going to be a long night so he needed what rest he could get.

He was dozing when he heard Harper return in the pick-up. Standing got off the bed, picked up one of the Glocks and peered through a gap in the blinds, only relaxing when he saw that it was Harper, carrying four large bags.

He opened the door. Harper hurried in and Standing closed the door behind him.

'Got everything?' asked Standing.

'Take a look for yourself,' said Harper, dropping the bags onto one of the beds. 'I went to three different dive shops, I figured buying it all in one place might raise a red flag.' He went over to the fridge and took out a beer.

Standing emptied the bags. There were two dark blue wetsuits, two sets of fins, two masks and snorkels, and two large waterproof storage bags. 'Perfect,' he said.

Harper opened his beer and drank, then wiped the back of his mouth with his hand. 'What time do you want to do this?' he asked.

Standing looked at his watch. It was just after seven. 'I'm assuming there'll be guards around all night, but we should wait until the lights are out. We can park up somewhere overlooking the villa.'

'We'll have to be away from the road,' said Harper. 'I saw three different black SUVs while I was out. They're still looking for you.'

'Okay, let's just aim for midnight, then. I think we can cross in about thirty minutes. The fins will speed us up but there'll be a lot of drag from the bags. But we should get there about twelve thirty.'

Harper nodded. 'Sounds about right. What equipment do we take with us?'

'We're going to be up close and personal, so while I love the Heckler I think we'll be better off with the Glocks and suppressors.'

'Yeah, I guess you don't want me letting loose with the Snake.'

'Probably attract too much attention,' said Standing with a grin. 'Ditto with the flashbangs. I think softly, softly is the way to go.'

'What about the Tasers?'

Standing shook his head. 'Tasers can be problematic at the best of times and besides, anyone in that villa is a valid target, whether or not they're holding a gun. They killed Pete and they killed Billy and they came bloody close to killing me, so I don't intend to cut anyone in there any slack.'

'No problem,' said Harper. 'What about night vision gear?'

Standing wrinkled his nose. 'The problem is if security is up then there'll be lights on in parts of the house. If we go in with night vision gear on and we hit a lit area, we lose any advantage. Our own night vision should kick in during the swim, so let's make do with that.'

'Okay, so Glocks and suppressors. Knives just in case?'

'Knives are good. And we should take our dry clothes with us, and towels. Wetsuits are great for buoyancy and they'll make us less visible in the water, but they'll hamper mobility when we're on dry land and we'll be dripping water everywhere. So we take our dry gear over in the bags and change under the jetty. We can stow the bags there and recover them when we leave.'

'Leave how? We swim back?'

'Let's leave our extraction options open,' said Standing.

'Fine by me,' said Harper. 'So what do we do for the next four hours?'

'If it's okay with you, I'd like to get some sleep,' said Standing. 'I didn't get a wink last night.'

'No problem,' said Harper. 'I'll sit outside on the porch. Guard duty.'

'Thanks for this,' said Standing. 'For everything.'

'No need to thank me,' said Harper. 'Any friend of Spider's is a friend of mine. Spider and I go way back.'

CHAPTER 32

Harper came back into the room just before eleven o'clock. Standing woke up as the door handle turned, and he was sitting up and reaching for the Glock on the bedside table as Harper stepped into the room. Harper put his hands in the air. 'I come in peace,' he said.

'Sorry. Force of habit.'

Harper closed the door. 'I gave this some thought while you were in the land of nod. How about we change into the wetsuits here and prepare the dry bags, then we can drive and park close to the water near Bang Bao Pier. There are a few dive places around there, and if we were unlucky enough to be spotted they'd maybe think we were doing a night dive.'

'With no tanks?'

'I'm just saying, there'd be a logic to us wearing wetsuits. Though hopefully no one will see us, so it's academic.'

Standing considered what Harper had said, then nodded. 'Yeah, it makes sense.'

He stood up and stripped off his shirt and shorts and shoved them in one of the dry bags. He looked down at his underwear. 'On or off?' he asked. 'What do you think?'

'You won't want wet underwear in the villa,' said Harper. 'So commando.'

Standing stripped off his underpants and put them in the bag, then pulled on a wetsuit and zipped it up.

Harper did the same, then they both put Glocks and silencers into the bags. The bags had double seals that would make sure that everything inside stayed dry during their swim over to the jetty.

'I'm going to leave the rest of the gear in the truck,' said Harper. 'In case something goes wrong.'

'Nothing's going to go wrong,' said Standing. 'But yeah, better to have the gear close by and not on the other side of the island.'

Harper packed the rest of the gear into the black holdall and then nodded at Standing. 'Good to go?'

'Let's do it,' said Standing.

CHAPTER 33

It took the best part of an hour to drive around the island to Bang Bao Pier. The roads were pretty much deserted but Standing lay on the floor in the rear of the cab, just to be on the safe side. There was a black BMW SUV parked outside the ferry terminal, even though it was closed. The windows were open and Harper caught a glimpse of two men inside, smoking cigarettes.

They passed another black SUV as they drove through White Sand Beach, and yet another parked near the entrance to the track that led to Best Friends Resort. There wasn't much traffic on the roads but Harper kept his speed down. The road was potentially lethal in places, twisting and turning as it made its way through the jungle. Occasionally they would pass roadside bars that were still open, mainly serving tourists, but as they approached the far south of the island it got busier, with upmarket resorts and restaurants. They followed the signs for Bang Bao Pier but then turned off onto a narrow track that led to the beach. They parked next to a dive shop that was in darkness and Harper switched off the engine. Standing sat on the back seat and pushed the black kitbag onto the floor and covered it with the blanket.

To their left was the pier itself, the first half cluttered with wooden shacks which gave way to the jetty lined with tourist and fishing boats. Ahead of them, less than a kilometre away across the bay, was Sammy Lee's villa.

There was a half-moon overhead and the water was calm. They sat in the cab, the engine clicking as it cooled, waiting until their night vision kicked in. They didn't see anybody walking by and the only vehicles that drove down the road were motorbikes and scooters. As the minutes ticked by they were gradually able to see more features on the peninsula and could make out the terrace and the jetty of Lee's villa.

'Okay, we're as good as we're going to be,' said Standing eventually. They climbed out of the cab. Standing pulled out the two dry bags and gave one to Harper, then took out the carrier bags containing the fins, snorkels and masks. They both took off their shoes and put them in the dry bags, then Harper locked the cab and placed the keys on the rear nearside tyre.

They walked barefoot down to the water's edge, then put the dry bags on the sand and prepared their facemasks by spitting on the glass and rinsing them in the sea. They put the fins on their feet and strapped their dry bags to their chests before wading out into the water. Once the water was up to their waists they put on their masks and snorkels, flashed each other an 'OK' sign, and lay face down and began swimming slowly towards the villa.

The water was pleasantly warm as it worked its way under the neoprene wetsuits. The wetsuits provided extra buoyancy to counteract the weight of the dry bags, but the dry bags themselves were awkward and made them less hydrodynamic, which meant they had to make more of an effort with the fins to propel themselves through the water.

Standing kept his face down, looking up every hundred metres or so to check his heading, keeping a slow and steady motion with his fins. It wasn't a race, what mattered was getting over to the jetty without being seen.

When they were a hundred metres from the peninsula shore they both trod water and checked out the terrace and jetty as best they could. The jetty was empty but as they watched, a figure emerged on the terrace and lit a cigarette. They watched him for the best part of two minutes before he flicked the remains of the cigarette away and went back inside. Standing gave Harper an 'OK' sign and they began swimming again, aiming for the end of the jetty.

They reached it and swam underneath the boards towards the shore. The seabed rose sharply and by the time they were halfway along the jetty, the water was only up to their waists. They stopped once they were out of the water, took off their equipment and stripped off their wetsuits, then opened the dry bags and towelled themselves dry before changing into their clothes and shoes. They took out the Glocks and screwed in the silencers, put the spare magazines into their pockets, then packed away their gear into the dry bags and stowed them under the far end of the jetty.

'Okay?' whispered Standing.

Harper nodded.

Standing took a deep breath and exhaled slowly. Everything up to that point had been planned for, but from now on they would be reacting to whatever happened. There was no way of predicting how many men they would be up against, where they would be, and whether or not they would be armed. Each room they entered would be a new challenge and one they would have to face blind. It was a task that Standing was up to – it was what he trained for – but he wasn't sure about Harper's skill set, and in a firefight an amateur, no matter how enthusiastic he was, could be more of a liability than an asset.

'The terrace looks clear at the moment, so let's check the front of the house first,' whispered Standing. 'We'll work our way around the house and make sure the outside is clear before we head inside.'

'Roger that,' whispered Harper. 'Shall I go right and you go left, meet you at the front?'

That was exactly how Standing would do it if he was with an SAS comrade, but until he knew how good Harper was he'd feel safer with him close by, so he shook his head. 'We'll stick together,' he said. 'You stay three steps behind me. Take care of anything I miss.'

'Got you,' Harper whispered. 'And I'll try not to shoot you in the back of the head.' He grinned and winked.

'That would be nice,' said Standing. 'Okay, follow me.'

Standing moved out from under the jetty and checked out the ground floor of the house. To the right of the area underneath the terrace was a large brick-built barbecue area, a metal table and two boxy sofas. Floor-to-ceiling sliding windows looked out over the garden and the jetty. He could make out several sofas inside and there was a big-screen TV on one wall. The room was in darkness and there didn't appear to be anyone there. He looked up and listened but couldn't hear any sound from the terrace, so he began walking along the grass, holding the silenced Glock with both hands and keeping it moving from side to side. Harper followed.

They reached the edge of the house, stopped and listened. Standing wrinkled his nose as he smelled smoke. Tobacco smoke.

He started moving again. They were still on grass and there

was a concrete wall about twenty feet to their left, about ten feet tall and topped with spikes. There were no windows in the wall of the house to their right.

He moved away from the wall as he reached the front of the villa. The smell of smoke was stronger now and he could hear voices. He raised his left hand and clenched his fist, telling Harper to stop. He couldn't see around the corner, so he listened intently as he tried to work out how many voices there were. All he could hear was mumbling but he figured there were two men. If they were both smoking then their hands would be occupied, but that was an assumption and assumptions could lead to mistakes.

He stepped to the side. The rear of a car came into view. A black BMW SUV. Then another car. Also a black SUV. He stopped as he saw the back of a man wearing a white shirt and jeans. The man was smoking and talking in a language Standing didn't recognise, Chinese maybe. As Standing watched, the man blew smoke into the air and laughed. Standing moved to the left. The man had a gun stuck into the back of his pants. Standing took a quick look over his shoulder. Harper had his gun in both hands, aimed away from Standing. He flashed Standing a quick smile, nodded and started moving to the left, getting closer to the concrete wall.

Standing took a deep breath, released half of it, then began moving forward. There was a second man next to a third vehicle, smoking a cigarette and listening to whatever the first man was saying. He was wearing a blue Adidas tracksuit top and baggy shorts and had an Uzi hanging from a shoulder strap. He opened his mouth when he saw Standing and the cigarette fell from between his lips. He scuttled backwards, reaching for his weapon. Standing shot him twice in the chest.

The suppressor kept the noise down to the sound of a balloon popping.

The man fell to the ground. The other man reached for his gun as he turned, but Standing had all the time in the world to put a bullet in the back of his neck and he fell forward, bounced off the SUV and rolled onto the ground. Standing aimed at the man's chest but he was obviously dead, so he cancelled the second shot.

Standing moved quickly, stepping over the two bodies and around the cars. He kept the Glock moving, ready for anything, but it was clear within seconds that there was no one else in the front yard. He nodded at Harper and pointed at the front door. Harper hurried and used his left hand to turn the door handle. The door opened. Standing moved to stand next to him, then as Harper pushed the door open, Standing moved inside.

The hallway was in darkness but they could hear music coming from upstairs. Ahead of them was the seating area with the floor-to-ceiling windows overlooking the jetty and the sea beyond. To the left was an open-plan kitchen. There was a corridor to the side of the kitchen and a door at the end outlined by a pale light. Standing pointed at the door and headed towards it. Harper tucked in behind him.

Standing reached the door but stepped to the side so that Harper could open it. The door opened inwards, so Standing had to step back. He frowned as he saw that it was a store room with shelves to the left and right and a single LED light overhead. He looked at Harper and shrugged. Harper frowned and pointed to the bottom of the wall facing them. There was a narrow strip of light bleeding onto the floor. 'Secret door,' he mouthed.

Standing used his left hand to push the wall and it clicked open revealing a flight of metal stairs leading down into a basement. He stepped through, his Glock at the ready. The steps turned to the left revealing a room some twenty feet square, lined with metal shelving units which were filled with stacks of cash wrapped in clear plastic. There was a table in the middle of the room and a Chinese man with rolled-up shirtsleeves was running banknotes through an automated counter. He had a pen in his right hand and was keeping a total in a notepad.

He looked up and his jaw dropped when he saw Standing coming down the stairs towards him. He reached for a Glock on the table but he was too slow and he hadn't even touched the butt before Standing had put two rounds in his chest.

A second Chinese man appeared at the bottom of the stairs. Standing's jaw tightened as he recognised him – he had been one of the men on the beach with an M16. Standing shot him in the face, blood splattered across the plastic packs of money and the man fell back against a shelving unit and slid to the floor.

'Well, this is interesting,' said Harper from the doorway, looking down at the money.

'Business is obviously good,' said Standing. He reached the bottom of the stairs, had a quick look around and then headed back up. Harper moved back into the corridor and Standing joined him.

'Okay, upstairs,' whispered Standing. 'And remember, three paces behind me.'

Harper nodded. They moved along the corridor and into the main seating area. To the side was a large spiral staircase leading to the upper floor. As Standing reached the bottom of the staircase they heard a toilet flush off to their right. They both turned to look at the door, guns at the ready.

They heard a tap run, and then the door opened. A fat man in a baggy linen shirt and cargo pants stopped in his tracks, his mouth open in surprise. He had an M16 hanging from a sling but he made no move to reach for it, instead he raised his hand. He said something in Chinese, which Standing figured was almost certainly 'don't shoot', but even before the words had left his mouth Harper had put two rounds in his chest and the man fell back, staggered against the wash basin and slumped to the tiled floor. Harper grinned at the dead man. 'Sorry, I don't speak Chinese,' he said.

They went back to the spiral staircase and looked up. They both flinched as they heard the rat-tat-tat of a semi-automatic but there were no rounds whizzing around them. Standing looked at Harper, shrugged and started up the stairs. There was another burst of semi-automatic fire, followed by laughter.

Standing and Harper continued up the stairs. They reached the top and stepped into a large living area that looked out over the terrace. There was a low modern L-shaped sofa and two La-Z-Boy reclining armchairs facing the windows. To the left was an open door that led to another room, the source of the gunfire and laughter.

They moved to the door and peered inside. There was a massive screen on one wall and two men were sitting on a sofa playing Call of Duty, jeering and laughing as fighters fell to the ground and died. The players had their backs to the door but two more men were standing to their left, waving their beer bottles at the screen and commenting on the action. Harper looked over at Standing, grinned and shook his head in amazement. The video game gunshots would have drowned out any sound they had made downstairs.

One of the spectators turned to look at the door and his eyes widened when he saw Standing and Harper. Standing put two shots in the man's chest and he slid down the wall, the bottle of beer still clenched in his hand. His companion turned to see what had happened and Standing shot him, too.

Harper hurried over to the sofa and slammed the butt of his Glock against the man sitting on the right of the sofa, then did the same to the man on the left. Both men slumped back, unconscious. 'You getting soft, Lex?' asked Standing.

'In your dreams,' said Harper. 'It's starting to look as if Sammy Lee and the girl aren't here, so at some point we might want to ask somebody a few questions. And we can't do that if everyone's dead.'

'Fair point,' said Standing.

Harper put his gun down on a side table and ripped the charging lead out of the PlayStation console. He pushed one of the men to the floor and used the lead to bind his hands behind his back. He yanked a wire from a standard lamp and bound the other man. Standing kept watch at the door until he'd finished.

'They'll be out for a while,' said Harper, as he collected his gun.

They moved back into the main seating area. There were three doors off to the right. Presumably bedrooms.

Harper went over to the first door, nodded at Standing and opened it. It was a big room with windows overlooking the sea, and a king-size bed with a mirror on the ceiling above it. Another door led to a marble bathroom with a whirlpool bath large enough for four people, and taps that looked as if they might be made of gold. 'I guess this is the master bedroom, but no sign of the master,' said Harper.

Standing nodded and went to the second door. He waited for Harper to open it. Harper turned the handle, pushed the door open and then stepped back. Standing went in, Glock at the ready. This room was smaller but the bed was also a king-size. There was a man on the bed, sleeping on his back, snoring softly. There was an M16 at his side and Standing's jaw tightened as he recognised him. It was one of the assassins on the beach who had been shooting at Green, maybe the one who had fired the killing shot. He looked left and right to reassure himself that the man was alone in the room, then jumped up onto the bed. The man's eyes opened and he gasped as he saw Standing looming over him. He tried to reach for his weapon but Standing kicked it off the bed and it clattered onto the wooden floor.

The man began mumbling in Chinese, clearly begging for his life, but there was nothing he could say or do that would change the outcome. The man looked over at Harper and said something to him, but Harper just shrugged. 'Not my problem,' he said.

'Look at me, you bastard,' Standing hissed at the man. 'Don't look at him, look at me.'

The man looked back at Standing. 'Please, don't!' he said, his voice trembling.

Standing held the man's look as he pulled the trigger and put a round into his stomach. He stared at the man and pulled the trigger again, aiming a bit higher this time but it still wasn't a fatal shot. The man gasped as blood pumped out of the wounds. Standing left it another few seconds before pulling the trigger a third time, an instantly fatal shot to the heart.

Standing stepped off the bed and realised that Harper had been staring at him. 'That was cold,' said Harper.

'He shot at Billy. Maybe even killed him.'

'I wasn't saying you did a bad thing, I just said it was cold.' He shrugged. 'Cold is good.'

They headed for the third bedroom. Harper opened it and Standing went in, but the room and the adjoining bathroom were clear. Unlike the master bathroom there was no whirlpool bath, just a walk-in shower. There were bottles of shampoo and conditioner in the shower and various hair sprays and gels by the sink. There were several long dyed-blonde hairs on the tiled floor. Standing went back into the room and pulled back one of the sliding wardrobe doors. There were a dozen or so items of girl's clothing on hangers and a hard-shell carry-on case at the bottom. He pulled it out. There was a luggage tag on the handle and he bent down to look at it. There was a name. KIM COOPER. And a phone number with a Vietnamese area code.

'She was definitely here,' said Standing.

'Well, she isn't now,' said Harper. 'And neither is Sammy Lee.' He went outside and looked out at the terrace. 'This is maybe for work. He's probably got a bigger place on the mainland. And probably a place in Cambodia. A guy like Lee will be on the move a lot.'

'He brought Kim here for a few days, maybe, and she saw what was going on. She calls her dad, Lee kicks off, and what? Takes her somewhere else?'

'I hope so, because the alternative isn't good, is it?' said Harper. 'But I think he does have somewhere else close by. The tiger cubs aren't here. Neither are those four girls we saw arriving on the boat. And there's cash here but no drugs. And there aren't the facilities here to keep a lot of girls. This is just a transit point.' He headed down the stairs and Standing followed him. Harper walked into the kitchen and opened a large stainless-steel fridge. He took out a bottle of beer and used the top of the fridge to bang off the cap. He drank from the bottle. 'This sort of thing always makes me thirsty,' he said.

'It's the tension. Anxiety. It dries the mouth.'

'You're okay?'

Standing shrugged. 'I don't get tense. The opposite, I switch into working mode and I'm totally relaxed. But I'll take a beer.'

Harper grinned and took out a second beer, banged off the cap and handed it to him. They clinked bottles and drank.

'The thing now is to find out where they took her,' said Standing. 'And where Lee went.'

'I'll handle that,' said Harper. 'Just give me half an hour or so.'

Standing frowned. 'What do you mean?'

Harper gestured upstairs with his bottle. 'The Call of Duty fans will probably know. And as they're not dead – no thanks to you – I can get them to tell me everything they know.'

'You'll do that?'

'You're good at clearing rooms and double tapping bad guys, I'm good at getting information out of people.' He shrugged. 'One of my many talents.'

Standing shook his head. 'No, it's down to me. I'll do it.'

'Have you tortured someone before?'

Standing forced a smile. 'No. But I'll do it.'

'Well, I've got form. Previous.'

'I'm a quick learner,' said Standing.

Harper smiled thinly. 'It's not about acquiring the skills, Matt. You could teach a monkey to do it. It's about how you deal with it afterwards.'

'You don't know what I've done, Lex. I've dealt with a lot over the years.'

'I'm sure you have. But deliberately inflicting pain for information leaves a lot of guilt. And the first time is the worst. It's like killing. The first time is the hardest, and then it gets easier. It just does. So I can go up there and do what has to be done and it won't change me in the slightest. But if you do it, it'll change you forever. You'll never be the same again. If I do it, it'll be business as usual.'

Standing nodded slowly. 'You're sure?'

'Absolutely. You wait here, okay?' He drained his bottle and put it by the sink.

'How long will it take?'

'It depends. There's a lot of factors at play.' He pulled open a kitchen drawer. He took out a pair of nutcrackers and a corkscrew. There was a knife block by the sink and he pulled out two knives, a small pointed one and a breadknife with a serrated edge. He bent down and opened the cupboard. 'There you go,' he said, and pulled out a bottle of bleach. He put everything into a blue plastic bucket, then picked up two tea towels. 'I'll keep the noise down to a minimum,' he said. 'But I'd keep the door closed if I was you.' He nodded at the bottle that Standing was holding. 'Maybe wipe the prints off when you're done. Just to be on the safe side.'

CHAPTER 34

Standing was just finishing his beer when Harper came down the stairs, holding the blue plastic bucket. He dumped the knives and the blood-stained tea towels in the sink. He put the bottle of bleach in the cupboard beneath the sink, then rinsed the towels and used one of them to wipe the knives.

'Lee is out looking for you,' he said. 'Apparently he said he wouldn't be back until he had your head on a stick.'

'What about Kim?'

'She was here, but he moved her just before they killed Pete. They took her and some other girls to a ship, called the *Galaxy*.'

'They're on a ship?'

'It's a cruise ship but the owners brought it onto dry land years ago and turned it into a hotel. It's abandoned now. There's half a dozen ships that they were using as hotels on a resort and the *Galaxy* is the biggest. It's the Grand Laguna Resort, not far from the pier where we left my truck. The girls are going to be trafficked to Dubai.'

'When?'

'Soon. But we don't have much time because the moment that Lee finds out we've been here he'll know we're onto him and he'll either move them out or kill them.'

'So what do you think, we go to this *Galaxy*?'

'It's your call. Your wish is my command.'

'We still haven't found Kim. And I really, really want to get my hands on Lee.'

'Then let's do it.' Harper had finished wiping the knives and rinsed the towels again.

'Can I ask you something?' said Standing.

'Sure.'

'Why did you knock out two of the guys? One would have been enough, right?'

Harper flashed him a tight smile. 'Two makes it easier. You work on one while the other one watches. Watching is worse because then you know what's coming.' He shrugged. 'Anyway, it worked.'

'They're dead now, right?'

'No, I said they can go, but they're missing most of their fingers and toes, so we'll have to drive them to hospital.' He chuckled at the look of surprise that flashed across Standing's face. 'No, they're dead, Matt. Dead dead.'

'You have a sick sense of humour, Lex.'

'That has been said,' he said. He wiped his hands on his shorts. 'Just give me a minute and we'll be off.'

'What now?' asked Standing, but Harper had already left the kitchen. Standing hurried after him. Harper walked along the corridor to the doorway that led to the basement. Harper went down the steps and put his gun on the table. There were several empty black nylon holdalls under the table and he grabbed two. He swung them onto the table and began filling them with bundles of hundred-dollar bills.

'Lex, are you crazy?' asked Standing. 'There's no way we can swim back with that.'

Harper continued to fill the bags. 'We don't have to swim,' he said. 'We can take one of their SUVs and drive back. If there are any guards at the entrance to the peninsula, they won't see us through the tinted windows. And we'll be coming from the villa, they won't be expecting that. Grab a bag and fill your boots.'

'And do what? They're hardly likely to let me on a plane with a bag full of hundred-dollar bills.'

'I can help you get into a bank,' Harper said. 'The banks here are very flexible.'

'Nah, mate. I didn't do this for the money.'

'Neither did I, but I've got expenses.' Harper finished filling the first bag and zipped it shut. 'If you're not interested in the cash, why don't you pop out to the jetty and collect the stuff we left there? No point in gifting them our DNA. I'll meet you outside by the cars.' He began shoving bundles of notes into the second bag.

Standing shrugged and went back up the steps. He stood in the hallway but everything was quiet, so he went to the kitchen and out of the door into the garden. He listened again but there was only the sound of the waves sloshing against the jetty. He kept his gun at the ready as he moved on the balls of his feet across the grass to the water's edge. He took a slow look around, scanning the water first, then the shore, then looking back at the villa, before satisfying himself that there were no threats in the vicinity. He ducked under the jetty and went over to the two waterproof bags. He grabbed them and made his way back to the garden. He paused again, holding his breath and moving his head slowly from side to side as he listened intently, then he jogged across the grass and around the side of the villa.

Harper had opened the rear passenger door of one of the black BMW SUVs and was shoving in the two holdalls. 'How much do you think you have there?' Standing asked.

Harper shrugged. 'Three mill. Maybe four. A million bucks in hundred-dollar bills weighs about ten kilos.' He grinned at the look of astonishment on Standing's face. 'What can I say, I've got a lot of expenses.' He took the waterproof bags from Standing, threw them into the back and closed the door. 'They left the keys in, which was nice of them,' he said. 'Now, the *Galaxy* is a fifteen- or twenty-minute drive from here, and we can pick up our big guns on the way. I'm guessing we'll be needing the night vision gear, but you're the expert at this sort of thing so it's your call.'

They climbed into the SUV. 'I'll gather some intel,' said Standing, twisting around and grabbing the waterproof bag that contained his phone.

Harper started the car. There was a sensor on the sun visor and he clicked it. The black gates slowly opened. Harper edged the SUV forward, looked both ways and turned right. He accelerated quickly, his eyes flicking from side to side.

Standing put down his phone and kept his Glock in his lap. He checked the window to his left. They reached the point where the land narrowed.

'Shit,' said Harper. 'Look.'

There were two men in tracksuits standing on the left side of the road. They were facing away from them but they looked like heavies and there was a black SUV parked off the road. The two men turned to look at the SUV. Harper and Standing pressed themselves back into their seats. The heavies didn't have guns in their hands, which was a good sign. The windows were heavily tinted, so Standing was fairly sure that they wouldn't be able to see inside.

Harper beeped his horn twice and the men waved.

Standing waved back as they drove by. The men might

see the movement but hopefully wouldn't be able to see their faces.

Standing checked the side mirror as they drove down the road. The two heavies were talking and neither reached for a phone or a radio. It looked as if they'd gotten away with it.

Standing tapped Galaxy Hotel Koh Chang into Safari but nothing came up. 'I'm not seeing anything about this ship,' he said.

'Try Grand Laguna Resort,' said Harper.

Standing tapped it into the search engine and got several hits. He scrolled through dozens of photographs of a white five-storey cruise ship surrounded by lush grass. There were several views of the rear of the ship that showed water in a channel behind it, but most of the vessel seemed to be on dry land. 'Okay, got it,' he said. There were a number of magazine and blog articles about the *Galaxy*, one of which said it had been abandoned for almost ten years, though rooms were being offered at 699 baht in 2012. One article claimed that there had been several suicides there, with people jumping to their deaths from the top floor, and the locals had started referring to it as the Death Ship and generally kept away from the place.

One of the photographs showed the main entrance, a doorway in the port side, with a wooden gangplank leading to it, sheltered by a canopy. It looked as if access was possible at the rear of the ship, too.

There were other buildings nearby, but they also seemed to have been abandoned. It would be the perfect place to keep trafficked girls away from prying eyes. He looked at his watch. Dawn was about four hours away.

'Have we got time?' asked Harper.

'We've got no choice,' said Standing. 'There's no way we can storm the place in daylight, and they're sure to find out what happened at the villa which means they'll be prepared for us. Or they'll move the girls out. Either way, we've lost. It has to be tonight.'

They drove into Bang Bao village. It was in darkness and only a pack of stray dogs paid them any attention. Harper headed for the dive shop and parked next to his pick-up truck. He switched off the lights and the engine. 'Okay, so what's the plan?' he asked.

'Drive as close to the ship as we can and use the night vision headsets to get up close and personal. Take out the bad guys and hopefully that will include Lee. There'll be an element of winging it, but I've done this sort of thing before, in training and in the real world.'

'Yeah, well I haven't. Just so you know.'

'Stick close to me and it'll be fine.'

'What gear do you want? Glocks and silencers again?'

Standing rubbed his chin. 'I think so, yes. But I'm going to take the Heckler as well.'

'There's no suppressor for that. And the flash will mess up the night vision gear.'

'If I have to use it, noise won't be the issue. Nor will vision. And we don't know what we'll be up against. There could just be a couple of hostiles there, there could be a dozen or more. Better safe than sorry.'

Harper grinned. 'I'll take the Gilboa Snake, then.'

'Go for it.'

'And if it's okay with you, I'd prefer to go in my truck.'

Standing nodded. 'That makes sense. This SUV sticks out, your truck blends. What about your ill-gotten gains?'

'You mean my expenses? I think I'll take everything in the truck.'

'That'll mean all your eggs in one basket.'

Harper grinned. 'I'll just make sure I take bloody good care of the basket.' They climbed out of the SUV and transferred everything into the cab of the pick-up truck. Five minutes later they were driving towards Bang Bao Bay.

CHAPTER 35

The GPS took them off the main road and onto a narrow track, barely wide enough for one vehicle. It had taken less than fifteen minutes to drive there from the dive shop. Harper stopped and switched off the headlights. 'They'll see us coming for miles,' he said.

'Do you want to use the night vision gear now?' asked Standing.

'There's starlight and a half-moon,' said Harper. 'Let's do it the old-fashioned way. If we wait a few minutes our own night vision will kick in.'

'You know that's why pirates used to wear eye patches,' said Standing.

'Say what now?'

'Pirates. Long John Silver and all. It takes twenty minutes or so to adapt from bright sunlight to near complete darkness, right? So if a pirate was fighting on deck in daylight, and then had to go below deck to carry on fighting, he'd be at a disadvantage. He can't see but the guys below deck, their night vision is working so the pirate is effectively blinded. So the pirates took to wearing an eye patch over one eye. That way, when it comes to fighting in the dark they take off the patch and that eye is good to go.'

'Nice one,' said Harper. 'But why didn't they wear a patch

over both eyes so that they'd both have night vision when they needed it?'

'Because . . .' Standing shook his head when he realised that Harper was joking. 'You're very funny,' he said.

Harper grinned. 'That's how I deal with tension,' he said.

'Me, I do square breathing. That's what calms me down.'

Harper frowned. 'I haven't seen you tense at all. Nothing seems to phase you. You're the bloody terminator.'

'In combat, sure. The training kicks in and my instincts are good. My problems arise when I'm not in combat and someone gives me a hard time. The instincts that protect me under fire tend to get me into problems back in the barracks.'

'You've got a short fuse?'

Standing laughed. 'I've got no fuse at all, that's the problem. Had an officer push me one time and before I could blink he was on his back with a broken nose.' He shrugged. 'Lost my stripes for that.'

'Well, you can't go around decking officers, obviously.'

'The fact that he was an officer didn't enter into it. There was no conscious decision to hit him, he hit me and I reacted. It's like when I'm in combat, I know what I have to do and I just do it. There have been times when an officer has told me what to do but I just ignored it because I knew he was wrong.'

'Your instincts are always right?'

Standing nodded. 'In combat, yeah. Always. I know where to go and what to do and it's almost as if it happens on autopilot. Everything seems to slow down and I have all the time in the world to do what needs to be done.'

'And what's this square breathing?'

Standing smiled. 'A trick that a therapist taught me.'

'You had a therapist? Seriously?'

'I didn't have a choice, it was either see a therapist or leave the Regiment. To be honest, she was good, taught me a lot. The square breathing technique is all about controlling your rate of breathing. You basically inhale for four seconds, hold it for four seconds, breathe out for four seconds, and then wait four seconds before breathing again. Repeat as necessary. The fact that you're concentrating on breathing means you calm down.'

'I can imagine you doing that under fire. The bullets are flying overhead and you're in-two-three-four, out-two-three-four.'

'That's the thing, right? They want me to be a killing machine under fire and a pussycat in the barracks.' He shrugged. 'I can understand why you turned down a military career. But you would have fitted right into the SAS.'

'Yeah, Spider used to say the same. I'm not sure if I could have got through Selection, though.'

'You look fit.'

'The physical side isn't a problem. I've done the Fan Dance a few times, usually for a bet. And I did the Long Drag when I was in the Paras. It wasn't a problem, But I always figured that the jungle phase would do for me. Weeks of cold nights and sweaty days, wet through twenty-four-seven with leeches sucking the blood from your balls. Why would anyone put themselves through that?'

'It demonstrates mental toughness,' said Standing. 'It's what most recruits fail at.'

'Because it's basically pointless. I'm mentally tough when I need to be, that's what counts. I don't see that I need to prove it by making myself miserable for six weeks. And at the end of the day, when you finally win the right to wear that beige beret, how much do they pay you? The equivalent of one kilo of the white stuff a year. It's an insult.'

Standing smiled. 'That's an interesting comparison.'

'It's true, though. You guys are the best of the best and they pay you less than a bloody train driver.'

'We don't do it for the money, Lex.'

'And they take advantage of that, don't they? Spider's the same. He relishes being the guy in the white hat, taking out the bad guys.'

'And what colour hat do you wear?'

Harper chuckled. 'Sometimes I wear a black hat, sometimes – like this time – it's white. So on balance, I guess, grey.'

'And your loyalties, where do they lie?'

'Not to my country, that's for sure. And not to the government, I stopped believing anything they told me years ago, Labour or Conservative. I'm loyal to my friends, Matt. And that's about it. Other than that, it's every man for himself.'

'Well, I'm just glad you're here.'

Harper grinned. 'Happy to help,' he said. He blinked and looked down the track. 'Okay, I think we're ready.' He put the car in gear and drove forward, keeping at just above walking pace. The path curved left and right as it cut through the undergrowth, a mixture of broad-leafed bushes, elephant grass and trees that restricted visibility to just a few metres either side. After about a kilometre they saw a wooden building on the left, and a red-and-white pole barrier blocking their way. There didn't appear to be anyone there, so they climbed out and looked around. The building was little more than a shack with a sloping tiled roof. Inside, a hammock was hanging from a roof beam and there was a faded sign detailing the rooms that were available, a hangover from the days when the resort had been open and welcoming guests. Now there was no question of guests being welcome – behind the barrier were oil drums that had been painted with red and white stripes and filled with concrete, and a sign warned that trespassers would be fined three thousand baht.

'Do you want to move the barrels so we can drive down?' asked Harper. He pointed to scuff marks on the ground. 'It looks as if someone has already done that.'

'Let's leave the truck here,' said Standing. 'We can approach on foot.'

Harper looked around. 'Okay, let me move it into the trees.' He got back into the cab, reversed a few feet and then drove off the track and eased the truck into the undergrowth. The trees were close together but he managed to get twenty feet or so away from the track. He climbed out and started grabbing handfuls of branches and foliage, which he stacked up against the back of the truck. Standing went to help him. After ten minutes or so they were confident that the vehicle wouldn't be seen from the path.

Harper opened the rear passenger door of the truck and unzipped the two dry bags. He gave one of the Glocks to Standing, along with a fresh magazine, then pulled the Heckler & Koch 417 out of the holdall. Standing slotted the new magazine into the Glock, then put it on the bonnet and took the Heckler. 'How many magazines for the Heckler?' asked Harper.

'Two should be enough,' said Standing.

Harper gave him two filled polymer magazines. Standing put one in his pocket and slotted the other into the weapon, then put it on the bonnet next to the Glock.

Harper gave Standing a suppressor, then reloaded the second

Glock and screwed in his own suppressor. He put the used magazine in the holdall, then he took out the Gilboa Snake and slotted in two full magazines. 'How many opposition do you think there'll be?' he asked.

'Probably less than at the villa,' said Standing. 'The guys there were to guard the money. All he's got in the *Galaxy* is the girls. Plus he's got guys out looking for me.' He shrugged. 'But who knows?'

'I'll take two extra magazines just to be on the safe side,' said Harper. He took two magazines from the holdall and put them into his pockets, then he put the weapon on the bonnet next to Standing's Heckler. He took the two sets of night vision headsets from the holdall, zipped it up and gave one of the sets to Standing before closing the door and locking up. 'Okay?' he asked.

'Okay,' said Standing. 'I'm thinking we go in at the rear. The front entrance is too easy to guard, the gangplank is the only way in. From what I can see on the satellite view, the rear is more open. We can work our way around and get the lie of the land before we decide for sure.'

Harper nodded. 'Makes sense.'

Standing slung the Heckler over his right shoulder and picked up the Glock and headset. He walked back to the track. Harper gathered his gear and followed him. They ducked under the barrier and started walking.

CHAPTER 36

Standing didn't see the dark shape looming over him until he was almost next to it. He swung his Glock up and his finger was tightening on the trigger when he realised it was a statue. It was an elephant. No, two elephants.

Harper cursed as he saw them, and then he chuckled. 'Bloody hell, that made me jump,' he said.

They started walking again. Three more elephants came into view on the left of the track. Standing turned his head as he walked, listening, but there was only the sound of night insects, clicking and whirring.

After a couple of hundred metres the track forked. Standing went to the left. There was enough light to see by, and as they followed the track they saw the *Galaxy* for the first time, a grey shape against the night sky. They stopped. If they could see the ship, anyone on the ship would be able to see them. Standing pointed to the left and they moved into the undergrowth. Their route took them to the starboard side of the boat, which meant they weren't able to see the gangplank or the entrance. They worked their way around to the stern. There was a small water-filled channel behind it, but then a strip of land and the beach beyond. Presumably the owners had dug a channel to sail the ship in, then filled in the hole once it was in place.

Standing stared at the stern of the ship. There was a deck area with seating around the edge, and as he peered into the darkness he was able to make out two figures sitting there. 'Do you see them?' he whispered.

Harper nodded.

'Okay, we're going to have to work our way around to the other side,' said Standing. 'We need eyes on the entrance.'

They retraced their steps through the undergrowth and got back to the fork in the track. This time they went to the right. After about fifty metres they came across a wooden building with a tiled roof. It was the resort's reception area, open to the elements and clearly unused. They stared at it for several minutes to reassure themselves that there was no one there, then moved forward. The ship came into view on their left and they saw more marooned boats to their right, all clearly deserted. They moved off the track to the right and kept in the undergrowth until the building was between them and the ship. They crept forward and took up position in the building. Much of the wood was rotting and at some point in the past someone had lit a fire there.

They had a good view of the gangplank and the entrance, which was about fifty metres away. A man was looking out from the ship, his M16 hanging on a sling. He was smoking a cigarette, and the red dot of the burning end moved up and down as they watched. 'I just see the one,' whispered Harper.

'I think there's another one, behind him and to the left,' said Standing.

Harper put on his night vision headset and switched it on. There was a brief flicker and then he was looking at everything with a greenish hue. There were two light green figures standing at the entrance. 'Two it is,' he said. He removed his headset and switched it off.

'We can't breach the entrance,' said Standing. 'Even if we take the two of them out, anyone else inside will hear the shots and come rushing.'

'Not if we use the Glocks and silencers.'

'They're too far away to be certain of a kill shot with a Glock. How about this? I work my way back to the rear of the ship. Once I'm in position, you take out these two with your big gun and hopefully that means the guys at the back will move forward. The only way off the ship at the front is the gangplank, so you can take out anyone who tries it. Meanwhile I'll board at the back and come up behind them.'

'And what about the girls?'

'With any luck they'll be on the ground floor. If not, we'll work our way up until we find them. How does that sound?'

'Sounds fine for me. I'll be here in cover shooting anyone who shows themselves. But you'll be in there on your own against multiple hostiles.'

'Sure, but I'll be coming up behind them while their attention is focused on you. It'll work.'

'Let's hope so,' said Harper.

CHAPTER 37

Standing looked at his watch. There were two minutes to go before Harper would take his shots. Standing was in the undergrowth overlooking the rear of the ship. Blank windows looked down at him. He had spent time looking up at all of them and seen no signs of movement.

From his vantage point, some one hundred metres from the rear of the ship, he could just make out one of the men, though it was nothing more than a vague shape and he couldn't tell if the man was armed or not. Not that it mattered. He was going in either way. He had put on a Kevlar vest because there wouldn't be much room to move once he was on board the ship and he'd need whatever protection he could get.

He put on the night vision headset and switched it on. It hissed and flickered into life. He could clearly see the man now, a light green figure sitting with his back to the sea. There was someone else with him, but from where he was crouched all he could see was the man's leg.

The Heckler was on its sling, over Standing's right shoulder. The fire selector lever was set to safe, but he could have the gun in his hands and the selector lever flicked to fully automatic in less than a second. He'd use the Glock and its suppressor for as long as he could, but if he came under return fire he'd need the Heckler.

He'd been counting the seconds off in his head and he knew that there was less than a minute to go. He checked the ground between his vantage point and the ship. Night vision gear could be a life-saver, but it was a nuisance when crossing rough terrain. The angle of the lenses meant that it was impossible to look straight down to see where your feet were, and an overlooked rock or branch could easily result in a twisted ankle or worse. The terrain was fairly flat, a mixture of grassy patches and stony soil, and he saw nothing large enough to give him any problems.

He took a deep breath and exhaled slowly as he ran through what he had to do. He'd earmarked the place where he would board the ship, close to where the railing joined the super-structure. He would be able to grab the railing and pull himself up and that would mean using both hands, but if all went to plan, the men on the rear deck would be rushing forward to the bow.

His internal count had reached twenty seconds to go. He took another deep breath and exhaled slowly. He had the Glock in his right hand but he wasn't planning on using it until he was on board the *Galaxy*. The Glock held seventeen rounds in the magazine, so eight kills with double taps and one left over. Before the Glock was empty he would switch to the Heckler. By then he'd have lost any element of surprise anyway.

Ten seconds. Nine. He took another look at his watch but his internal clock was on time as always. He counted the remaining seconds and as he got to two he heard two shots from the front of the ship. The shots were a second apart but Standing knew that he had actually heard four shots, two groups of two.

He lost sight of the figures on the rear deck and started

running. He was halfway there when he heard another shot, then shouts from the front of the ship. Three dead, possibly, depending on how good a shot Harper was. Standing didn't hear any return fire, so maybe Harper had taken out all three targets.

He reached the ship and tucked the Glock into his trousers before jumping up and grabbing the railing. He lifted himself up so that he could get his foot onto the lower railing, then he pushed and he was up and over. He grabbed the Glock again, keeping low as he looked left and right. There were walkways port and starboard and as the gangplank was on the port side, he figured that was the way the men would have gone.

To his right was a large room that had once been a restaurant or bar. Several broken chairs and tables were scattered around but most had been removed, and large sections of a blue carpet had been ripped up to expose the steel floor.

Most of the windows overlooking the restaurant had been smashed and broken glass crunched underfoot as he headed down the corridor. At the end of the restaurant was a steel door with a sign that said STAFF ONLY and beyond that was a wide wooden staircase. Standing ducked back as he heard footsteps and a second later a man appeared on the stairs, an M16 clutched to his chest. Standing stepped forward and put two rounds at the top of the man's chest, then moved to the side, both hands on the Glock. A second heavy was on the way down, a revolver held above his head. Standing shot him twice in the chest and the man pitched forward and fell on top of the first body. Standing heard shouts from the floor above. Then he heard another shot from the front of the ship.

He made a snap decision and headed up the stairs. If he

continued towards the bow then anyone coming down the stairs would be behind him and that would be dangerous. Best to neutralise them before they became a threat. He reached the first floor. There were corridors running up and down the ship, and more stairs heading up. The walls were panelled and there were jagged holes where light fittings had been ripped out. There was no outside light, so the space was in darkness. He squinted at the stern of the ship and as he did, he heard a door open behind him. He whirled around just in time to see a man emerging from a cabin. The man's night vision hadn't kicked in, so he showed no sign of seeing Standing as he headed towards the stairs, an M16 at his side. Standing could see him clearly, a light green figure walking straight towards him. He raised the Glock and put two rounds in the man's chest. He slumped against the wall and the carbine clattered onto the floor.

Standing moved down the corridor, towards the bow. He heard a woman crying and stopped and listened. It was coming from the room that the man had come out of. He opened the door and stepped inside. The windows had been covered with sheets of plywood and the room was in darkness. There were screams and shouts, but he realised immediately that there were only crying Asian women there, maybe a dozen of them, four sharing two single beds, the rest of them lying on the floor. 'It's okay, it's okay, I'm here to rescue you!' he shouted. 'Stay here and don't come out until you hear my voice again.'

The women continued to cry as he closed the door. As he moved down the corridor another door opened. A man emerged, short and stocky with slightly bowed legs. Standing fired as the man turned towards him and both shots thudded into his chest. An Uzi fell to the floor as the man slid down the wall and died. Standing hurried over to the door and opened it. There were more women inside, crying and holding each other. 'Stay here, don't leave the room until I come back and tell you it's safe.' He had no idea if they understood what he'd said, but he pulled the door shut and headed down the corridor.

He heard more shots from the front of the boat as he reached the end of the corridor. There was another staircase there and he stopped and listened. There were more shots from the entrance, but he needed to be sure that no one was coming down the stairs, so he waited.

A round missed him by inches, smacking into the panelling by his face and peppering his cheek with splinters. The shot had come from behind him, so Standing bent down as he twisted around but the shooter had anticipated the move, because the next shot hit Standing in the centre of the chest. The round hit with the force of a hard punch and made him gasp but the Kevlar did its job and stopped it from doing any real damage.

The shooter was crouched down with both his hands on his gun and was about to fire a third shot when Standing pulled the trigger twice in quick succession. Both rounds smacked into the man's chest and he fell back and hit the floor hard. Standing figured he had lost the element of surprise and that it was time to switch to the Heckler. He dropped the Glock and reached for his carbine, and once he was sure that the corridor was clear he turned back to the stairs.

He decided to go down. He sighted down the Heckler as he took the stairs one at a time, feeling with the toe of his trainer before transferring his weight. Night vision headsets were great in the dark on the straight and level, but stairs were problematical because they didn't allow him to see where he was putting his feet.

He was on the third stair down when a pale green figure burst into view, holding a carbine. Standing aimed at the centre of the figure's chest and his finger was tightening on the trigger when he realised that the man was wearing a night vision headset. It was Harper. Standing relaxed his trigger finger. 'Bloody hell, mate.'

'Yeah, yeah, it's me,' said Harper.

'Well, I know that now,' said Standing. 'What happened to the plan?'

'I got them all,' said Harper. 'The two who were on guard duty and two more turned up. Then it went quiet, so I thought I'd improvise.'

'You nutter. I could have double tapped you. And more importantly, you could have shot me.'

'Nah, I knew you had everything in hand and that if I saw anyone it would probably be you,' he said. 'How many did you get?'

'Five,' said Standing.

'I got four,' said Harper. 'Not that it's a competition. Do you think that's the lot?'

'It's a tough call,' said Standing. 'Anyone on board must have heard the shots, so if they didn't come forward they must be hiding.'

'Do you want to search the place, top to bottom?'

'I think we've got to. Just in case. But there's what, four floors with twenty cabins on each floor? So eighty cabins?'

'The alternative is having someone up there with a gun who could come out any time. So yeah, we should check.'

Standing nodded. He gestured at the corridor behind him. 'I found girls in two cabins down there.'

'Is Kim there?'

'I didn't stop to look, I just told them to keep their heads down. Come on, let's clear the top floors and then we'll see what we need to do with the girls.'

Standing headed up the stairs and Harper followed.

The top floor contained the bridge, another restaurant, a gym, sauna and a large swimming pool, though anything of value had been ripped out long ago, including most of the tiles that had lined the pool.

The floor below was filled with cabins that were considerably larger than the ones Standing had seen, but they had been stripped bare and it took only seconds to check each one.

The third floor had more, smaller cabins, but it was clear that no one had been there recently. They checked each room, working their way methodically down the corridor. Harper would open the door, Standing would go in, gun to his shoulder, he'd move quickly to the bathroom, and back. All the furniture had been removed and light fittings had been torn out, along with most of the toilets and washbasins. They moved quickly and efficiently and in less than half an hour they were back on the floor where the girls were.

Standing pointed at the two doors where he'd seen the girls, then they checked the rest of the remaining cabins. All were empty. He knocked on the door of the first one he'd entered, then opened it. 'It's okay,' he said. 'We're here to help you.'

He let his Heckler hang from its sling and took off his night vision headset. There was some light coming from a small battery-operated lantern in the corner of the room. He held up his hands. 'It's okay,' he repeated. He did a quick head count. There were seven women in the bedroom and another two sitting on the bathroom floor. 'Does anyone speak English?'

One of the women raised a hand. 'A little,' she said.

'Where are you all from?'

'I am from Vietnam. Three more here are from Vietnam also.' She pointed at a young girl, and another. 'They are from Laos. The girls in the bathroom are Thai. The rest are from Cambodia.'

'Can you tell everybody that you're going to be okay, the bad guys are dead and we'll get the police to come and collect you.'

'I can tell the Vietnamese girls, yes, but I do not speak Thai or Lao.'

One of the girls sitting in the bathroom held up her hand. 'I can speak English. And I speak Thai and Lao. I will explain.'

'That's great, ladies. Just sit tight while we arrange transport for you.'

He closed the door and went along to the other cabin. Harper took off his night vision headset. Standing opened the door. He smiled and held up his hands. 'It's all over, ladies. We'll have you out of here as soon as possible.' He looked over at the bathroom where an Asian girl with dyed-blonde hair was standing with her arms folded. 'Are you Kim?' asked Standing. 'Kim Cooper?'

The girl frowned. 'Yes. I am. Who are you?'

'It's a long story,' said Standing. 'But I'm glad we found you.'

'I can go home?'

'Of course. That's why we're here. How many of the girls here speak English?'

They all raised their hands and Standing smiled. 'Well, that makes it easier,' he said. 'Look, everything is okay but I need you to stay in the room for a little while longer while we arrange transport. But there's no need to worry. You're safe now.' He nodded reassuringly but the girls still looked fearful.

'What about Sammy?' asked Kim. 'Where is he?'

'We're not sure. But we've taken care of all his men here and at his villa.'

'He has another place in Cambodia. And another on one of the Cambodian islands. He's always moving around.'

'Don't worry, he won't ever be in a position to harm you again.'

Kim winced. 'You don't know him,' she said. 'He's a very powerful man.'

'I've come up against some very powerful men in the past, and trust me, it doesn't make them bulletproof.' Standing fished his mobile phone from his pocket, scrolled through until he found Dean Cooper's number. He wasn't sure what time it was in Vietnam, but he figured that the American wouldn't mind being woken up for some good news. It took almost thirty seconds for Cooper to answer. 'Hi Matt,' was all the American said, but Standing could hear the apprehension in his voice.

'It's good news, Dean,' he said. 'There's somebody here that wants to talk to you.' Standing handed the phone to Kim and headed out into the corridor with Harper.

'What do we do now?' asked Harper. 'We've got twenty or so girls here who need looking after.'

'When Kim has finished talking to her dad, I'll call Fah. She's a local cop who was showing us around. I'll ask her to arrange transport for them.'

'You're sure that's the way to go?'

Standing nodded. 'I'm sure.'

CHAPTER 38

Standing saw the three sets of headlights carving through the night sky as they made their way along the track. Then they stopped as they reached the barrier. Standing could picture the barrels being rolled out of the way and the barrier raised. Hopefully they would be so busy clearing the path that they wouldn't notice Harper's pick-up truck parked in the undergrowth.

After a few minutes the headlights began to move again. Standing turned to look back at the cruise ship, a huge dark shadow against the stars. He was holding his Heckler, with a fresh magazine locked and loaded.

He turned back to look at the track. The first of the vehicles appeared, heading directly towards him. Then the second. Then the third. Black SUVs. They fanned out across the grass and came to a halt about a hundred metres away. Their headlights remained on, casting long shadows behind Standing.

Standing narrowed his eyes against the glare of the head-lights, his Heckler across his chest. His breathing was slow and even, and if anyone had taken his blood pressure they'd have found it to be that of a resting athlete, his pulse slow and steady.

The rear passenger door of the middle SUV opened and a figure climbed out. The door closed and the figure walked to

the front of the vehicle. All Standing could see was the silhou-
ette, but he realised it was a woman. And as she continued to
walk forward, he saw that it was Fah. She was wearing jeans
and a Liverpool shirt and had a Liverpool baseball cap on her
head, back to front. Despite not wearing her uniform, she had
her Glock in a brown leather holster on her hip. She stopped
when she was twenty feet or so in front of the SUV. 'You need
to put your gun down, Mister Matt,' she said. 'We will handle
it now. There is no need for you to be carrying a weapon.'

'Who is "we", Fah?'

'What do you mean?'

'Those aren't police vehicles,' said Standing. 'Who did you
bring with you?'

'Please put the gun down, Mister Matt. We don't want anyone
to get hurt.'

'Hurt?' shouted Standing. 'People have died, Fah. A lot of
people have died.'

Fah looked around at the middle SUV and shrugged. The
front passenger door opened and a figure climbed out. Standing
squinted, but the headlights meant that he couldn't see who
it was. The rear doors of the SUV opened and two other figures
emerged. They walked together to the front of the SUV. Fah
turned back to look at Standing. 'Please, Mister Matt, put
down the gun.'

The three figures walked to stand alongside Fah. They were
all holding M16s. The man to her left was Sammy Lee. He
was wearing a black suit and a white T-shirt and had a thick
gold chain around his neck. 'Do as she says, Mister Matt,' he
shouted. 'There is no need for anyone else to die tonight.'

The doors to the other SUV opened and closed and more
men appeared, fanning out in a large semicircle facing Standing.

'That's bollocks and you know it!' Standing shouted. 'You killed Pete, you killed Billy, and the moment I drop this gun you'll shoot me too. Why did you kill Pete in the first place? You could have just warned him off.'

Lee sneered at him. 'He wasn't the type to be warned off,' he said. 'But the plan wasn't to kill him like that. My men were questioning him. They wanted to find out who he was and why he was watching my house.' He shrugged. 'They left the bag on for too long. Shit happens.'

'And then when you found out that Billy and I were watching you, you sent your men again?'

'Billy?'

'Pete's brother.'

Lee laughed. 'Oh yes, the twin. It's not often you get to kill the same man twice, is it?'

'You think this is funny?' shouted Standing.

Lee's face hardened. 'No, I don't think it's fucking funny. There is an expression – "Don't break another man's rice bowl." Have you heard that? It means don't fuck with another man's livelihood. That's what he was doing. He was threatening to break my rice bowl. And now you're trying to do the same.'

'So when Fah told you that Billy and I were staying at the same hotel as Pete, and that we were watching you from Rasta View, you just decided to cut to the chase? You sent men to kill us?'

'You were threatening to break my rice bowl. You left me no choice.'

Standing looked from left to right, scanning the faces of the men facing him. There were eight in all, plus Lee, plus Fah. Fah's gun was still in its holster. Lee and four of the heavies were holding M16s, one man who stayed by his vehicle was holding what looked like an Uzi, and the remaining three had handguns. Standing recognised two of the men, he'd seen them on the terrace through the binoculars.

Standing was already in combat mode. This was only going to end one way, the only question was who would live and who would die.

Standing doubted that Lee would be proficient with the M16, he was carrying it for effect, to show what a hard man he was. The three handguns were too far away to be accurate, even if the shooters were in range mode with both hands on their weapons, which they weren't.

The Uzi was a wild card. It fired at a rate of six hundred rounds a minute and the guy appeared to have a 32-round magazine rather than the 25, but either way the gun would empty in less than three seconds on full automatic. Spray and pray. The Uzi wasn't accurate beyond thirty feet or so but sheer chance meant that one or two of the 9mm rounds might hit home.

That left four M16s. One of the men was holding his weapon down at his side as if he wasn't sure what to do with it. The other three had their carbines across their chests. One had his finger stiffly down the side of the lower receiver as his instructor had obviously taught him. But the other two had their fingers ready on their triggers. They were the dangerous ones. All they had to do was point and pull the trigger, and a pro could do that in less than a second. Both men also had their feet in the correct positions – left foot ahead of the right, feet shoulder-width apart. They were pros, so they would have to be dealt with first. So the pros, then the Uzi, and the guy with the stiff finger. Bish, bash, bosh.

Lee wasn't an issue. Lee would be the first to die, no matter how it played out.

'Do you want me to count down from three?' shouted Lee. 'Or are you going to do the sensible thing and throw down your weapon?'

'I'll throw it down, but I have your word? Your men won't shoot?'

'You have my word!' shouted Lee, but the way he grinned and looked at his men showed beyond doubt that he was lying.

'Okay,' said Standing. He slowly raised his Heckler until it was above his head. In his mind he began to count. One thousand and one. One thousand and two. One thousand and three. On three he moved his right foot back and then moved his weight forward onto his left foot as he swung the Heckler down, his finger already curling around the trigger.

A shot rang out from behind Standing, to his right. Actually two shots, but they sounded simultaneously. Both rounds hit Lee in the centre of his chest. The perfect double tap.

Standing already had one of the M16 experts in his sights and he squeezed the trigger twice. Both rounds slammed into the man's chest and he staggered back.

Lee was still on his feet as if he didn't realise he was already dead, but the gun fell from his hands and blood was pouring from the two holes in his chest.

Fah began to scream and she put her hands up to her face.

The man on the far right, holding a handgun, stiffened as two rounds from the Gilboa Snake smashed into his heart as Harper followed their plan – take out Lee first and then take out hostiles from right to left.

Standing took aim at the second M16 expert, who was just about to squeeze his trigger. The man fired but his shot went high, and almost immediately Standing put two rounds in his chest.

Harper shot another of the heavies and this time both rounds went into the man's skull, blowing blood and brain and skull fragments across the grass.

The man with the Uzi used his left hand to support the barrel as he took a step away from the SUV. Standing knew immediately that it was going to end in tears, the man's stance was all wrong and he had the weapon down at his waist as he pulled the trigger. He had it on fully automatic, so the sound of the shots blended into each other. *Brrrrrrrrrrt.* The gun pulled to the right and up. A pro would have taken his finger off the trigger and aimed again, but this guy was no pro and he fought to pull the gun back but it was already out of control. Bullets raked across Lee's back and then thudded across Fah's shoulders before the magazine emptied.

Lee finally fell to the grass, and a second later Fah slumped down next to him.

The man dropped the Uzi and ran to his car. Standing shot him twice in the back and he fell against the vehicle and rolled onto the ground.

The remaining men with handguns turned to run back to their vehicles, but Harper took them both out. Shooting them in the back wasn't an issue, neither side had intended to take prisoners.

Standing took aim at the final M16 heavy, who still had his gun at his side. His mouth was open wide in shock and he wasn't a threat, but this was no longer about threats, this was about taking out the opposition, so Standing fired twice, one shot to the heart and a second to the face. The man crumpled and hit the ground.

Standing took a deep breath and let it out slowly. It was over and had taken less than five seconds from the moment he had first raised his Heckler above his head.

Harper appeared at the prow of the *Galaxy*. 'You okay, Matt?' he shouted.

'Good as gold.'

'I'll be right there.' Harper disappeared from the prow and after a couple of minutes came jogging out of the entrance and along the wooden gangplank. He grinned as he walked up to Standing. 'They thought they had you by the short and curlies.'

Standing shrugged. 'They thought it was all about numbers,' he said. 'Ten of them and one of me. But I do this for a living.'

'Plus you had your ace in the hole,' said Harper, raising the Gilboa Snake. 'I love this gun.'

'It did the job,' agreed Standing.

Harper rested the gun against his shoulder and surveyed the carnage. 'You were right about Miss Fah,' he said.

Standing shrugged. 'Lee had to have had someone on his payroll,' he said. 'I thought it might be Benz or Somchai that Pete had spoken to when he phoned the Tourist Police number. But Fah was the only one who knew that Billy and I had been to Rasta View. So it must have been her who tipped off Lee. And it explains how they were able to get into Pete's room. Pretty girl like Fah knocks on your door, you're going to let her in, right? Especially when she's a cop.'

'Can't argue with your logic,' said Harper. 'Mind you, she was obviously a Liverpool fan, so she wasn't all bad. So, what do you want to do?' He gestured at the bodies. 'We've a lot of explaining to do. Or digging. How do you want to handle it?'

Standing looked at his watch. 'The first ferry leaves for the mainland in about an hour,' he said. 'You've got plenty of time to get there. Take your guns and the cash. As soon as you're on the mainland, call me and I'll call Colonel Kittisak.'

'Who's he?'

'He's one of the top cops in Trat. I'm fairly sure he's honest, but even if he's on the take, his paymaster is dead, so that should end any loyalty. He should get here about ninety minutes after I call him. I'll tell him that we've got the girls and that there was a shootout.'

'He's going to want to know who shot Lee. And his men.'

'I'll plead ignorance. I'll tell him another gang showed up, that they did the dirty and left.'

'He's not going to believe that.'

'No, but when I tell him about the vault in the villa and all the money there, that might be enough of a distraction.'

Harper laughed. 'It might at that. You sure about this?'

'I don't see I've got a choice. The Best Friends Resort has all my details, as do the cops. If I try to leave the country they'll stop me, guaranteed. So at the end of the day I'm going to have to talk to them. Best I do it here. And if I'm the one to tell him about the money in the vault . . .' He shrugged. 'That's got to win me some Brownie points.' He gestured at the *Galaxy*. 'Plus I've got to tell him about the girls. And about Kim Cooper. Somebody's got to take care of them.'

'You can sell it to him that if you're left out of the picture, he can take all the credit.'

'That's what I'm hoping.'

'And he can keep the money.'

Standing grinned. 'Exactly. There's no upside to charging me with anything, especially if that means me telling my side of the story in open court.'

Harper nodded. 'Well then, I'll be going. It's been a pleasure doing business with you.' He held out his hand and Standing held out his to shake. Harper laughed. 'I meant give me the gun,' he said. 'But yeah, I'll happily shake your hand.'

They shook hands, and then Standing gave him the Heckler. 'Thanks for everything, Lex,' he said.

Harper winked. 'Mate, the bags of money are all the thanks I need.' He shouldered both guns and headed to his truck.

After a few minutes Standing heard the engine start up. As the truck disappeared into the distance, he looked up at the night sky. He'd taken no pleasure in killing, but there had been no alternative. It had been kill or be killed. There was never any question that Sammy Lee wanted him dead, and the men who had died with Lee were hired hands and they deserved what they'd got. Miss Fah had been collateral damage, but she had made her choices and it was only fair that she paid the price. He took a deep breath and exhaled slowly. Sammy Lee's death had in some way made up for what the man had done to Pete and Billy Green, but it would never bring them back, so Standing didn't feel victorious or that he had in any way won. He had lost two comrades, and nothing he did could ever change that.

CHAPTER 39

Alan Sage parked the Nissan Qashqai close to the iconic red phone box next to the Storey Arms outdoor education centre. It was the starting point for the SAS's Fan Dance, usually heralded by a flashbang or a training grenade, but today wasn't a march against the clock. Standing was sitting in the front passenger seat and Terry Ireland was in the back with Jack and Joe Ellis. They had left the Stirling Lines barracks at seven o'clock in the morning after a breakfast of bacon rolls and coffee, and the drive had taken just over an hour.

Standing climbed out and stretched. He was wearing tracksuit bottoms and a North Face fleece over a black polo neck. The weather forecast was good with almost no chance of rain but it could change quickly in the Brecon Beacons, so they had packed wet-weather gear in their rucksacks just to be on the safe side.

Sage popped the lock of the rear door and Standing pulled out his rucksack. Ireland and Sage joined him with Jack and Joe Ellis. As they prepared their gear, two young guys with large Bergens walked over to their car, an old Honda Civic. From the way they were panting and sweating they had clearly just come down off the mountain, and by the look of their gear they were soldiers training for the Fan Dance. Smart recruits always came to the Brecon Beacons to train before attempting SAS Selection. They were both young, barely in their twenties, whippet thin with not an ounce of fat between them. They both had short haircuts and Standing would have bet his last pound that they were Paras. 'All right, guys?' asked Standing. 'How are the winds up there today?' On a bad day the winds at the peak could gust at more than sixty miles an hour.

The taller of the two shrugged. 'Not too bad, sir,' he said. 'How did it go today?'

The squaddie shrugged. 'It was okay, sir. It's Jacob's Ladder that always takes it out of me.'

Jacob's Ladder was on the far side of the mountain, a steep descent with massive boulders close to the summit that could be treacherously slippy in rain or snow. Going down was bad enough, but coming back up for the return leg was pretty much the hardest part of the Fan Dance. A true stamina-sapper. Standing wasn't sure if the lad was saying 'sir' out of politeness or because he thought Standing was an officer. It was probably the former.

'Do you guys have a date yet?' asked Joe Ellis.

The SAS ran two selection courses, one in the summer and one in the winter. Both had their issues. Dehydration was a big problem in the summer, which meant having to carry more water. Winter often meant rain, sleet or snow, and one slip could mean a twisted or broken ankle.

'We're up in three months,' said the shorter of the two. So that would be summer.

'Plenty of time to put the work in,' said Ireland. 'What's your time?'

The taller squaddie looked at his watch, a black Casio. 'Just over three and a half hours,' he said.

Standing nodded. 'That's good.'

'Yeah, but the weather's pretty much perfect today. We were aiming for three hours fifteen but Raz here kept cramping up.'

Standing nodded. 'Try scoffing a couple of bananas about an hour before you start,' he said. 'Gets your potassium, calcium and magnesium levels up and that prevents any cramp.'

'Thanks, I'll try that next time,' said Raz. 'Got any other tips? We need all the help we can get.'

'I tell you what I always used to do,' said Sage. 'Release the waist strap and chest straps on your Bergen while you're going up. Helps you breathe better and there's less hip flexor activation. Tighten them again when you want to run or when you're descending.'

The two squaddies looked at each other and nodded. 'Thanks,' they said in unison.

'And get yourself a camel bag full of water and fix it to the top of your Bergen,' said Ireland. 'That way you've got a drink whenever you need it and there's no faffing around with bottles.'

'That's allowed?' said Raz.

'Sure, it's all extra weight so they don't care. You're allowed between four and five litres. I did my Selection in the summer so I took five litres and drank a litre on the ascent.'

'Brilliant, thanks,' said Raz. They both fist-bumped Ireland, then did the same with Standing and Sage and the Ellis boys.

'Good luck, guys,' said Standing. 'Train hard, fight easy.'

The two squaddies gave him a thumbs up and started loading their gear into the back of the Honda.

Jack Ellis chuckled as they walked away from their SUV. 'Train hard, fight easy? That's your advice?'

'He's quoting Mike Tyson, right?' said Joe Ellis. 'Train hard, fight easy, and take a bite out of the opposition's ear if you get the chance.'

'It was said by a Russian general,' said Standing. 'Alexander Suvorov.'

'Yeah? Was he one of those that died in Ukraine?' asked Sage.

Standing shook his head sadly. 'You guys clearly don't know your history. He was around in the seventeen hundreds, fighting the Turks. Once he'd beaten them he set about the Poles. "Hurrah, Warsaw's ours!" is another of his quotes.'

'How would you know that?' asked Sage.

'I read,' said Standing. 'You should try it some time.'

They headed up the west slope, keeping a steady pace on the stony track, and within an hour they had the summit in sight.

'Nearly there,' said Ireland. 'How about the last one there gets the beers when we get back?'

'How about you get fucked?' said Sage. 'Slow but steady wins the race.'

'That is pure bollocks, slow but steady tends to come last,' said Standing. 'But I'm not racing. Tell you what, Paddy, let's make it first one that gets to the top buys the beers and you can start running. We'll see you there.'

'I was just trying to make it more interesting,' said Ireland. 'You guys are no fun.'

They had made an early start so that they would be alone on the peak, and the plan worked. There was no one else there when they arrived at the white-and-green National Park plaque that marked the summit, atop a pile of large stones. They took off their rucksacks and looked around. The sky was a clear blue with only wisps of cloud in the distance and they could see all the way to the Bristol Channel, the Gower Peninsula, the Black Mountains, Exmoor and much of South Wales. Usually when Standing was at the summit there was no time to admire the view, he would be straight down the other side, against the clock. It was a pleasant change to stand there with all the time in the world and just enjoy the view.

'Let's do this,' he said eventually.

The men took off their rucksacks. Standing had been carrying the box containing Billy Green's ashes, and Pete's ashes were in Sage's rucksack. They took out the boxes and placed them on the ground.

Standing had flown with the boxes from Bangkok, packed into a hard-shell suitcase. He had been escorted to the airport by Police Colonel Kittisak and three burly officers and whisked through security and immigration. They didn't leave him until he was on the plane and the door was closing. Standing hadn't actually been deported and had had to pay for his own ticket, but he had the distinct impression that his departure wasn't a matter of choice.

Kittisak had been happy to take the credit for the release of the trafficked women and for the breaking up of Sammy Lee's criminal empire. His men had found computer records at the Koh Chang villa that detailed Lee's criminal activities and which had led to police raids on more than a dozen properties, most of them in and around Trat. Huge amounts of heroin and methamphetamine had been found, along with half a dozen live tigers, cratefuls of rhino horn and ivory, and several hundred rare turtles. More than fifty men had been arrested, most of them Chinese, and Kittisak had appeared on television in front of a stack of money that came up to his waist. The police were claiming that they had seized four million dollars in cash from Lee's house on Koh Chang. Standing had smiled at that – there had been at least twice as much in the strongroom when he and Harper had left.

There had been interviews with the women who were being trafficked – mainly from Vietnam, Laos and Burma – and shots of Kim Cooper at the airport, posing next to Kittisak as she was about to fly back to her father. She had thanked him and given him a very respectful wai, which he had accepted magnanimously with a nod and smile. Later Kittisak had posed with the Thai SWAT team who were taking credit for storming Lee's house and the *Galaxy*. There were condolences for the sad death of Tourist Police Corporal Fah, killed in the crossfire, with no mention of the fact that she had been on Sammy Lee's payroll.

Standing's rapid departure from Thailand was obviously due in part to Kittisak's fear that Standing might contradict the official account of what had happened, but that was never going to be an issue. So far as Standing was concerned, Police Colonel Kittisak could take all the credit and as much of Lee's ill-gotten gains as he wanted. All that mattered to Standing was that he had avenged Billy and Pete, and that he had most definitely done. All that remained was to scatter their ashes and have a final drink with them.

Ireland opened his rucksack and took out a bottle of Johnnie Walker Black Label, a bottle of Smirnov vodka and seven plastic tumblers.

'What's your pleasure?' asked Ireland.

'I'll take a whisky,' said Standing.

'Vodka,' said Sage.

'Whisky,' said Jack Ellis.

'Yeah, whisky,' said his brother.

Ireland poured whisky into four tumblers, and vodka into the remaining two. The men picked up their drinks and raised their tumblers in salute to the boxes.

'Pete and Billy, you'll be missed, guys,' said Standing.

'Amen to that,' said Sage.

'The good die young,' said Ireland.

'Don't cry because it's over, smile because it happened,' said Jack Ellis.

'A drink to the living, a toast to the dead,' said Joe Ellis, raising his tumbler.

They drained their tumblers and put them into Ireland's rucksack. Standing knelt down and opened his box. He pulled out the cloth sack, tied at the mouth with a red rope. Sage did the same.

'Make sure you don't throw them into the wind,' said Ireland. 'I really don't want either of the Green boys in my mouth.'

Sage and Standing undid the ropes around the necks of the cloth sacks, then moved to stand with their backs to the wind.

'Be seeing you, lads,' said Standing. He shook the bag and a cloud of white dust erupted into the air. It was quickly whipped away by the wind. Sage did the same with his bag and another white cloud of dust burst forth. As Standing shook the bag, pieces of bone tumbled out and hit the ground. Sage tilted his bag and chunks of bone fell out, more than a dozen in all, landing around his feet.

'Well, that's not what I expected,' said Joe Ellis.

Standing knelt down to examine the pieces. There were several curved sections that had once formed part of the skull, a large piece of jawbone and a dozen or so chunks of bone. 'Yeah, I guess the Thai cremation system isn't as efficient as it is here.'

'I thought it would just be ashes,' said Ireland.

'You and me both,' said Standing.

'We can't just leave the bones here,' said Sage. 'It looks like a bloody crime scene.'

'Maybe we can,' said Standing. He stood up and gestured at the pile of stones. 'You know this is a Bronze Age burial mound?'

'I did not know that,' said Ireland.

'All those times you went by here, you never wondered what it was?'

Ireland shrugged. 'I figured it was just to mark the summit.'

'Give me a hand,' said Standing. He picked up one of the larger stones and took it off the pile. Then another. And another. Sage, Ireland and the Ellis twins helped, and after a few minutes they had taken a couple of dozen stones away and had made a deep hole in the stack. 'That'll do,' said Standing. He began picking up the bones and pieces of skull and dropping them into the space. Ireland and Sage picked up Pete's remains and put them in the hole. They ended up having to go down on their hands and knees to pick up the smaller pieces.

'If they could see us doing this, they'd piss themselves laughing,' said Ireland.

When they had finished, Standing picked up the remaining two tumblers and poured the contents into the hole. 'Cheers, guys,' he said. 'Next round's on you.'

He put the empty tumblers into Ireland's rucksack, then the five men replaced the stones and made the mound complete again. Standing and Sage packed away the bags and boxes and shouldered their rucksacks.

'How about last one back to the phone box buys the drinks,' said Ireland. 'And the petrol.'

'Sounds good to me,' said Standing.

As he spoke, Sage moved behind Ireland and dropped into a crouch. Standing pushed Ireland and he yelped and fell back, toppled over Sage, and hit the ground with a dull thud.

Sage sprang to his feet and started running down the path. The Ellis boys grabbed their rucksacks and ran after him. Standing followed, laughing out loud.

'Bastards!' shouted Ireland, still sprawled on the ground, then he burst out laughing. 'I'll get you for this.'

'You're not the first person to say that,' shouted Standing, who was already fifty metres down the hill. 'But you'll have to catch me first.'

Don't miss Stephen Leather's next explosive
instalment in the Spider Shepherd series

CLEAN KILL

A plane is shot down and the crew are taken hostage . . .

Bloodthirsty terrorists have shot down a British helicopter in
West Africa and taken the crew hostage. Their lives hang in the
balance and the British government is refusing to negotiate.
The pilot is Liam Shepherd whose father Dan 'Spider'
Shepherd of MI5 is the only man that can help.

Spider Shepherd is dispatched to rescue them . . .

Shepherd and an SAS team are immediately dispatched
to fly out to Mali to rescue the kidnapped Brits.

**At the same time, a high security prison
is moments away from violence . . .**

But the mission takes Shepherd away from an
investigation of a high security prison that is seconds
away from exploding into violence.

**With hundreds of lives at risk,
Shepherd is running out of time . . .**

Available to pre-order now

HODDER &
STOUGHTON